T0385310

In The Shadows

Also by Anna Smith

In The Shadows

ANNA SMITH

A BILLIE CARLSON THRILLER

QUERCUS

First published in Great Britain in 2025 by

QUERCUS

Quercus Editions Limited
Carmelite House
50 Victoria Embankment
London EC4Y 0DZ

An Hachette UK company

The authorised representative in the EEA is Hachette Ireland,
8 Castlecourt Centre, Dublin 15, D15 XTP3, Ireland (email: info@hbgi.ie)

A CIP catalogue record for this book is available
from the British Library

HB ISBN 978 1 5294 2 898 8
EB ISBN 978 1 5294 2 899 5

2

Typeset by CC Book Production

Printed and bound in Great Britain by Clays Ltd, Elcograf S.p.A

Papers used by Quercus are from well-managed forests and other responsible sources.

For Cillian. Look for the magic in every day.
Be happy. Be grateful. But most of all, be kind.

PROLOGUE

Pitch black. She's running, her heart bursting in her chest, her lungs burning as she tries to gulp in air. She's running for her life. And she can hear his footsteps behind her, the snapping of twigs as he tears through the woodland after her. She knows this stretch of wood well, and she knows she has nowhere to go, and that if she keeps running further and further away from the house, he will catch up with her and then it will be over. She stumbles, twists her ankle and falls, searing pain surging through her, but she clambers back up, because she can hear his voice now.

'You fucking bitch! I'll get you!'

Over her shoulder she catches a glimpse of him racing towards her, and she turns away. Through the trees, not too far, she can see the light in the kitchen window of her cottage where she bolted from after he attacked her. She has to go back. There are places she can hide, outbuildings. She breaks into a run again, gasping as the pain from her turned ankle shoots up her leg, adrenalin and fear driving her on.

When she gets to her yard, she glances behind her but she cannot see him now. She reaches the barn door and drags it open, stumbling inside into the darkness and the stillness before pulling the door closed. She seldom goes in here. It's mostly used for storing gardening tools and stacking chopped firewood. She bolts the stable door top and bottom and manages to squeeze herself in behind the boxes. She crouches down, trying to slow her breathing, her body soaked in sweat from the terror and the exertion.

In the silence she can hear her heartbeat. She strains her ears and can hear footsteps outside in the yard getting closer. Then they stop. He's outside. She knows it. She's barely breathing. She hears the barn door being dragged open. He's inside. The stable doors rattle as he tries to slide the bolts but he can't as it's locked from the inside. She can hear the steps walking away, and she dares to take a breath. Then suddenly the crashing sound of an axe on the door. Christ almighty. The door splinters and he keeps on smashing until there's a big enough hole in the upper door for him to push his arm through and open the lock. Some light comes in, but she stays statue still, hoping she's invisible. She can sense him glancing around, scrutinising every corner. Then she hears him snigger.

'There you are, bitch!'

He crosses the floor and pulls back the boxes, exposing her. She looks up as he stands with the axe in his hand. *This is it,* she thinks. *He's going to swing that down on me and it will be over. What will they say when they find me?* He stands that way for a long moment. Then suddenly, he reaches down, grabs her by the hair and drags her out of her hiding place as she yelps in pain. He pulls her to her feet. But then, from somewhere, she finds the strength to raise her leg and knee him squarely in the balls. He buckles over and she tries to free herself from his grasp, but he's too strong and pulls her back and she stumbles onto the floor. Now he's straddling her, punching her face one way then the other and for a second, she can see stars. His hands go around her neck, and he squeezes. Her eyes are open and she's gasping as he presses the wind out of her body, and she knows if she can't get out of this then very soon, she'll die. She thrashes her body violently, kicking her legs, then turns her head and somehow manages to sink her teeth into the back of his hand, and she holds on like a rabid dog as he screams in pain. Then with a final heave she forces him off her and she wriggles free as he is on his knees trying to scramble up after her. She looks around, her eyes falling on a garden spade. She picks it up, and then it's like slow motion, and she can see herself raising it and bringing it down on his head with a sickening crack. He falls face down. She lifts the spade, ready to go again. But she can see he's unconscious, blood beginning to seep from the back of his head. She stands over him, breathing hard, her mouth half open in shock and terror over what she's just done. He's not moving. At all. She stands and watches for maybe a minute, then she reaches her fingers down to feel his neck for a pulse. There's none. He lies there, his dark eyes wide open, staring, dead.

CHAPTER ONE

Elizabeth Fletcher turned on the cold water tap and stood at the kitchen sink, watching the water run over her trembling hands. She could feel her knees shaking and her teeth chattering as she looked out of the window at the still dark night, her mind a blur of panic and shock. She tried to take slow breaths to control herself, to find some kind of recovery that would focus her mind so she could work this out. She had just killed a man. He was out there now, lying in her barn, blood spreading across the stone floor.

It was self-defence, of course. She knew that, and anyone who investigated the death would absolutely agree, once they looked at the red welts on her neck where he'd tried to strangle her and the swelling on her cheek where he'd punched her hard. She was the victim, not this stranger who she didn't even know anything about, yet who she'd drunkenly brought to her home for sex. She could call the police, but she wouldn't. God almighty! How could she call the police and explain that? But even if she could find a way to admit that she had a drink problem, and had made a dangerous and stupid decision to pick up a stranger in a bar, she still couldn't tell the police. It wasn't what she'd done; it was who she was. Who her husband was. Christopher Fletcher was a university lecturer, a hugely respected figure widely quoted in the media for his expertise, who was fluent in several languages, his political lectures translated across Europe and beyond. She would find a way through this. She had to. But right now, there was a body in her barn that she had to get rid of.

She splashed cold water on her face and wiped it gingerly with a tea towel, glimpsing at her puffy cheek in the small mirror in her kitchen. The bloodshot eyes staring back at her with a shocked, almost crazed expression told their own story of too many boozy nights, and sometimes days. The years of alcohol abuse were beginning to show the ravages on her once beautiful face.

She stood for a moment, her breath coming a little easier now as she focused on what to do next. She went into the hall and pulled open the cupboard, and from the bottom shelf she dragged out a large tarpaulin they'd used to cover the barbecue, but which she'd kept for some inexplicable reason even though they'd got a new one. It was strong and thick. She folded it quickly, then went into the utility room, pulled on her wax jacket and put on a pair of light gardening gloves. She picked up a torch and headed out to the barn.

The door was still half open, the way she'd left it when she ran in horror a few minutes ago after what she'd done. Now she crept inside, somehow half expecting him not to be there, some faint hope that this had all been a terrifying nightmare and she'd wake up any moment in a fevered sweat. She switched on the torch. He was there all right, the pool of blood from his head now wider on the floor. She looked down at him, not really even sure how to start doing this. He wasn't a big man, but he was muscular and he'd be heavy. She was fit too, from lifting weights in the gym over the years and keeping herself in good shape, but she wouldn't be able to lift the dead weight of a grown man.

She put down the torch and left it on. Then she crept towards him, trying to keep her eyes from looking at his dead stare. She bent down and managed to turn him over. She went into the back pocket of his jeans and pulled out his mobile phone, making a mental note to pick up his shirt and jacket from her house before she moved him, if she was able to move him. She had to. She knelt down, hooked her arms under his and tried to budge him. Not a chance in hell. She shone the torch around the barn. She suddenly remembered there was a contraption somewhere, a jack kind of thing that had been left by the previous owners, and she'd seen guys working on the house last year lifting blocks of bricks with it. She went out of the stable and shone the light across the barn floor and spotted the jack at the other side. She had no idea how to use it but went over and pressed what looked like the power button. It sparked to life with a mild humming noise. She pressed the lever up, down, and finally up again to see how high it would go. High enough, she decided. She had to work fast, efficiently; make sure everything was done, cleaned up.

She opened the barn door wide and walked quickly to her Land Rover Discovery, climbed in and reversed it slowly up to the open barn door. She got out of the car, and pulled the jack into the stable, surprised at how easy it was to operate, then turned it around so the two long forks jutting out from the bottom faced the dead body. She pushed the button, and it moved forward, the forks making the dead body flinch eerily when they bumped against it. They were moving it but couldn't get underneath properly. These things were for moving pallets and bricks, not dead bodies. She needed a board to put beneath him. All she could see in the barn was a wide length of ply-wood but that might be strong enough. She dragged it across the floor and put it down beside him. Then she knelt down and, with everything she had, she rolled his body onto it. He was on his back now, eyes staring up at her, a trickle of blood sliding down his nostrils. *Don't look,* she told herself. *Just get it done.* Once he was on the board, the forks slipped beneath it and secured it. She pulled the lever to raise the board, surprised it was actually moving it. She kept raising it until it was at the height of the open door of the Land Rover boot. Then she stood back, wiped sweat from her brow and moved towards it. She tried to push the body into the boot, but it wouldn't budge. Then again, with every scrap of strength in her body, she heaved it and it rolled into the boot. He was still supple enough for her to push his legs into a position so she could get the door closed. She then picked up the barbecue cover and tucked it around him, and pulled back the cover of the boot so he was hidden. Then she got into the car and switched on the engine. Where the hell was she going to go?

She sat for a moment, scenarios and scenes of where and how she could dump the body flashing like a macabre list. She could drive all the way out of the village along to the cliffs and reverse the car close enough to open the door and hope for the best. Or she could drive a few miles away to the river – but someone might see her going through to the next town. She checked her watch. It was three thirty, still dark, but there were CCTV cameras in the town so that wasn't an option. She reversed out of the yard and turned the car down the long driveway and out onto the open road. There was no traffic and the night was still, the sky dark in the moonless night. She took the small lane off the main road, which was narrow and grassy and mostly used by walkers, not cars, but the four-wheel-drive car could handle it. She drove along slowly and managed all the way up to the lower part of the cliffs. She had to be ultra careful here. One slip of the clutch and she'd be over along with the car and the dead body. She slowed down, found a way to reverse and went close to the edge, then got out and opened the door, the wind whipping up.

She dragged the body out with the cover, catching his legs, and he hit the earth with a soft thud. She could hear the roar of the ocean. In the distance she could see the lighthouse flashing. She dragged the body to the edge, but she dared not take another step in case she slipped. She sat down, and pushed with her feet, inch by inch, till he was closer to the edge. Then one final heave and he went over.

She could hear the thud of him hitting the craggy rocks, and she closed her eyes to blot out the grisly images the sound conjured up. She just hoped he went all the way down to the foot of the cliffs and into the sea. She crept on her hands and knees to the edge, shone the torch and peered over. He lay on the rocks at the bottom of the cliff, his body small in the distance, the waves crashing in against him. She dared not look at his face, but watched for a second as the waves became deeper, and she hoped that very soon they would carry him off. She pulled herself onto all fours and crawled away, then got into her car and drove fast back to her house. When she got inside, she ran to the toilet and threw up, kneeling on the floor with her hands clasped around the toilet bowl. It was over. For now.

Elizabeth stirred in the grey morning light and opened one eye. Her head was thumping, her neck stiff, and every muscle in her body ached. She wasn't even sure if she could get out of bed. She checked the clock at her bedside. She had been asleep for around two hours, but it was not sleep, just the turmoil of nightmares and terrors after having finally collapsed with exhaustion. She pushed through her pain and eased herself to a sitting position, massaging the back of her neck and her head. Then she fell back on the pillows, her head tight as she tried to get some kind of perspective on what she had done last night, how she would find a way through it. She told herself she might never have to worry about it because by now his body would be long gone, carried away by the waves, and if he ever did wash up, it might be far away and there would only be what was left of him.

When she'd come home after throwing him over the cliff, she had cleaned the whole house of any evidence that anyone other than herself had been here. She'd washed the bedding, the glasses; cleaned the floor, sanitised the kitchen. Then she'd gone to the barn and washed down the jack she'd used to raise him into the boot of her car. There was nothing left to do. All she had to do now was convince herself that none of it had happened.

She'd taken his passport out of his jacket pocket. Who was he? His name was there, a citizen of Russia, the passport stated. She remembered the USB stick she'd taken out of his pocket earlier, and how she had slept with it under her pillow as she'd been too tired and frazzled to look at it. Then she scrolled through his mobile phone, messages in Russian, before going into his contacts list. To her horror she found her husband's mobile number. She recognised it straight away. But the name alongside it was not his.

CHAPTER TWO

Six weeks later

I was wrapping up a call with a woman who wanted me to uncover the truth as to why her mother had been found dead on a Spanish beach. I had listened to her story, and it was all over the place as she rattled it out at a hundred miles an hour, breathless and sounding overwhelmed by the whole ordeal. I wanted her to calm down and give me a step-by-step account of what she knew, but that was not going to happen, not right now anyway. I told her it would be best to come and see me in my office where we could go through everything she knew about her mother, an ex-pat in her early sixties living on the Costa del Sol, who had gone for dinner one evening and never come home.

'I just know she's been murdered,' the frantic woman said, her voice cracking with emotion. 'I know it in my heart. She was found on the beach with a head injury, her clothes soaking wet. That's just not my mum. She would never go onto a beach at night. Never. Somebody knows something.'

It's always hard to find the words to console someone when they've lost a loved one in circumstances that rouse suspicion. Even if there is a genuine explanation and it is obvious that there was no foul play involved, they don't want to believe it, so lost are they in their shock and heartbreak from the sudden and tragic loss. Sometimes it looks as black as they paint it, and I can see why people cling to the notion that a third party is responsible. I'd seen it before, whether it was a teenager who inexplicably walked into the sea, or a stag weekend where the groom simply disappeared only to be found weeks later at the bottom of a river in the Czech Republic. There were no answers. Somebody must have done it. No way would the grief-stricken families want to accept a drunken stumble or even that the person was desperate, trapped and depressed, and took their own life.

So here I was, listening to this sad woman having to face an ordeal that would shape the rest of her life. I knew what that felt like. I'd been there, even if I was so very young when my father jumped off a bridge in Glasgow into the River Clyde. There was no way I could reason with her now, so I suggested she find a time when she could come and see me.

I hung up the phone and sat back on the leather rocker in my office three floors up in the heart of Glasgow city centre. From here I can see life as it unfolds on the streets below, from the apparently homeless Romanian man wrapped in a sleeping bag who turns up to the same spot each day, to the upwardly mobile young thrusters striding to and from their offices, headed for coffee shops, bars or rushing to get in and out of the city. On days like this, when I'm a little tired, I can lose myself in the scenes below, imagining their lives, what stories they have to tell.

The door to my office opened and Millie stuck her head around.

'That girl just phoned back, Billie,' she said. 'Wants to see you tomorrow. You're clear in the diary.'

I turned my chair around to face her.

'Sure,' I said. 'I will have to see her anyway to decide whether I take her case. She sounded really agitated.'

'I know,' she replied. 'She called just before you arrived earlier, told me about her mother dead in Spain. Convinced someone is involved in her death. I just let her talk and told her you'd be in shortly.'

'Yes,' I said. 'She's frantic – in that way where she doesn't want to hear any probable explanation. Poor girl.' I sighed. 'I'll make my mind up once I see her.'

Millie stood a moment longer.

'How was your weekend?' she asked, giving me a knowing smile.

I know Millie so well. She's much more than the front of house lady I hired when I started this private investigator business over two years ago. She's become a rock in my life when it was well short of stable, when I waded through misery every day in search of my toddler son Lucas, snatched away from me by his father and taken to America. It's only a few months since I finally found him, but for a very long time before that, when I had to dig deep to stay in any kind of game, Millie was always there for me. And now, since I brought Lucas home to my Glasgow flat and so much has changed in my life, Millie is there like the mother I lost far too soon. Lucas loves her and I do too.

'It was really great,' I said, sipping my coffee. 'Lucas had a terrific time and was buzzing so much all the way home last night I thought I'd never get him into bed. But when he did go, he collapsed and was asleep in five minutes.'

I knew Millie would also be wondering how it went with Scanlon, my friend for years since we were young cops together at police training college. Like Millie, he had picked me up from the darkest places in recent years, and although I was always determined that we had to be friends and nothing more, it had strayed further than that. I wouldn't say I regretted it, because I didn't. But I'd moved into territory I wasn't used to, and I was still treading very carefully. I smiled to Millie.

'And yes,' I said, knowing she was waiting. 'Scanlon was on top form. He's so good with Lucas and they're great together. We had a laugh, some lovely food, and it was the best weekend I've had in a very long time.'

She raised her eyebrows enthusiastically.

'Glad to hear it.'

There was a call coming in on her desk, and she turned and left.

I thought for a moment about the weekend with Scanlon and Lucas. We'd stayed in a small apartment overlooking the seafront, eaten terrific food, and snuggled up on the couch, all three of us watching a movie after going out for pizza. It was a proper family outing like normal people have, but I've never experienced that before because of the way my life had been in recent years, so I wasn't really sure if I was doing everything right. We stayed up after Lucas went to bed and once he was asleep we cosied up together in the bedroom next door and made love and everything seemed just about as good as it gets. Even if there was always this niggling doubt that I had to watch my step because this kind of thing wasn't supposed to happen for me. Or was it?

My phone buzzed.

'Woman on the line, Billie. She doesn't want to say what it's about but wants to talk to you.'

I blew out a sigh and shrugged. *Good start*, I thought.

'Okay, Millie. Stick her through.'

I let the phone ring twice, then picked it up.

'This is Billie Carlson,' I said. 'How can I help?'

I heard her take a breath.

'I would like to meet with you, if possible. As soon as possible.'

The voice sounded clipped, posh.

'Can you tell me what it's about?'

Silence.

'Not on the phone, I'm afraid. I mean, anyone could be listening.'

Here we go, I thought. For all the sad cases that rocked up to the half frosted-glass, half wooden door in my office, most of them were genuine cases who'd come to me as a last resort. I wouldn't want to glamorise my job because it is far from glamorous. Many of my clients are betrayed spouses, business partners who have been cheated and robbed, and occasionally some desperate girl or man in search of help when they have nowhere else to go. But now and again, there are nutters who are up to their eyes in paranoia, and little by little I have learned to let them down and tell them I can't help them.

'I don't really see people without an appointment,' I said. 'And then it is normally in my office.' I paused. 'I've had a couple of dodgy encounters with people outside of my office, if you get my drift.'

I waited, sensing her turning over her options.

'I understand. Look, I'm not a threat to you or anything. I've got a problem. I can't discuss it on the phone.'

I didn't reply, waiting for more information. Eventually she spoke.

'My ... er ... Billie ... I knew your family. Your father – Anders Carlson.'

The words – his name – hit me like an explosion, and for a moment I wasn't sure if I'd heard her correctly. I hadn't heard anyone say my father's name for over twenty years.

'What?' I asked, incredulous.

'Sorry. My husband. He worked alongside your father in the university. Years ago, of course.'

Still my mind lurched, my heart suddenly racing, a flush of heat creeping up my chest. So few people had ever spoken about my father since the day he was buried and I'd stood there in the rain, a lost, bewildered twelve-year-old girl, clutching my weeping mother's hand, wondering what my life would be now that he was gone.

CHAPTER THREE

Now and again, someone walks into my office and within fifteen minutes of listening to them, I know that even if it sounds like the ramblings of the desperate, they're a hundred per cent right. Proving it and getting a conclusion is another matter. Most of the time I tell people straight up that I hear what they're saying, and I sympathise with them, but I lay it on the line that they will probably get nowhere in their quest for the truth.

As I listened to Gina Evans tell me about her mother, Cathy, who died in Spain, I couldn't help feeling she was on a mission that would haunt her for the rest of her life, but one that would most likely never find any closure. But as she told the story there were tiny shafts of light that a good investigator might be able to drag out to get to the truth. And on top of that, I couldn't help but feel sorry for her as she sniffed and poured out her heart, her face flushed and tired with the look of a woman who hadn't seen six hours' sleep in a while. So far, she had told me that the Spanish police – the Guardia Civil – on the Costa del Sol had had the case wrapped up by the time she flew over to Malaga, within forty-eight hours of her mother's body being found on the beach in the popular Brit tourist town of Fuengirola.

'They didn't give a damn,' she said. 'They more or less dismissed me and said she had a lot of alcohol in her system and had most likely wandered onto the beach and just died. But she had a head injury. There was blood on her hair and at the back of her head. Somebody must have done that.'

'What about the autopsy report?' I asked. 'Did you see it?'

'Yes. It said the cause of death was cardiac arrest. That there were drugs and alcohol in her system. They said the head injury might have been caused by a fall.' She shook her head. 'Drugs? My mum would never in a million years have taken drugs. She wouldn't even have known where to start. Sure, she liked a drink – sometimes maybe a bit too much. She could be silly sometimes with drink. But drugs? No way. And I don't believe she fell.'

I looked at her, tried to choose my words carefully.

'Gina, what do you mean by "silly"?' I asked. 'Do you mean your mother sometimes made bad judgement calls on a night out that could lead her into danger, maybe by getting into the wrong company?'

It had to be said and I could see by the look on her face that she was recalling things from her mother's past. She spread her hands.

'Look,' she said. 'My mum had a hard life. She brought me up in an abusive marriage until my dad died eight years ago. It was only then that she began to live, and I was glad that she did, because she'd had a horrendous time for so long. My dad was a drunk and could be brutal to her, and I grew up with bad memories that I'm still dealing with. But she deserved some happiness. She was in her early sixties and had started to go to Spain three years ago, and it was perfect for her. She was enjoying herself. She'd made friends with ex-pats out there and took three or four trips a year, sometimes renting an apartment for two months at a time in the winter. Then she got a long-term rental and stayed. I was happy for her.'

She was telling me of her mother's life, but she wasn't telling me enough.

'But you said she could sometimes make decisions that weren't all that good. What do you mean?' I asked.

She hesitated a moment, then pushed out a sigh.

'She got involved with a guy a couple of years ago. He was from Liverpool. I saw pictures of him. Good-looking, in his forties. And she seemed to be having a good time with him. I mean, it's her life. I didn't want to ask too much. If she was happy, I was happy.' She paused. 'But then it all ended in tears. She'd loaned him money – quite a lot of money for her, about four grand – and that was the last she saw of him. He disappeared. So, she got her fingers well burned there. And to be honest, I think that was all because she was swept up in the life, maybe having too much to drink, and making rash decisions. She would never have done that a few years ago. But I think she was enjoying being taken out, wined and dined by this guy and made to feel like a woman again. When she told me about it, she vowed she would never get involved with anyone again, and she would be more careful about the company she kept. This was over a year ago, and since then she's been fine. Until now.' She stopped, swallowing her emotion.

We sat for a while not saying anything, Gina blinking back tears, looking beyond me out of the window into the street, then back at me, waiting, hoping for an answer. I'd heard stories like this before, sat opposite heartbroken parents whose son never came home from a stag weekend in Spain, or whose daughter had died in a fall from a balcony in one of those high-rise hotels in Benidorm. You never could get to the bottom of what actually happened, and Spanish police were always quick to get the case wrapped up and the body sent home, writing it off as an accident where alcohol played a huge part. Brits dying abroad in mysterious circumstances was not good for tourism, and the object was to have the case done and dusted before anyone started with the lawsuits.

I'd seen it before as a police detective when I was sent to Spain after a twenty-year-old lad died in a street brawl with rival football fans. Nobody saw enough to make a statement to us or the Guardia Civil. But this was the Costa del Sol, and among the tourists and party weekenders, there lurked a vicious underworld controlled by ex-pat Brits and Irish cocaine kings who ran their empires, and grassing anyone up would be a death wish. But from that trip I'd been on with my detective sergeant, we had made good contacts within the Guardia Civil, and also a local fixer with his ear to the ground and a wealth of connections, most of them on the other side of the law. It might be worth a punt, I was thinking. But these days, my life was different. I had Lucas to think about. And traipsing over to Spain without him was not something on my agenda. I took a breath and explained this to Gina and could see the crestfallen look on her face.

'I can understand,' she said. 'But is there any way you could take my mother's case forward?' Her voice sounded pleading.

After a moment of considering, I spoke.

'What I can do, Gina, is I have some contacts on the Costa del Sol, people who will be closer to the case than most, so I can ask one of my friends there if he can make some discreet enquiries. I'm not promising anything by any means, but if they can come up with something that is worth going over there for, then I can look at that. How does that sound?'

She nodded, brightening.

'I'll pay you whatever your daily rate is,' she said. 'And if you do go over there, I can pay your expenses.'

I put my hand up.

'Well. Let's not get ahead of ourselves just yet. I'll take your case as far as I can, and we can talk money in due course. But first I need to contact my source over there and get him to do some digging.'

I pushed my chair back. The meeting was over. I was concerned that I'd taken on something that I wouldn't be able to really run at. But I know what it feels like to have nowhere else to go, and to need someone to fight your corner. She stood up and stretched her hand across my desk.

'Thank you so much. I'll email you everything I have: all the details from the Guardia Civil officers and the police report and autopsy report. I'll do it this afternoon.'

'Great,' I said. I raised my eyebrows. 'But Gina. Please. Don't go getting your hopes up at this stage. There's a long way to go.'

'I know,' she said, smiling for the first time, then she turned towards the door.

When she left, I let out a long sigh. I knew she'd only heard what she wanted to hear, that someone was taking on her case, that someone would tell her that her mother did not stumble full of drink and drugs onto a beach to die alone. Nobody ever wants to believe stuff like that.

CHAPTER FOUR

The mystery woman who wouldn't give her name yesterday called again around midday as I was scrolling through online newspaper clips about Cathy Evans' death in Spain. It had been front-page material the first few days after she'd been discovered, but like everything else, the news agenda moves on. And in the absence of anything juicy to add to the story, Cathy Evans had become just another Brit abroad who had died in unexplained circumstances. Millie was downstairs picking up sandwiches for lunch, so I took the call myself in my office.

'Billie Carlson Investigations.'

Silence, and I waited rather than repeat myself.

'I called yesterday,' she said. 'We spoke briefly.'

I recognised her voice straight away. In fact, her clipped tones had rattled around in my head most of last night after I'd put Lucas to bed and lay in my bath, the brief conversation we'd had unleashing a raft of memories. I knew if I even started to go down that road, I'd never get any sleep.

'Who is it, please?' I knew who it was, but I wanted it to come from her.

'My name is Elizabeth Fletcher. Could we meet as soon as possible?'

The name rang no bells, not that I'd have expected it to. Many of my childhood memories had faded, and though I recalled my parents sometimes having people at our home for dinner, I never knew who they were. It didn't matter. They were grown-ups with conversations that didn't interest me, and when they did have people over, I would have spent most of the time watching television in another room or reading a book.

'Elizabeth,' I said, 'can you give me an idea what it is you would like to see me about? It's important that I know some brief details.'

Nothing. Then she cleared her throat and spoke.

'I'm in trouble.'

I gave it a second to sink in.

'What kind of trouble?' I asked.

'I . . . It's not something I want to talk about on the phone. Can we meet? Away from your office?'

'Elizabeth,' I began. 'I'm sorry, but you must understand that I need to at least have some details before I agree to meet you, or anyone else, in any circumstances.'

I heard her breathing, then after a moment she spoke.

'You may have seen the police investigation into the body washed up on the rocks near Portpatrick?'

I had indeed. Around a month ago, it was in all the newspapers, about the mystery man discovered by fishermen off the coastal town of Portpatrick in the heart of Dumfries and Galloway. I recalled that they thought the man was in his late thirties and that nobody had come forward to claim him. The police investigation into the body had found a gaping head injury but suggested it could have been caused by washing against rocks. Police were around the area but because there was no immediate ID, there was nothing to go on. Portpatrick was a quiet town, busy in the summer, but in the spring there were not too many visitors. One hotelier had given a name, saying a man fitting the description cops had issued had come into the village and booked to stay overnight but hadn't turned up. And the name was untraceable, foreign, possibly Eastern European. Police enquiries around the village asking if anyone remembered the man had drawn a blank. It was one of these stories that interested me, because of the mystery, but that was about it. Who knew these days – he could have been a drugs gangster dumped by his cronies, anything like that, or just someone who had run out of luck.

'Yes,' I said. 'I do remember. Has this got something to do with you?'

I waited a long time for an answer.

'I'm afraid it has,' she eventually said.

My mind was full of questions now, too many to ask here. And, really, the main question I wanted to ask was how she knew my parents. It was that more than the intrigue of a mystery man that made my decision.

'Okay, Elizabeth. Where are you?'

'I'm at my house down the coast. In Portpatrick.'

'I see,' I said, even more intrigued now. 'Are you able to come to Glasgow?'

I didn't have the time or inclination to drive two hours for a meeting, and with Lucas to pick up mid-afternoon, it was too tight.

She seemed to hesitate, then answered.

'Yes. I could. I don't live here all the time. It's a holiday cottage. I live mostly in London . . . and Berlin, you know. I'm abroad a lot of the time.'

Whoever she is, she's not poor, I was thinking. A holiday cottage on the Scottish coast as well as living in London and Berlin. I was even more fascinated.

'When do you think you'd be able to come to Glasgow?' I asked.

'This afternoon? I could leave now and be there within a couple of hours, maybe a bit longer.'

I checked my watch automatically. I could ask Millie if she would pick up Lucas and take him to my house if need be. She was always pleased when she got to spend some time with him.

'That's good for me. If you call me when you're in Glasgow, then we can arrange to meet.'

She took a moment to answer then spoke.

'Actually, if I'm coming to Glasgow, I'll book into the Hilton. Too long a journey to come up and go back. We could meet there.'

'Perfect,' I said, picturing a woman of some means and determination, wondering what her involvement was with this mystery dead man.

It turned out she wasn't going to be in Glasgow until nearer four in the afternoon, so I had time to pick up Lucas from nursery. I was glad, because even though Lucas loved it when Millie picked him up, I wanted to keep his life as even and as simple as possible so that he was with me every hour of every day that I could manage. It had only been a few months since I'd brought him back from the USA, after a tortuous hunt lasting more than eighteen months, because my husband snatched him away from me without warning. Sometimes that hell seemed like a long time ago, as though the nightmare was something rooted in my past, and who I was now – happier, calmer – was completely different from who I had been then. I promised myself almost every day that I would never, ever take having Lucas for granted again. And I wouldn't.

He was thrilled when I went to the door of the nursery as

the kids stampeded out and he ran into my arms. *I will never get tired of moments like this.* I explained to him as he skipped along, clutching my hand, that Millie was in the car and we were going to our flat and she would make him something to eat in case I was a couple of hours, as I was working late. I seldom did this, as I liked my nights to be spent with him, and often these days with him and Scanlon, which had become the new equation in my life. But even if I worried about it, Lucas was always completely unfazed. Whatever happened to him in the USA I might never know, and I didn't think I wanted to, but he was a resilient, incredibly tough little dude who had been passed from pillar to post over there. He was an adorable little boy.

Millie helped strap him into the back seat and we headed for the flat. I went in along with them and took something out of the fridge I'd taken from the freezer this morning. Lasagne, shop bought, but it was a favourite. And I told her there was garlic bread. I changed him out of his nursery kit of white polo shirt and blue sweatshirt and made sure he was settled, and once he was happily ensconced in the living room with the TV on, my mobile rang.

'I'm just pulling into the Hilton now,' said the voice of Elizabeth Fletcher.

'Great. I'll be there in around fifteen minutes.'

'Thank you.'

She hung up.

I stepped into the marble-tiled foyer of the Hilton through the revolving door, taking in the warmth and anonymity of the hotel. Apart from a couple of men checking in at reception, the place was deserted and the cocktail bar off the main area was empty except for the barman in his navy waistcoat behind the bar, polishing glasses to keep busy. As one of the biggest hotels in the city, no doubt it would be busy in the next couple of hours with overnight hotel guests or stragglers from lunch elsewhere arriving. Hotels like this had a million stories, from the corridors of the rooms to the bars and restaurants, and for a moment I thought how lovely it would be to just pitch up at the bar, order a large gin and tonic and chill out for an hour before an exquisite dinner here. I'd been here. Many times, and it was always good. But not today. Today was about Elizabeth Fletcher.

Who was this woman, this voice on the phone whose words 'I knew your father' were echoing again and again in my head? What would she tell me today about this friendship? Did I dare to ask in case I would hear something I didn't want to hear? In case something would distort the image I had cherished of my loving father and mother and the times we used to have before it was all taken away one winter's night?

I took a seat on a small sofa opposite the fake fire, and when the barman looked across at me, I ordered some tea. I was thinking about sending Elizabeth a text to tell her where I was when I was suddenly conscious of a tall, slender woman at the entrance to the bar. Bathed in the soft light, she looked quite striking. She stood for a moment then caught my eye and walked across.

'Billie?'

'Yes.' I stood up and stretched my hand and she shook it in her long, cold fingers.

'Thanks for seeing me at such short notice.'

'No problem. Thanks for coming all the way up.'

I offered her a drink and she asked for a gin and tonic. Long drive, I thought, or maybe she needed it before she could impart what had brought her to this moment. The barman, eavesdropping, nodded when I looked at him and he prepared her drink, the clinking of the ice hitting the glass the only sound in the bar. She sat down, long legs in trousers and soft leather ankle boots, slipping off her navy cashmere coat and pushing back her dark brown hair. I pitched her at early forties or fiftyish, well preserved and looked after with smart clothes, perfect make-up and dark eyes that were watchful. But I could see the tiredness and something like shock or worry in them. The barman came over and set down a gin and tonic on the copper-top table. She picked it up and took a decent swig, before taking a breath, her nostrils flaring slightly. I looked at her inquisitively.

'So,' I said, spreading my hands. 'Here I am. How can I help you?'

I said it but I was thinking that if she really did have any-thing to do with a dead body on the rocks, then there wouldn't be much I could do. But I couldn't think of any other way to say it.

She picked up her drink and took a small sip, but I had the feeling she could easily have downed the lot in one go. Her tongue darted out to lick her lips, and she took a breath and pushed it out, her head shaking a little.

'Well,' she said. 'Where to begin.'

I watched and waited, said nothing. She looked at me, then at the fake flames.

'As I said to you, that man who was found on the rocks. I . . . I know him.'

I raised my eyes, surprised.

'You know him?'

'Well. Not know him. But I . . . I was with him. Before.' She swallowed. 'Before he was found.'

My heart skipped a beat, and even before she went any

further, I had the feeling that it was the police she should be talking to.

'What do you mean, Elizabeth, by before? You mean days, weeks?'

She sat for a moment, the fake crackling of the fake fire the only sound. I waited as she stared at the table, then she opened her mouth to speak, her brow knitted, her voice a whisper.

'He attacked me. He tried to strangle me.'

She lowered the polo-neck sweater, but there was nothing to see. Then she touched her face with her fingertips.

'He punched my face over and over again. The bruises are gone now. It was weeks ago.'

Weeks ago. It was four weeks since the body was found. What was she telling me?

'Elizabeth,' I said. 'Whatever you are going to tell me, I can see it's difficult for you. So, it might be better if you just start at the beginning. Tell me everything. How did you meet? When? What happened?'

CHAPTER FIVE

She began. I listened. And the more I listened, the more I had the feeling I knew how this story would end. But I let her speak.

'I come to Portpatrick sometimes on my own, or with my husband, Christopher, depending on when he's in the country. He works away a lot.'

There was a hint of resentment in the way she said it.

'What does he do?' I asked.

She took a moment to answer, then whispered, 'He was a university lecturer, as I told you, and still does some lecture tours. But he also works for the Foreign Office. That's how we met. We both worked in the Foreign Office in Ukraine a very long time ago.'

I must have looked impressed because she glanced at me, then looked wistfully beyond me.

'I suppose it sounds quite exotic in a way,' she continued. 'You know, the travel, the sometimes exciting postings to far-flung places, the whole vista of a life that is so different from other, dare I say, normal jobs. But the truth of the matter is that often as a junior Foreign Office official you do all the dogsbody jobs, you know, everything from preparing the way for diplomats higher up the chain to engaging with diplomats from other countries. It was hard work. And then there was the everyday stuff – liaising with families whose relatives had been killed or had gone missing, or, more often than not, dealing with twentysomething Brits getting arrested and banged up abroad. I'm sure you've read all these things in the newspapers.'

I nodded. I had. But it was good she was building up a picture for me of who she was, and what kind of life she'd led.

'Are you still working in the service?'

'No.' She shook her head quickly. 'I gave it up years ago. Had enough. I thought I might write a novel or something.' She half smiled. 'But, of course, I haven't. Not yet. Too lazy.'

'Where is your husband now?' I asked. 'Is he aware that you've been attacked?'

She looked at me, surprised.

'Oh, good God, no! Absolutely not.'

'Why not?'

She blinked a few times before she answered.

'Because . . . it would ruin him if it got out, the details of how I was involved . . . That's why I can't go to the police.'

'Why would it ruin him if you've been attacked?' I asked. 'I have to say, the normal course of action would be to go to the police, would it not?'

She shook her head, closed her eyes briefly as though trying to shut out an image.

'It's too late for all that. I can't go to the police. Not now. Not ever.'

I sat forward and looked her in the eye.

'Why?'

She held my gaze and bit her bottom lip, then picked up her glass and took a long drink.

'Because . . . because . . .' She paused. 'I killed him.'

Her words, delivered deadpan with no hint of terror, exploded in the air, and even though I'd half expected she had something to do with this man's death, it was still a shock. Alarm bells were ringing all over the place, and my gut instinct was to stop her right there and tell her the meeting was over. Then she suddenly put her hands up to her face.

'It was self-defence. Totally. He was trying to strangle me. It was him or me . . . He—'

'Elizabeth,' I interrupted. 'You need to go to the police, not to a private investigator. Honestly. You have to go to the police.'

She spread her hands.

'I can't. I can't go to the police. They don't know who he is, they're still trying to find out from forensics. But I do. I know who he is. I didn't at the time, when I killed him, but I know now. I have his mobile phone, and also a USB stick I found on him. I haven't looked at that yet, but I'm sure some people will be looking for him.' She paused, swallowed, lowered her voice to a barely audible whisper. 'He's . . . I think he must be a spy.'

'A spy?' I replied in a whisper. 'How do you know? What kind of a spy?'

'I don't know yet – Russian. He's – he was – Russian. But I'm trying to figure it out. And also, on his mobile, my husband's number is there. But the name beside it is not his. Something is going on.'

That was putting it mildly, I wanted to say. Either I told her right now that I was out, that no matter what was going on, her first stop had to be to go to the police. This was not for me. But then I thought of my main reason for seeing this woman – that she'd told me she had known my father. I wanted – needed – to know more about this. And why did she even tell me that in the first place? Did she know more about my father than I did? These were questions not for now, so I put them aside.

'Elizabeth,' I said. 'Look. I don't know what you think I can do for you, and I stress again, you need to go to the police.' She shook her head and I put my hand up. 'Hear me out,' I said. 'You have to. But right now, I want you to tell me the whole story of how you met this man. What happened that night. Can you do that?'

She waited for a moment then spoke.

'Okay. I will tell you everything. I'd gone out to the village for an early bite to eat and then ended up in one of the pubs. I get bored being in the house all day and sometimes I just need to get out, have a couple of drinks. I . . . I drink a lot. I spend a lot of time on my own. My husband, well, we're not really together as we once were. You know, it's like the light has gone out of the romance we once had all those years ago.'

She looked down at the floor, then at me.

'I get lonely, so I sometimes go to a bar. But this time I stayed longer in the pub than I meant to. And that's because after a couple of drinks sitting at the bar, this guy came in and I noticed how good-looking he was. He was at the other end of the bar and was on his own. The place was busy with tourists and early evening locals, I suppose – I don't really have much to do with the locals. I like to keep a low profile and just keep private. You know what villages are like.'

She took a breath and looked into the middle distance as though she was remembering.

'Then this guy smiled over to me, and I smiled back. I know it sounds clichéd but that's what happened. After a couple of minutes, he went away, maybe to the loo, and when he came back, he sat on the bar stool next to me and said hello. I did the same and we got chatting. He asked whether I lived here and said he was passing through on a business trip and had been staying in Stranraer. He didn't say what kind of business, and I didn't ask.'

She shrugged and said he bought her a drink, and they both got chatting.

'He had an accent. Eastern European or, from my experience, Russian I would say, but he spoke very good English, and from his conversation I could see he was intelligent and educated, but he never spoke at all about his life. He said he was Serbian, but I suspect that's not true.' She shook her head. 'So damn stupid now when I think about it, but it was the alcohol. It was flowing and we were talking and laughing, and it was like being free and young again and being chatted up by a handsome stranger. Just ridiculous that I would get involved in that. I don't normally do things like that, but I . . . well . . . sometimes I don't know when to stop with the alcohol, and between the wine with dinner and the four or five gin and tonics I really felt I was getting quite drunk. I told him I'd have to go as I needed to walk back to my house – it's only a few minutes off the main road and up the track. He offered to walk me home, and I stupidly agreed. I admit I was attracted to him, and thought why not. And that was my biggest mistake.

'We left the pub and headed to my house and he walked me to the door, then we stood for a moment, and he suggested he would love a coffee. We went into the house and that was it.' She blew out a breath. 'I won't go into the detail, but we ended up in bed. We had sex.' She looked embarrassed.

I was trying to work out why an intelligent woman of the world like her would get involved in something like this. I wasn't judging, because that's what happens sometimes when people are lonely – they make choices that they might regret. She looked back at me.

'I know I must sound like a slut to you, but I'm not. This is the first time I've done anything like this. I don't know what I was thinking about. I was drunk.'

'I don't judge people, Elizabeth. Everyone does things once in a while they might regret. It's part of life,' I said, and I meant it. She nodded.

'Anyway, at some point in the night we must have fallen asleep, and with me being drunk I must have been in a deep sleep. Then I woke and I heard someone moving around the house, and I listened and wondered what he was doing. I got out of bed and saw him opening drawers in my husband's study as though he was looking for something. At first I thought, *Is he robbing me?* but I just wasn't sure, and when I heard him come back down the hall towards the bedroom, I pretended I was asleep. I heard him go into the bathroom and then I heard the shower being turned on. I tiptoed out of bed and saw his mobile phone on the dressing table. Something took over – instinct, suspicion – and I picked it up and scrolled through it. Some messages were in English and others in what I think was Russian, so I don't think he was Serbian. Then I looked through photos and then his contacts. That's when I saw my husband's phone number, under the name Sergei. I stopped in my tracks, shocked, abruptly sobered up. Something was very wrong.

'But I was so absorbed in this that I didn't hear him come out of the bathroom. Suddenly he was standing there, stunned, a look of rage on his face. He shouted something like, what the fuck are you doing? And that was it. He was over in two strides and had grabbed the phone off me, and he slapped me so hard I fell onto the floor and tasted blood. He then started to beat me and kick me. I screamed, "What are you doing? Who are you?" and he dragged me by the hair and tried to choke me. I managed to wriggle out of his grasp, and ran from the bedroom, pulled on a coat and ran out of the house.

'I knew I could run to the woods at the back of the house, but it was pitch black and I knew he would be right behind me. I tried to hide in bushes, and then run again, but he caught up with me, and again tried to strangle me. I hit him with a piece of wood, and he fell off me, and I ran. But he got back up. Eventually I ran back to the house, and into the barn, into the stable, and locked it. He smashed through the door with an axe and grabbed me, and we grappled on the floor, him trying to choke me. I wriggled free, then I picked up the spade and hit him as hard as I could. Afterwards, once I'd calmed down enough, I knew I had to get rid of him. I got him into my Land Rover, then drove to the cliffs and pushed him off.'

I listened, as shocked at what she'd been through as I was stunned at what she'd done. While she told me, she hadn't cried, not once, as though she was still fired on adrenalin but had to offload this grisly tale to someone. I wasn't sure what to say to her. Eventually I spoke.

'That's some story.' It was all I could think of saying at that moment.

'I know,' she replied. 'Horrific. Believe me, I'm totally traumatised by it all, and don't know where to turn.'

There was a short answer to this, and it had to be said.

'You have to go to the police, Elizabeth,' I said, looking straight at her. 'I mean, what else do you think you can do here?' I paused. 'The police must have been making enquiries around the area once the body was discovered. Did they speak to you?'

She shook her head.

'No. I left the village the morning after I killed him. I had to get out of there.'

'Why did you come back?'

She sighed and shook her head.

'Because I forgot that I left the USB device under my pillow. I had to come back to get that.'

I raised my eyebrows.

'That was risky.'

'I know.'

'Was the USB stick still there when you got back?'

'Yes.'

'So you haven't looked on the device to see what's on it? Not at all?'

'No.' She shook her head, angry with herself. 'How stupid is that! I just wasn't thinking. I was in such a flap. I just wanted out of the house fast and to get as far away as I could. So bloody careless!'

'Where is it now?'

'In a wall safe in my house.'

'Have you any idea what could be on that device?'

She shook her head, pushing out a sigh.

'Could be anything. That's what worries me.'

'What do you mean?'

'What if it's something that could be used against my husband? I just don't know.'

'Why would someone use something against your husband?' I looked her in the eye. I knew she was holding stuff back. 'You need to be straight with me, Elizabeth. A hundred per cent straight. You got that? Otherwise I'm out of here right now.'

She held my gaze for a long moment, and I could see in her eyes the ravages of alcohol that women over forty experience if they're boozing big time, and although she was good-looking, under the veneer there was a story of a rough life. She didn't reply for a bit and sat picking at the skin on the back of her hands. Eventually she looked up at me and spoke.

'My husband is a spy.'

She said it so matter of factly. The words hung in the air. I kept my expression deadpan, then asked, 'You mean, he's not a university lecturer?'

'No,' she said. 'I mean, yes, he is a university lecturer. But he's also a spy.'

'A British spy? You mean, for the UK government?'

She nodded slowly. We sat for what seemed like an age not speaking, mostly because I didn't quite know where to go from here with my questions, never mind whether I wanted to go anywhere near this case. Then I asked, 'So, have the police talked to you at all if they were doing the rounds in their investigation into the body that washed up? I mean, since you got back?'

'No.' She shrugged. 'I only got back two days ago. I think they might have moved on a bit, because there was no ID on the man. It's a mystery to them and to everyone who he is. But I hear they are still asking questions, so I'm hoping they don't come to me.' She paused. 'Whoever sent him to me will know.' Her face tightened. Then the words came tumbling out. 'Whoever he is working for sent him to my house. He was looking for something. I think he knew who I was, and he targeted me because maybe he wanted to find something in my house – something connected to my husband. I don't know.' She stopped, swallowed. 'That's why I can't go to the police. Whatever my husband is involved in, he can't be seen to be connected to this in any way. He's respected, a revered academic across the UK, Europe and beyond. Nobody knows about the other side of his life.'

'Why do you think anyone would send an agent to your home in Portpatrick, instead of tracking your husband to wherever he is? Is it not a bit odd that they were in the village where you and your husband have a holiday home?'

She shrugged.

'Yes, I suppose. Who knows. Maybe they had some information that he would be coming there at some stage and they wanted to recce the place. Maybe they were planning to kill him or something. I just don't know.'

I was fascinated by her story, but not sure what she thought I could do for her.

'Elizabeth, what is it you think I can do here? Everything you've told me makes me really think this is a matter for the police and not for me.'

She pushed out a sigh as though she was trying to figure out an answer.

'I thought . . . I thought perhaps you could make very discreet enquiries in the area to see if there is anything about this man, when he arrived, any details of what his business was here. Anything like that. And perhaps find out what the police view is, like how far are they going to investigate this? Is that a possibility?'

I considered this for a moment, then replied.

'Yes, I think I can put some quiet feelers out to contacts in the police who may know the status of the investigation. And I suppose I can look at any background locally to see if anyone else had any contact with him.'

'Thanks,' she said. 'I'd appreciate that. You can let me know your daily rate and I'll deal with it.'

I glanced at my watch. There wasn't much more to say here, apart from addressing the elephant in the room – that she had known my father. I decided to leave that for another day.

When I left, I walked to my car, questioning myself as to why I didn't bring up her claim that she knew my father. Why?

What was the matter with me? It was the only real reason I was there, the only reason I'd agreed to meet her. Yet when it came to the crunch sitting facing her, I couldn't bring myself to ask. What was I hiding from?

CHAPTER SIX

From what I could glean from my Spanish police contact, the case of Cathy Evans was more or less closed. Of course, like police the world over, they always keep an open mind if someone comes up with evidence to the contrary, but right now there was no reason for them to keep digging. Cathy's death was more likely the result of too much alcohol followed by a fall which caused a head injury, and she ended up somehow on the beach until she was found dead the following morning. It happens, Detective Pablo Sanchez said, and I could almost see him shrug in that way the Mediterraneans do when emphasising a point.

'But how can they just write it off so easily?' I asked, leaning back on my chair with the phone to my ear. 'I mean, how far did they look into her background, like how she lived out there?'

I could hear him sigh. It wasn't so much that he was bored, but when I'd called him yesterday evening, he told me he hadn't been on the case but would see what he could find out. I'd known Sanchez from being sent to the Costa del Sol on an enquiry while I was a police detective, and he'd been a big help then, making sure I'd had everything I needed on the case. And he'd also smoothed the way so that I didn't have much to do with his macho bosses, who hadn't taken kindly to a British cop making enquiries on their turf – never mind a woman.

'Yes, I think they did. But I think they find she is just like a lot of Brits over here. You know, they go in the bars, they drink maybe too much, then can't look after themselves.'

'But she was a woman in her early sixties, Pablo. She's not going to be living like that,' I said. 'Well, at least I think not.'

'You'd be surprised what we find with many people who come here.'

I knew he had a point, but I didn't like him generalising foreigners the way he was doing. I didn't reply, then he asked, 'So. You coming here to investigate?'

'Not at the moment,' I replied. 'I'm a private investigator now. Not a police officer.'

'I see. You leave?'

'Yes. A couple of years ago. I work as a private eye now. And the daughter of the woman has asked me to look into her mother's death.'

'A private eye,' he said. 'Like in the movies?'

'No,' I said, rolling my eyes. 'Nothing like in the movies.'

I could imagine him smiling.

'Okay,' he said. 'I saw somewhere in the file that she was friends with a Scottish woman here, but when the Guardia Civil went to the address, she is not here now.'

'You mean, she's left Spain?'

'I don't know. But she is not in her apartment any more. Neighbours said she may have gone home – back to UK.'

'Do you have a name?'

'*Momentito*,' he said. 'I look.'

I pictured him scrolling down the screen, then eventually he spoke.

'*Sí*. Here is the name of her. Jane M . . . Mc . . . McAllister.'

He stumbled a little trying to get the name out. 'Is that how you say?'

'Jane McAllister,' I repeated. 'Yes. That's it. I don't suppose you have an address in Scotland?'

He was quiet for a second as though he was reading.

'No. Only she is in Glasgow.'

'It's a big city. A common name. You have any idea of her age?'

'Not for sure. But the neighbour say she was like fifty or something.'

I stifled a sigh. That didn't give me much to go on, but it was a start. I was going to have to do this the hard way.

'Okay, Pablo. That helps. Maybe I can track her down here.'

'Good luck with it. You think you come here?'

'Not at the moment,' I said. 'But you know what would be really helpful, Pablo?'

'What?'

'Well, if there was any chance you could maybe find out a little more about Cathy Evans – you know, like where she used to drink and eat or who else would know her, who she may have been friends with? I'm thinking that with the police enquiry at the time, maybe they were satisfied with what they saw, you know, on the face of it, but perhaps it needs more looking at. I mean, just if you could find the time.'

He didn't answer at first and I hoped I hadn't overstepped the mark.

'I will see,' he said. 'But I cannot promise. I am working different times each day and night. But I see. If I find anything, I let you know.' He paused. 'And maybe you come over and buy me dinner?'

I could hear the mischief in his voice, and I knew that I had him on board, at least for the moment.

'Thanks, Pablo. I really appreciate it. For sure, I'd be happy to buy you dinner.'

'Okay, Billie. I must go. Good luck.'

'*Muchas gracias*,' I said in my best Spanish.

'*De nada, guapa*,' he replied as he hung up.

I smiled at his parting comment – 'You're welcome, beautiful.' It wasn't the kind of throwaway line I got if I ever called my old police boss DCI Harry Wilson for help.

My next call was to Tom Brodie, my lawyer friend who had dug out information for me on cases where most of the doors looked firmly shut. A hotshot lawyer in his day, Tom had fallen hard after his only son died from an accidental heroin overdose when he was trying to get clean. After the tragedy Tom hit the bottle even worse than usual, and in a few short years he'd lost everything – his marriage, his partnership in a top Glasgow law firm, and on top of that his confidence. The vicious circle of drinking to get him through a day in court spiralled out of control, and the word got around that Brodie was yesterday's man. I'd always found him an easy lawyer to deal with when I was a cop, even if he was defending whatever villain I had collared. So, when he was down on his luck we remained friends, and in fact he was a huge support to me when I went into meltdown myself after Lucas was taken. It was people like Brodie who got me through it, and I wouldn't forget it.

I'd used him in a couple of recent cases, though, and found that little by little he was beginning to come back to the Brodie I used to know. He knew how to strip down an investigation, to analyse, and he still had friends in all sorts of places. I'd told him on the phone about Cathy Evans and he said he would get to work finding names and connections that might lead us to her. When he called towards lunchtime to report what he had, I told him to come into the office and we could discuss it over a sandwich. While I was waiting, I put a call in to Gina.

'Gina,' I began. 'Did your mother ever mention a friend called Jane McAllister?'

'Jane McAllister?' she said, repeating the name.

I told her that the police in Spain had mentioned the name to me. I heard her pushing out a frustrated sigh.

'Well, they never mentioned the name to me.'

'Did your mum ever mention her?'

She took a couple of seconds to answer.

'I think I've heard the name before. But Mum had a few different friends – people she'd met in the area where she lived or in bars and things. I think I've heard her mention someone called Jane, but I don't know if that's the second name.'

'Can you remember if she said anything else about her? Like where she was from? Was she Scottish?'

Again, a couple of seconds as she seemed to be recollecting.

'I think she knew a Jane from Scotland. Glasgow, I seem to remember. But I never met her. Mum would mention various friends who she used to meet, but never really elaborated about them. She used to go to keep fit classes over there, and she met a few people through that. She seemed happy enough and that was all that mattered to me, that she wasn't alone out there and had friends.' She paused. 'I wish I'd paid more attention to everything now. I feel guilty.'

I knew all about guilt, about taking your eye off the ball and suffering the consequences. And perhaps she should have listened more to her mother, learned more about her friends. But I wasn't about to say that to her.

'Don't feel guilty, Gina. Your mum seemed to be having a happy enough life. It's not like having a twenty-year-old working and living in Spain, where you'd be asking more detail. Your mother had lived a life, and she would know from experience who she could make friends with.'

I said it more to make her feel less guilty. But my gut told me that there was something about her mother's life in Spain that she'd kept hidden from Gina, something that had consequences which led to her death that night. And the more I thought about it, the more I really wanted to find out.

Brodie was full of business when he breezed through the door, and I could hear him chatting to Millie from my office. I came out from behind my desk and went through to see him, glad that he was looking clear-eyed and healthy. He seemed upbeat.

'I decided to go to Martha Street,' he said. 'I thought I might as well see what I could dig out from the registry office on any Jane McAllister who may fit the bill.'

I nodded my approval. Martha Street was the place to register births, marriage and deaths in the city centre, and despite all the digital searches these days on social media, it was the old-fashioned way to find a birth or marriage certificate and take it from there, and sometimes it was the best.

'Find anything interesting?' I asked hopefully.

'Well,' he replied. 'Going for someone around the age of fifty, I managed to dig up three Jane McAllisters, all in Glasgow. And also marriage certificates for two of them. The assistant up there is great, and she went through all the Jane McAllisters from around forty, and there were only the three, so you have to hope that one of them is the right one. I know it's a long shot, but something to start with.'

'Of course,' I said. 'I wonder if McAllister is her own name, though, or her married name.'

Brodie raised his eyebrows as though anticipating the question.

'Yes, and if it's her married name, that narrows it down to two McAllisters. When I got the marriage certs out there were only the two, who had married in the seventies. So, we have two addresses to start. Of course, they may not be there now or haven't been for years, but you never know. A neighbour might know any background – such as if she has gone to Spain or something like that.'

I knew it was a long shot and was going to involve knocking on doors and following leads, but it had to be done.

CHAPTER SEVEN

By the time I'd knocked on a couple of doors of neighbours for the first address in Rutherglen in the east end of the city, it was clear I was drawing a blank. The Jane McAllister who lived there was married and working in the local baker's. When I began to question a little further, asking if they knew if she spent time in Spain, the neighbours eyed me with suspicion, asking me what this was all about. I told them I was trying to track someone down and that I was a private investigator and that seemed to calm them a little. But no, this Jane didn't go to Spain – she and her husband had a static caravan in Ayrshire and that's where they spent their holidays. I sighed to myself. That's how it goes sometimes.

I checked my watch as I made my way to my car. I had an hour before I was due to pick up Lucas, so I still had time to hit the second address. I was keen to get them done today, so that I could establish quickly if I was anywhere close to the right track.

The second address was on the opposite side of the city, a new-build estate of terraced and semi-detached houses up off Maryhill Road. I parked outside the house where there was a yellow citroën in the driveway and hoped for the best. No answer, and no sign of life behind the white door with the stained-glass inset window. I stood for a few moments, then a car pulled into the driveway two doors down. I waited until the woman got out and was unstrapping a toddler from the back seat.

'Excuse me,' I said as I approached.

She turned around, inquisitive.

'Sorry to disturb you, but I'm looking for Jane McAllister.'

She glanced over my shoulder to the house where I'd been.

'Yeah. That's Jane's house there,' the twentysomething woman said, lifting the child into her arms. 'But she'll be at work, I think. She works in the café down the road part time since she came back from Spain.'

I hoped my face didn't show the little surge of elation in the Spanish connection.

'Yes, she lived in Spain for a bit?' I said.

'Yeah. On and off for a while, after her man died. They had an apartment out there. Still got it, I think. But she's back now.'

Now and again, you do get a break in this job. I didn't want to push my luck by asking any more questions of this helpful young woman, as it was looking like this Jane was the woman I was after.

'Right,' I said. 'Thanks. I'll maybe pop back, or ... where does she work?'

'It's the Busy Bee Café just at the top of Byres Road.'

I thanked her and smiled at her toddler, who was waving to me, then turned and went back to my car.

The café was one of those trendy craft shops dotted around the west end of the city that are easy on the eye while you sit and enjoy a coffee. From the window it looked like there were only a few tables near the front, but I could see beyond that people were also seated towards the back. I went inside and had a look around the shelves while keeping an eye out for the staff behind the counter and waitresses who might be Jane McAllister. There were two women working on the counter, one who might have been in her fifties, and another who seemed to be waiting tables and looked too young. I took a seat as far away from the front as I could and waited. Within a couple of minutes, the young waitress came up and I ordered a flat white. When she brought it and placed it on the table, I looked up at her.

'Is Jane in just now?' I asked.

She glanced at me.

'Jane?'

'Yes,' I said. 'Jane McAllister.'

'Oh, right. I'm new here,' she said. 'Jane works in the kitchen. Do you want me to get her?'

'I don't want to disturb her if she's busy,' I said. 'But maybe if she had a moment?'

'Okay. I'll say to her.' She paused. 'Who will I say is looking for her?'

'If you say it's Billie. Billie Carlson.'

'Billie,' she said, giving me the look I'd seen many times when people can't quite figure out why a girl is called Billie.

She went, picking up empty cups from nearby tables and stacking them onto her tray. Then she disappeared through an archway that I assumed was the kitchen.

I didn't have a script for how I was going to handle this, because I had no hard evidence to be suspicious about the death of Cathy Evans. But my gut had told me there was something not quite right about it, and I was hoping that her friend might throw some light on her life on the Costa del Sol. I was halfway through my coffee when a woman came out from the arch and glanced in my direction, then walked from behind the counter, wiping her hands on a towel as she came towards me. Her cheeks were a little flushed, I assumed from working in the warm kitchen, and she looked a well-preserved fiftysomething woman, slim, with reddish hair and pale blue eyes made up with dark mascara and liner. She pulled her lips into a friendly smile but eyed me curiously.

'You're asking for me?' she said. 'I'm Jane McAllister.'

'Hi,' I said. 'Sorry to disturb you at work, but I wondered if we could have a chat some time? It's about Cathy Evans.'

Her expression changed from curious to cautious, and she automatically glanced over her shoulder.

'Cathy? Are you a friend of hers?'

'No,' I said, keeping my voice low. 'Her daughter, Gina, asked me to look into her death.' I searched her face. 'I'm a private investigator.'

She looked surprised, troubled, her brows knitting into a vertical line between her eyes.

'Really?' she said, seeming stuck for what else to say.

'Yes,' I said. 'At the moment I'm just contacting people who knew her. And looking into the circumstances she was found in. On the beach. The head injury.'

She shook her head sadly.

'I know,' she said. 'It was such a shock. So sad. We were good friends out there, and quite close. I was shattered when it happened.'

So far, so good. At least she wasn't asking to have me thrown out.

'Is there a time we could maybe have a chat?' I asked, looking her in the eye. 'I'm trying to get a picture of her life out there, who she was friends with, where she went. It would be great if you could help.'

She stood for a moment not answering, biting her bottom lip as though she was contemplating whether to get involved. Then she spoke.

'I get a break in about ten minutes,' she said. 'Maybe we could talk then. But not here. I could meet you up the road a bit.'

'Great,' I said. 'How about the entrance to Kelvingrove Park?' I gestured, nodding in the general direction.

'Okay.' She glanced around again. 'I'll see you there.'

I walked up Byres Road and crossed to the entrance of Kelvingrove Park and stood at the gates for a moment, gazing across the sweep of the hill and pathways. In an instant I was taken away from the rush of the city traffic to the tranquil, lush gardens in the shadow of Glasgow University, and where the River Kelvin winds its way down to the River Clyde. It felt like a lifetime ago when as a student I would spend long summer afternoons in the park, studying alone or along with other students, or walking hand in hand with whoever was my current boyfriend during those heady days when we were on the cusp of life with so many hopes and dreams. My reverie was broken by a voice from behind.

'Hi.'

I turned around to see Jane McAllister, her eyes watchful, a half-smile as she greeted me. I smiled back.

'I was daydreaming there,' I said. 'I used to love this park when I was at uni here.' I turned back to the entrance. 'You want to go up and have a seat on one of the benches?'

She nodded and we walked up the steep hill and sat down on a bench. Jane sat with her hands folded across her lap, looking straight ahead, waiting for me to start.

'So, Cathy Evans,' I began. 'Her daughter thinks there is more to her death than what the police have told her. They said it seems she had a lot of drugs and alcohol in her system and maybe fell and hurt her head and ended up on the beach. But her daughter is not convinced.' I paused, glancing at Jane for a reaction. There was none. 'What did you think at the time?' I asked.

She sat for a long moment not speaking, then took a breath and glanced at me sideways before staring straight ahead.

'It's . . .' She paused, then turned to me. 'I'm a bit worried to talk about it,' she said.

'Worried?' I asked, feeling a little twist in my gut. 'Why?'

She shook her head slowly and sighed.

'Cathy was a lovely woman. But she was naive. She made friends easily, probably because she was on her own in Spain, and like that, we became good pals. We would go to the same pub where karaoke and stuff was on some nights, and have Sunday lunch, and go to some beach bars. We had a good laugh, and talked about our old lives and how great it was to be living in the sun now.' She smiled, turning her gaze to me. 'That's the kind of woman Cathy was. She was obliging, trusting, that kind of thing. But you have to watch yourself over there. Some people are not what they seem, and you have to be careful who you mix with – that's how I've always been.'

'Did you see a lot of Cathy? How did you meet?' I asked.

'We lived in the same block of apartments,' she said. 'I had my own place, and Cathy was doing a long-term rent. I think she'd been over a couple of times to the area and stayed in hotels, but decided she wanted to live like the ex-pats, so she rented. That's how we met. By the pool one day, and we became instant friends.' She smiled. 'We used to go for early tapas in the evening and she would tell me all about her life. She had a hard time, you know, with her husband. And I think she just wanted to let her hair down now and live her life.'

'Understandable,' I said. 'Her daughter told me that her husband was cruel to her, so I can see why she would want to put all that behind her.'

'Yes,' she said. 'But, as I said, she was too trusting.'

'Do you mean with men or other people in general?'

'Both. She was easily taken in. One guy took a lot of her money. His name was Tony. He was a bit younger than her and good-looking, and she was infatuated, I suppose. She loaned him some money for a business deal he said he was doing – and that was the last she saw of him. And then . . .' She glanced at me, then away, sighing. 'Well, this is the bit I'm worried about talking about.'

'What do you mean?'

She took a breath.

'The people she became friends with. I just didn't like them. This couple. They were English but had Scottish friends too. We met them in a bar one night when the place was in full swing, and we all had a good laugh. They had a house there, an apartment or villa or something. They seemed to have a bit of money, always travelling to exotic places. Cruises and such. Very well-heeled.' She paused. 'But I didn't really fancy their company.'

'Why?' I asked.

She shrugged.

'I just felt it was a bit false. They were always buying drinks for us when we met them, or picking up the tab if we were having dinner. I mean, I liked them a bit, but I wouldn't class them as great friends. But I think Cathy was quite taken in by them.'

'Do you know the name of these people? Where exactly they live?'

'Marsden, they were called. Steve and Marilyn. Not sure where exactly they lived, but it was near Marbella.'

'What kind of ages were they?'

She screwed up her eyes.

'I think forties, maybe mid-forties. They looked well. Good clothes, and well-groomed and stuff. They were retired estate agents or something. Said they'd had their own business back in Manchester or somewhere. Said they were now living the good life.' She paused. 'They definitely had money. They were always going somewhere. Flying off to Dubai or going on cruises to the Caribbean or other places.' She stopped again, and swallowed. 'They even invited me and Cathy to go with them.' She turned to me. 'I mean, who does that? Invites anyone to join them on a cruise? All paid for? I wasn't even tempted. But Cathy was.'

I looked at her, surprised. Her daughter hadn't mentioned any of this, nothing about a couple who had befriended her mother to this extent.

'Did she actually go on a cruise with this couple?'

Jane nodded but didn't reply.

'What, like one time?'

She shook her head.

'More?'

'At least twice on a cruise, and a couple of times to Dubai when they invited her to a friend's birthday party.'

Alarm bells were going off all over my head. Jane's mobile rang and she took it out of her pocket.

'Look, Billie, that's the kitchen. They're really busy and asking me to get back. I have to go.'

She stood up, and I got to my feet, disappointed but intrigued by what she'd told me.

'Okay. But Jane, is there any chance we could talk again? I'm fascinated about these friends, and want to know a bit more.'

'I'm not sure,' she said. 'I . . . I'm not sure I should even have told you what I have.'

'Why? Are you afraid of these people?'

'I don't know. I just know that Cathy was fine until she met them, and now she's dead. I might be paranoid, but I just don't get it.' She stepped away. 'I have to go.'

'Can I call you?'

'I'll call you,' she said. 'I'll call your office.'

And she was off, quickening her step down the hill and out of the gate towards the traffic lights at the top of the road.

CHAPTER EIGHT

Elizabeth opened the windows to let out the smell of disinfectant. It was everywhere. The floors, the sinks, the bathroom, the bedroom. She'd bleached and scrubbed and cleaned every corner of the house so much since she'd come back that her fingers were beginning to feel raw. And all the time she was working, the flashbacks kept bombarding her – the expression on his face when he'd come out of the bathroom and caught her with his mobile phone in her hand. The slap, the beating, the running through the woods. She'd barely slept more than a couple of hours at a time since it happened, and she was at the stage where all she could do was try to keep a step ahead. Even when her husband had phoned her last night, she had to put on an act because he kept asking her if she was all right. He must have detected the stress in her voice. 'I'm fine,' she'd told him. 'Everything is fine. Just a little tired, that's all.'

In all their years of marriage, Elizabeth had known not to ask about Christopher; about his life outside of the university lecture tours and the sabbaticals he spent apparently teaching philosophy. She knew there was a double life, she'd known it from the very start, but they had made a pact never to speak of it, that she was never to ask, and she stuck to that. It had been a good life in many ways – the money, the lifestyle, the intellectuals they met, the old friends from the embassy days in far-off lands, and the visits and parties. But it wasn't honest, because nothing was ever as it seemed. When he was going off on a lecture tour of two or three European cities, often he told her that she couldn't come, and she wondered if it was during these tours that his secret life happened. What did he do? What did he spy on?

They'd been invited to dinners in Whitehall with top civil servants – but none of it felt honest, because she had to just be there, and these people probably knew she didn't know what went on, and was kept in the dark. Almost like an accessory to Christopher. So over the years, she drank too much. She never had an affair, although once or twice she'd come close. She wasn't even sure if she still loved Christopher or if he still loved her, because they were not the people they had been all those years ago. But the encounter of a few weeks ago was so far away from who she was. She could never forgive herself for the betrayal more than anything. Killing him was about survival and she could justify that to herself.

She hadn't seen the car heading down her driveway but caught the rear end of the dark blue vehicle as it left and turned right onto the road. She stood looking at it for a moment, watching as it disappeared, and she could only see the top of it over the hedge. She wondered if someone had been at the door, and she hadn't heard as she was at the back of the house. Perhaps it was a delivery of some sort? She often forgot when she'd ordered something, and a package turned up.

She went out into the hall, and there was a white A4-sized envelope on the doormat. It must have been pushed through the letter box. Curious, she picked it up. There was no stamp on it, so it had been hand delivered. She walked down the hall and into the kitchen carrying the envelope and placed it on the island worktop, then stood staring at it. *You're being silly,* she told herself, before walking across the kitchen and flicking on the kettle. She stood listening to the kettle warm up and prepared a mug of instant coffee, standing with her arms folded looking across at the envelope. The kettle pinged and she poured boiling water into the mug then carried her coffee over to the worktop, pulling up a stool to sit at the breakfast bar. She picked it up, sniffed it, half smiled to herself. What was she going to smell? she asked herself. *Just open the bloody thing.* Then she tore open the corner of the envelope and slid a fruit knife across the top, making a neat line. She peered inside, then turned it upside down and emptied the contents onto the worktop. Her stomach dropped. It was one sheet of paper. On it were letters that had been cut out of a newspaper, some capitals, some small letters. The letters danced in front of her eyes as she peered at them, putting them together, holding her breath.

YOU *WER*e SEEN. *in the* **woods**. Two oF *YO*u. THERe aRE P*i*cT*U*Res.

Terror lashed across her gut. She felt sick rising and rushed to the sink on shaky legs as she retched. When she composed herself, she stood up, wiped her mouth with a paper towel and ran the cold tap to fill a glass, her hands trembling. She took the glass and went across to the easy chair by the window and sat down. After a couple of deep breaths, she managed to get the glass to her lips and drink some water. Her head was swirling with all sorts of possibilities.

The car. It must have been that blue car that delivered the

envelope. She closed her eyes, trying to picture the car again as she'd seen it going down her driveway. What kind of car was it? She racked her brain trying to get a full picture of it. *Just slow down*, she told herself. *It will come to you.* She took herself back to the moment when she saw the car. The number plate. Did she even notice that? They do in the movies, but right now she was just seeing herself standing idly staring at the car before it was gone. Then it came to her. There was something on the back parcel shelf that she remembered. She closed her eyes tight. A rucksack. Yes. That was it. A green-coloured rucksack, like the kind you took if you were out for a hike. She didn't know why that was coming back to her now, in the midst of all these thoughts, but she definitely saw it. Now the car. What kind of car? It wasn't a big, luxury car, and not a tiny little run-around either. But she couldn't think what it was. She'd seen it a little from the side, enough to know that it wasn't small. Maybe like a family saloon car. But they were everywhere, and even if she did remember it, what could she do about it anyway? It's not as though she could go up and ask the driver if he or she had delivered something to her house.

She sat for a few minutes until she was fully calm, thinking straight. She drained the glass of water and stood up. She would go into the village and look around. Yes, it was probably ridiculous, but she had to do something. Sitting here going over and over the note that had been put through her door would drive her nuts. She would go down to the village for the first time since all this had happened and just walk around, maybe go for a coffee, pick up some things in the supermarket.

A few minutes later, she checked herself in the mirror in the hall as she pulled on a jacket and stepped out of the house, locking her front door and heading to her car. She took her car – she had used the Land Rover to drive to the cliffs, but the Merc was her own car. The old Land Rover sat in the yard, close to the barn, like some chilling reminder of what she'd done. She hadn't looked inside it since she'd bleached it from top to bottom, and she reminded herself that she would open its doors when she got back home just to let the smell of bleach out. Just in case anyone came snooping and wondered what she'd been bleaching.

The village was quiet as expected before the tourist season. Still a few cars parked along the front and a few more in the supermarket car park. Elizabeth found a parking space close to the exit, then grabbed her carrier bag as she got out of the car and headed for the supermarket. Inside she took a wire shopping basket and walked up the aisles, no clue what she was really there for, but she picked up one or two ready meals and some cold meats and salad stuff. She stopped at the fish counter and browsed the fresh fish all laid out on a bed of ice and stared at it as though she couldn't quite figure out what to do. She thought of buying a couple of salmon fillets and some hake that she could use in the next couple of days. Yes. That would do. She was about to smile up to the assistant behind the fish counter when a voice from behind made her freeze.

'Something fishy going on here, is there?'

'What?'

She felt the colour draining from her, then she turned, startled, but relieved to see the beaming face of her window cleaner standing grinning at her.

'Fishy,' he said, scanning her face, looking a little surprised at her reaction. He pointed to the counter. 'Fishy, I mean. The fish. Loads of it.'

Elizabeth managed a chuckle.

'Oh, right.' She smiled at him. 'I was miles away there, wondering what I'll have for dinner.'

'That salmon looks just the ticket,' he said. 'Fresh in this morning, eh, Tam?' He looked up at the assistant.

'It is that,' he said. 'Some fine fillets there.'

'You've talked me into it,' Elizabeth said, asking for two fillets, as well as some hake.

'How're things?' the window cleaner said. 'I'm due out to your place on Monday.'

'All fine,' she said. 'Looks like the weather is picking up.' Elizabeth tried her best to sound cheery.

'You around for long?' he asked.

'Not sure,' Elizabeth said. 'A few things going on. Might be heading back down south shortly.' She flashed her credit card onto the machine and put the items in her basket.

'Aye, back down to the big smoke. I don't know how you can stand it,' he said. 'All of them people. This is the place to be. So peaceful and beautiful, especially now the spring is nearly on us.'

'Yes,' she agreed. 'I do love it. But you know how these things are. Work and stuff.' She wanted away from this conversation right now. 'Oh well. I must get on,' she said, turning away from him.

'See you Monday,' he said, and she could feel him watching her as she left.

Elizabeth felt as though she was scurrying to her car to get as far away from the supermarket as possible. It was absurd and she knew it. She would have to calm down. She put her shopping in the car and walked to the end of the road and around to where her favourite café overlooked the water. It was quiet inside, only a few people having coffee and a couple braving the chill outside on bistro tables. She sat down, checking her phone and trying to put things in perspective. Somebody was out there who saw her that night. That was for sure. They saw her in the woods, as they said in the note. But what were they doing in the woods at three in the morning? Was it kids? Was it one guy, campers, a couple having a secret assignation? And it must have been someone who knew her, otherwise why would they even go to the trouble of leaving a message like that, menacing, making it look as though there were going to be more to follow? She would have to tell Billie Carlson and see what she said about it.

'Afternoon, Elizabeth.' The middle-aged waitress smiled down at her.

'Hello.' Elizabeth looked up, pushing her hair back and smiling. 'I was miles away there.'

'Yeah, we're all guilty of that, so we are.' Elizabeth had known the waitress, Maggie, for a couple of years since they'd met at a yoga class.

She ordered a coffee and scrolled through the messages on her phone. After a few minutes the waitress came back and set down her coffee, then looked at her.

'So,' she said. 'What have you been up to?'

Elizabeth's stomach lurched and she looked back, confused. 'What?'

'What you been up to?' Maggie repeated.

'I . . . er . . . Nothing.' Elizabeth was flustered and could see Maggie clocking her. She recovered quickly. 'Well, I was down the road a few days and glad to be back here in the peace and quiet.'

Maggie raised her eyebrows.

'Peace? Here? You missed all the action.'

Elizabeth looked at her, knowing she would have to say

something because the story had been all over the news. She nodded.

'Oh, yeah, the body that washed up. I saw that on the TV.'

'Place was busy with cops everywhere.' Then she lowered her voice. 'Nobody knows who he was. Some foreigner. Was in that hotel one night, but seems he never actually stayed there. Booked in and didn't come back. There are only a couple of people who saw him. Nobody else seemed to see him or even speak to him.'

'How strange,' Elizabeth said, her head cocked a little to the side, curious. 'Nobody knows who he was? Poor man.'

'Might have been drugs related,' Maggie said. 'That's the chat anyway. Maybe was dumped up the road a bit and washed up here.'

Elizabeth nodded but didn't answer. She took a big gulp of her coffee and tried not to wince as it burned the back of her throat.

'Police were in here at one point. Said to keep our eyes and ears open in case any scuttle comes up about this guy.' She paused. 'Were you away when this happened?'

Elizabeth swallowed hard, trying to stay calm. She had to.

'I can't remember,' she said. 'I can't remember exactly when it happened, but I think I was down in London. I just saw it on the news.'

'Yeah. Well, the police are still looking for clues. But to be honest, if they think its drugs related, they'll not be busting a gut. You know how it is.'

Elizabeth nodded but didn't answer and was glad when the waitress turned to leave.

'Anyway, duty calls. Enjoy your coffee, Elizabeth.'

Elizabeth slumped in her seat and let out a sigh. She was desperate to get out of here and run all the way back to her car, but she knew she couldn't. She sat for a few minutes until she finished her coffee, scrolling on her phone, then got up and left, leaving some coins on the table.

She walked along the street towards the car park, her eyes everywhere, glancing over her shoulder, feeling as though she was being followed. But there was nobody. Behind her dark glasses she peered at every car that passed to see if they were looking at her. Off-the-scale paranoia, she knew. But someone was out there, that was for sure.

In the car park she was glad to open the driver's door and sink into the seat, feeling the safety of isolation. She took a long breath and let it out slowly as she gazed out of the window at the sky changing colours, the puffy white clouds drifting away in the distance. Then she saw it. She was about to switch on her engine when a car glided past her and headed for the exit. From the corner of her eye, she spotted that there was a green rucksack on the parcel shelf. That had to be it. She quickly took a picture of the number plate because she knew in her rush she would never remember it. Then she waited for another car to pass in front of her before she pulled out behind it. She kept well back, and even allowed another car to pull out as they went onto the main road, and she began to follow. She had no idea where this would lead or how long she could afford to follow without being detected, but she had to give it a try. She had to find out who this was. It might not even be the right car. Plenty of people would have various items like rucksacks on the parcel shelf. But instinct told her she was doing the right thing.

She followed as the cars headed towards the traffic lights and all of them went straight ahead. Along the road a little and one of them turned off, so now there was only one car in front. She followed, well behind, but could still see the car, which looked like a blue Ford Focus or Fiesta or something similar, and it definitely rang bells with what she remembered seeing earlier. She strained her eyes to try to see if she could make out if it was a male or female driver. But she couldn't see. Then at the edge of the shore road, the car turned up to the right and pulled in at a mechanic's workshop. She slowed down and pulled into the kerb where she could see the car go into the small forecourt which had a couple of cars parked, and signs for MOTs, new tyres and budget tyres.

She watched as the driver's door opened and a woman climbed out. Then from a bay beyond, a guy came out from beneath a car that was jacked up and stood up, wiping his hands on a grimy cloth from his pockets. He went across to her and gave her a hug, but as he did, the woman pulled back and wiped her clothes as though to gesture to him not to get so close because he was filthy with oil and dirt from work. He wiped his forearms, and she followed him into the makeshift office attached to the workshop.

Elizabeth waited a few moments, read the sign on the front of the garage and took a couple of snaps of it, then sat wondering if that was them. They looked like a couple; there was obviously some romantic involvement. She wondered if perhaps they'd been on an illicit tryst in the woods late that night; wondered if they were both married. She couldn't recall ever seeing them around, but then again, she spent so little time in the village or in the pubs or cafés, was mostly away, and this place was really just a bolthole for her, and especially for her husband. Because of what he did, he needed somewhere off the grid a little.

So, she had nothing more than a deep suspicion. She needed more evidence. But she would call Billie Carlson with the information and the number plate and then it was a question of just watching and waiting. She had the feeling she hadn't heard the last of this pair yet – that's if they were the ones who had sent panic through her with that note.

CHAPTER NINE

I couldn't stop thinking about what Jane had said about the couple in Spain who had befriended Cathy Evans. Who takes people they barely know on lavish holidays for free? There's no such thing as a free holiday, and whatever Cathy was doing swanning around on cruises with this couple, I was convinced it wasn't innocent. The Costa del Sol was full of a myriad of ex-pats, most of them glad to have reached a stage in life where they could quit the rat race and kick back to enjoy the delights of the endless sunshine, hazy siestas and the pavement café lifestyle they only ever dreamed about when they were traipsing around their homeland, hunched over and stressed by heavy workloads. Those were the lucky, legit ones – and there were many of them.

But there were also just as many career criminals who had poured into the Costas from the seventies, and retirement was the last thing on their minds. There were the low-rent hoods who carried drugs across from Amsterdam and beyond, but also the big shots lording it in their lavish villas, where they could see the coast of Africa on a clear night, knowing there was a whole network of people working to bolster their empires while they never got their hands dirty. The top-drawer gangsters ploughed dirty money into bars and restaurants and property along the coast from Marbella to Torrevieja and beyond so that everything looked legit, and they employed clever accountants and lawyers to cover every track and make them untouchable. And they were, really. The united police forces of the UK and Europe trapped a few now and again, swinging onto yachts stacked with millions of pounds worth of cocaine destined for the streets of the UK. But for every haul seized, another one was on its way. And over the years, criminals had to seek out new ways to not just bring their drugs in, but to hide their money, stay one step ahead of the law.

Dubai, South America, Switzerland, Liechtenstein were full of grubby money. Gangland bosses outwitted the National Crime Agency at every turn. They used impressionable people to hide their money, and sometimes the simplest way was to pack it into a suitcase and travel to a foreign land where authorities didn't ask too many questions. I suppose we'll never know how high up the level of corruption went, but cops chasing the proceeds of crime would tell you it went all the way to the investment banks, who turned a blind eye to where money came from as long as it was being deposited in their bank. That's what makes the world go round, a gangster up to his neck in it once told me. Nothing to do with hard work.

So, what was the story with Cathy Evans? My gut feeling was that she was being used for something – smuggling, carrying money, or as some kind of decoy to make the big guys look innocent. But I hadn't a single piece of evidence to back any of that up. I didn't even know anything about the couple, who they were or their history – they could have been philanthropists who wanted to give something back. And even if I did find them, it wasn't going to bring Cathy back. But I couldn't let this go. My cop instinct told me there was more to it. I had to find out who exactly Steve and Marilyn were before Cathy's case disappeared off the radar for the cops in Spain.

I picked up my phone and pushed Tom Brodie's number. We spoke for a few minutes as I outlined everything I knew about Cathy Evans, and he too thought it was suspicious. Especially about the cruises and the trips to Dubai. While we were talking, I could hear him tapping keys on his computer.

'Hmmm,' he said. 'I see a Steven and Marilyn Marsden here with a host of credit cards – Visa, Mastercard, Amex.' He paused. 'Oh, and here's one with a Spanish address.'

'You're kidding me, right?' I said. 'Where are you seeing that?'

'If I told you, I'd have to kill you.'

'But have you actually found a Spanish address?'

'Well, yes. Oh, wait. Sorry. No. That's the address of the bank.'

'But there is a bank they have an account with somewhere in Spain?'

'Yes. Marbella. Banco Sabadell.'

'I'm more than impressed, Tom. You'll have to show me how you do this.'

'Not a chance,' he replied and I could see him grinning on the other end of the phone.

'I need more, though. I need to know where they live and any details of bank balances and stuff like that.'

'Well,' he said. 'I'd have to advise you as your lawyer that what you are requesting is highly illegal, madam.'

'Yeah,' I replied. 'But if they take me away in handcuffs, I know a shit hot lawyer who will bail me out.'

He chuckled.

'Okay. Leave it with me, Billie. I'll see what I can find, short of going out there and investigating.'

'Yeah, best to do what we can from here – for starters anyway. If we're going to be trampling over bank accounts, it's better we do it somewhere far away from people who might not be happy.'

'Correct. I'll keep digging and see what I can come up with.'

I thanked him and he hung up. I was pleased with what he had found so far, and just as glad for the way he sounded buoyed up for finding the information. It was good to see him emerging out of the depression that had dogged him for years, and that in itself was worth a lot to me.

My mobile rang on my desk, and I glanced across and saw Elizabeth Fletcher's name on the screen. I picked it up and pressed it to my ear.

'Elizabeth,' I said. 'How are things?' It was a routine greeting of mine, but as soon as I said it to her, it felt a kind of flippant question to ask someone who had just clubbed a man to death and pushed his corpse off a cliff.

There was a pause at the other end of the phone, then she spoke.

'Things, Billie,' she said, 'are more stressful by the minute.'

There was a little tremor in her voice. It was difficult to know what to say given how deep in the shit she was because of what she'd done, but I had agreed to take on her case, even though I couldn't see how there was ever going to be any kind of happy ending for her.

'What's going on?' I asked. 'Something happened?'

'Yes. Someone saw me that night.'

'What? Where?' I asked, trying to get a handle on how anyone could have been where she was in the middle of the night.

'I don't know. But maybe they were in the woods or something, you know, near my house. When I was running away from that bastard. He was chasing me, and I ran a good bit into the woods, and then realised I was going nowhere and that he was catching up, so I turned back and ran towards my house.'

'But it was about three in the morning, was that not what you told me?'

'Yes. But maybe someone was in the woods. There's a lovers' lane kind of spot off the road where the teenagers go for illicit sex so nobody can see them. Maybe someone was in there.'

'But how do you know you were seen? What's happened?'

'I got a letter. Shoved through the door of my house. Yesterday. I nearly died when I opened it.' She paused. 'I think I'm going to be blackmailed.'

'Shit. What did the letter say? Handwritten? Typed?'

'It was in an envelope. It was written using letters cut out of newspapers. All it said is "you were seen in the woods. There are pictures."' She paused. 'Pictures. I mean, Christ almighty, who takes pictures in the woods in the middle of the night? I'm totally wired here. I think I have an idea who did it . . . I've been watching all over the place.'

'Hold on, Elizabeth,' I said, trying to sound calm. 'Let's just take this stage by stage. No point in getting hysterical about it right now. What have you done so far? Did you see anyone at your house delivering the note?'

'No. I've been cleaning and bleaching for days to get rid of any signs that forensics might find if they come in here. Which they might, you never know. I need to get out of here. My husband will be back in a few days, but I don't want him here. I'm going to get him to come to London. Anywhere but here.'

She sounded close to the edge, and it was easy to see why. She'd told me about her lifestyle, the money and the wealth and travel and her respected lecturer husband. She didn't know what he had been involved in in recent months, but he had probably been working for the security services. Maybe he had become trapped in something, because why would some Russian guy have his mobile phone number under a different name? But whatever it was, now everything was in tatters because she'd got drunk and picked up a man, who may well have been there seeking her out for another reason. I was nowhere near finding anything out about this guy as he was still unknown to the cops and they didn't appear to care that much, with newspapers saying that it seemed likely it had been a hit from a drugs gang, and he'd been dumped into the sea somewhere and had washed up at Portpatrick.

'So, what makes you think you know who sent the letter?' I asked.

'I remembered the car, and that it had a rucksack on the parcel shelf. So, in town I've been watching all the cars over a day or so, and suddenly I saw this car in the supermarket car park. I followed it. It was a woman driving and she drove into a garage forecourt and went towards a guy who came and hugged her, and they went through the back.'

'Do you know these people?'

'No. But there is some kind of relationship there. He kissed her on the lips. Maybe they're having an affair. Maybe they're both married. Maybe that's why they were in the woods that night. You know, meeting in secret.'

'At three in the morning?'

'Well, I was running through the woods at three in the morning being pursued by a man, so it's not unheard of,' she said.

I didn't want to argue the point, but I thought she was right. She was about to be blackmailed.

'Can you come down and see me? See what you can find down here?'

I thought about it, the journey, the possible stay overnight. Could I take Lucas and maybe Millie down for a couple of days and see her? Or maybe I should just leave him with Millie and go down by myself, do it in one day, have a dig around and see if I could come up with anything?

'Are you there, Billie?'

'Yes. I'm here. Was just thinking of the logistics, Elizabeth. I have a three-year-old son, and I don't like leaving him overnight. I have to think how I can do it. I may have to leave him with a friend who can take care of him and come down for one day. Maybe early in the morning and come back in the evening. I should be able to get a handle on this couple if you think that's who it is. Meanwhile, I think you are right about the blackmail. Someone is chancing their arm. You'll probably get another letter very soon.' I picked up my pen. 'Can you tell me the name of the garage and I can find out who owns it, works there and stuff? And what about the car you followed with the woman in it. Do you have the reg?'

She reeled off the name of the garage and the registration.

'I'll get on this and see what I can come up with. Let me look at coming down in the morning. Very early on.'

'Thanks, Billie.'

'And let me know if there is any other contact. Anything at all.'

'Okay. I will.'

'I'll text you once I'm near the village.'

CHAPTER TEN

After I hung up I sat for a while at my desk gazing out of my office window at the early afternoon sky, glimpses of blue in between the broken clouds, my thoughts drifting to how different my life was these days. Until I had Lucas back in my life, waking to his sweet smile and the warmth of his hand in mine as I walked him each day to the doors of his nursery, everything I had done seemed to be on autopilot. I didn't realise that at the time – you don't think about these things when you are just trying to survive, put one foot in front of the other each day, get through until the part of me that was missing was finally found.

It had only been a few months since I found Lucas and brought him home, yet in the times I had looked back at who I was before this, I can hardly believe it was me. I had completely thrown myself into work, once Scanlon had convinced me and cajoled me that I had to pick myself up or it was sink or swim time. In those days, to keep my depression and desperation at bay, I took on cases, difficult ones, all sorts that would keep me occupied. I seldom turned down a case, whether it involved leaving town for a few days or digging in and staking out a house or premises overnight. But things were different now. I had Lucas to consider at every turn, and although I wouldn't change it in a million years, it restricted how I did business.

Having had the conversation on the phone with Elizabeth, I'd normally have driven down to the Ayrshire coast tonight, set up in a hotel and stayed for a few days making discreet enquiries. But I didn't want to leave my son. I thought of taking off with him for a couple of days down the coast, maybe taking Millie with me, booking into a small hotel, and she could look after him while I went about my investigation. But something niggled me about this whole Elizabeth affair, and my instinct told me not to take Lucas anywhere near a situation that might become dangerous. The guy she killed – perhaps he was there to find something out about her husband through her. His bosses would have sent him there. They would know by now that he was dead, even though no one had claimed the body. Perhaps this wasn't over yet for Elizabeth, and I had to deal with things one step at a time.

The people who were obviously planning to blackmail her with the menacing letter would have to be tracked down. In a small village it would be easy to find out where I was staying and all the stuff that would identify me, and the last thing I wanted was for Lucas or Millie to be anywhere near that. But I also didn't like leaving him overnight. I talked to Millie about it, and she agreed with me, and offered to pick him up from nursery tomorrow, give him dinner and put him to bed at my flat in case I wasn't home by the end of the night. My mobile rang and brought me out of my reverie. It was Elizabeth again.

'It's me,' she said. 'You'll not believe it, but I just got another note through the door. Must have been while I was on the phone to you from the kitchen and I didn't even hear anyone coming up the driveway. Jesus!'

'Have you opened it?'

'No.'

'Do you want to open it now?'

'You think I should?'

'I think you have to, Elizabeth.'

'Okay.'

There was the sound of paper being scraped and then rustling. And then a gasp on the other end of the phone.

'Fuck! It's a photograph. My God. I can't believe this.'

'Just take a moment,' I said calmly. 'Look closely at them.'

'I don't need to look closely to see that it's me running in my pants and vest through the bloody woods, and this bastard behind me. It's as clear as anything. You can see my face from the side, and him, he's bare chested and in jeans.'

'Is there a note?'

'Yes. Shit.'

'What does it say?'

'Hold on. Let me read it again.'

'Christ. Here's what it says: "If you want to get rid of these pictures, it will cost you. Phone this number for a meet."'

'Give me the number.'

I knew it would be a burner phone unless the people were completely stupid. She gave me the number and I wrote it down.

'Okay. I'll check it out, but I'm sure it won't be traceable. Don't phone the number tonight. I'll get down early in the morning and you can call it then. Arrange a meeting. See what they say.'

'What will you do? We can't go to the police?'

'I know. We'll see. I'll come down tomorrow. We can't decide now. Just stay in the house tonight. Lock all the doors and stuff. Don't go out.'

'You're scaring me now.'

'Sorry. I don't think these people are threatening, they'll just want money. But best to stay out of sight for now. I'll come to your house if you text me directions. Or better still, meet me outside the village somewhere, so you're not seen with me. I'll see you tomorrow.'

I hung up. I called Scanlon and he answered after two rings.

'Telepathy, Carlson. I was going to call you just this minute.'

'You must be thinking about me all the time,' I said, smiling to myself.

'Of course!' he replied.

I could hear him chuckle. I loved the sound of his voice more these days than I ever believed was possible just a few months ago. He was always my biggest supporter and shoulder to cry on in the bad times, but lately whatever it was we'd had between us over the years had grown into something bigger. He'd been spending some nights sleeping over at my house and although I had been reluctant to let anyone else into my life now that I had Lucas all to myself, it just seemed to work between us. Lucas was crazy about him and was thrilled every time I told him he was coming over and we would be eating out or staying home together. I had really no idea where this was going but this was the happiest I'd felt in any time I could ever remember as an adult. If I was going to have a proper grown-up relationship with Scanlon, I wasn't even sure how we would do it, but for the moment it felt good.

'You go first,' I said. 'What did you want to call me about?'

'I finish early today and was going to see if you wanted to take Lucas out to eat.'

'Or we could eat in,' I said, 'maybe go for a walk in the park first if the weather keeps up, then go home and get a takeaway. I've an early start in the morning so need to get stuff ready.'

'What you up to?'

'You wouldn't believe it if I told you.'

'Yes, I'm sure I would, Carlson.'

'Okay. Meet me at nursery when I pick Lucas up and we'll go for a walk, and I'll tell you then. How does that sound?'

'Are you going to stress me out?'

'I hope not. But first, can you do me a favour and check out a car reg for me?'

'Okay, let's hear it. I'll try and get it before I meet you.'

'You're the best, Scanlon.'

'I know. I've told you that many times. See you later.'

Lucas came running towards me as soon as the double doors opened and the nursery children spilled out. It always amazed and delighted me that every day he was so thrilled to see me even though we'd only been apart for around four hours. I wondered if there was a little trigger inside of his head some-where that made him think back to a time when he'd been taken, and perhaps he'd looked for me and I wasn't there. I'd asked the child psychologist about this, worried that maybe he didn't trust me to not be around, because even in the flat, if I'd go into another room and he couldn't see me, he'd be calling out after me. He wasn't upset or stressed, but there was always the odd hint that the scars of being snatched from me so young and without warning would take some time to heal.

'Hey, wee guy,' I said, ruffling his hair. 'You want to go to the park? Danny's coming to meet us.'

'Yeah, yeah!' He was bouncing. 'Danny's coming! When? Is he coming to the park too, Mummy?'

'Yes, darling. We're going together. Then we can get dinner at home later. How do you like that?'

'That's a great idea, Mummy.' He squeezed my hand as we walked out of the gate.

As we approached my car, I saw Danny casually leaning against the bonnet, a smile spreading across his handsome face when he saw us. Lucas broke away from me and raced towards Danny's outstretched arms, and he picked him up and swung him around.

'All right, wee man?' Danny said, planting a kiss on his cheek.

'We're all going to the park, Mummy says.'

'Well . . .' Danny put him down on the pavement as I opened the car. 'If Mummy says it, then it must be true.'

He opened the back door and strapped Lucas into his seat. Then he came around the car to me and kissed me lightly on the lips.

'You okay, Billie?'

'Yes. All good,' I said. 'I've a few things to tell you.'

He gave me a sideways glance as he opened the passenger door and got inside and we drove up towards Byres Road and Kelvingrove Park.

We walked up the path to the top of the park and I sat on a bench for a bit while Scanlon played chase with Lucas, running after him as he bolted across the grass and hid behind the shrubs. He was shouting, 'You can't find me, Danny!' and I laughed as he was easy to see even from where I was sitting a few yards away. Danny had to go through the motions of trying to work out where he was, and then Lucas shouted, 'I'm over here!' It made me chuckle, the logic of kids playing hide-and-seek, who tell you where they're hiding before they start. After a while, Danny went to the ice cream van and bought a cold drink for Lucas and coffees for us, and we all sat on the bench watching the people up and down the park, dog-walkers, tourists, students on the way to university.

'So, what's the sketch with this car?' Scanlon said. 'I've got the details for you.'

'Great stuff, Danny. Thanks.'

'The car is a Ford Focus. Belongs to Theresa Doyle. Address in Portpatrick. She's thirty-eight years old.' He looked at me. 'What's she done?'

I took a breath and puffed as I glanced at him then straight ahead.

'Where do I start?' I shook my head.

'She in trouble?'

'It's a long story, Danny,' I said, knowing that I would have to tell him and aware that he would go off the edge when I did. I was also considering not telling him, because he's a cop, and once I told him he would then be in possession of crucial information about a crime and having the knowledge of it placed him in a tricky position. But I couldn't leave him out of it as I'd done before and keep things secret. It wasn't fair to him. 'Well. She could be. But she's not the big player in this case. The main woman is a lady who has a house in Portpatrick – she's English but she and her husband have a holiday home there. And she got in touch with me last week.' I shook my head. 'It's crazy.'

'What's she done?'

I took another breath.

'You remember that guy who washed up a few weeks ago on the beach down there? Wasn't a huge story as his body was never claimed.'

Scanlon narrowed his eyes as though trying to recall the case.

'Yeah, I do remember it. Word was that he might have been some guy dumped over a drugs deal gone wrong or something. He had a Russian passport but was never identified by anyone and police couldn't track relatives. Probably a false passport.' He turned to me. 'What's he got to do with your client?'

I waited as long as I could before I answered but I knew I had to come out with it because there was no easy way to say this.

'My client. Her name is Elizabeth Fletcher. Posh, middle class – I'll tell you her background later over dinner. But, well, how can I put this without alarming you?'

He raised his eyebrows in anticipation.

'She killed him,' I said in a low voice.

'What?'

'Yep. She killed him, because he was trying to kill her. Then she drove his body to the cliffs down at Portpatrick and pushed him over.'

'Oh, Christ, Billie!' Scanlon shook his head and rolled his eyes to the sky.

Lucas pulling at his arm, broke into the moment and I was glad.

'Come on, Danny. Come on, we'll race.'

'Okay, kid. Let's go.'

Lucas was off like a shot, looking over his shoulder, his voice lilting as he sang, 'You can't catch me, Danny!'

We bought fish and chips from the Italian chip shop near my flat and ate our dinner straight from the paper, washed down with milk for Lucas and sparkling water for Scanlon and me. Afterwards, as I ran a bath for Lucas, Scanlon helped him build a jigsaw then carried him to the bath on his back. By the time I got Lucas ready for bed he was so tired he wasn't even protesting or asking to stay and play with Scanlon. I tucked him in and read him a story, and he was asleep by the second page.

Scanlon was standing in the kitchen.

'You want some tea?' he asked.

'No. It will keep me awake and I want to be on the road early in the morning as soon as I drop Lucas at nursery.'

'So,' he said, coming into the living room and putting his arms around me. 'Are you going to tell me what's going on?'

I hugged him then we sat down on the sofa, and I turned to him.

'To be honest, Danny, I really don't like telling you any of this because it involves a crime, and I don't want to put you in a difficult position.'

He nodded.

'I understand that, Billie. But if you're getting mixed up in something that involves a murder, then you really need to think twice about what you're doing. And I know it puts me in a difficult position, but I see things a bit different between us these days.' He took hold of my hand. 'I care what happens to you. Everything. I worry if you're going down one of these rabbit holes you tend to seek out without thinking because who knows how it will pan out.' He sighed. 'I just wish you wouldn't get involved at all with whoever this woman is in the car or who-ever this woman is who said she killed that man. Do you think she's telling the truth? I mean, why didn't she go to the cops?'

'Because she feels she can't. She's, well, she's something of a . . . what can I say? Not a public figure, but her husband works for the security services. Both of them worked for the Foreign Office in various countries over the years.'

'She's a spook?'

'Not sure. I don't think so. But she says her husband is. And he's also a very well-known and prominent university lecturer in politics all over the world.'

'They'll both be spooks,' he said.

'Yes, maybe,' I agreed. 'She told me he was a spy.'

He was silent for a moment. 'So, this dead guy with the Russian passport – it's not a coincidence she encounters him in a place like Portpatrick?'

'She met him in a bar. She was drunk and she took him home.'

'What?'

'Yes. So she says.'

I told him everything that Elizabeth had told me, blow by blow, and then about the menacing letters shoved through her door and the photographs. I'd seriously considered over the last couple of days telling him about the connection Elizabeth claimed to have had with my father. But it just didn't feel right to be taking as gospel that she was telling the truth. So, for the moment I'd keep it to myself. There was already enough meat on Elizabeth's story for Scanlon to pick away at.

'And these chancers are going to blackmail her?'

'Looks like it.'

'What are you going to do tomorrow? Front them up and accuse them?'

'I'm not sure how I'm going to do it. I'm taking Dave Fowler with me. I asked him earlier and he's keen to go. It's good to have him, though I'm not expecting any strong-arm stuff from anyone. But I want it wrapped up in a day as I don't want to leave Lucas overnight. Millie is picking him up and I hope to be home by the time he's in bed. It's just a run down there to see the lay of the land.'

'And what about this Elizabeth woman? What is she going to do? Just get away with murder and bolt somewhere?'

'It was self-defence, Danny. Not just cold-blooded murder.'

'If she'd talked to the cops after the attack, she wouldn't be in this mess. But once you start dumping bodies, everything else in your defence goes out of the window. You know that.'

'Yes. And so does she. She doesn't want to tell the police and drag her husband into it. She thinks this guy was sent to her to find something out, but she doesn't know what. And she has this USB stick she took from his pocket.'

'What?'

'I don't know what's on it, but she said she saw her husband's phone number on his mobile with a different name – it was a Russian name – so she feels there is something very scary going on and she just wants away from here quickly before anyone starts blackmailing her and she ends up trapped.'

Scanlon was silent for a while. He sat back, his hands behind his head.

'You know what you should do, don't you, Carlson?'

'Yes. But I can't go to the police, Danny. You know that.'

CHAPTER ELEVEN

I was glad Dave Fowler suggested taking his car for the trip to Portpatrick as it's big and comfortable. Plus he was driving, which left me free to make the odd phone call or read an email. As well as that, I wanted him to meet Elizabeth and see what his take on this woman was and if she was everything she said she was. Fowler had been helping me on investigations since coming back down to Glasgow from the Highlands, where he'd been living a quiet life as a retired detective. He was an old-school cop at heart, and in one encounter not long ago he saved my life after a thug tried to throw me over a staircase in a block of flats.

I already had Brodie trying to dig up anything on Elizabeth Fletcher, but so far there was nothing, only that she was the wife of a respected university lecturer and they had both worked for the Foreign Office in the past. If people work with the Foreign Office, you tend never to know much about what they do for security reasons. But I know that for many of them, even if they seem to have minor diplomatic meet and greet roles in far-flung embassies, there is much more to it than that. Foreign Office staff in places like Moscow or Bogotá are not there to fill in forms for tourists who may get into difficulty. If they are working in Africa, South America or in Russia or any other British embassies, they are there principally to gather intelligence. Nobody in authority would ever admit that but it was a given.

'So, this Elizabeth woman. Do you think someone is after her because of the guy she killed? What about this USB stick? How come she doesn't let you have it?'

'She told me she wasn't ready to hand it over, but she would the next time we met. We'll see.'

When I'd told Fowler the grisly details of Elizabeth's case, he had the same reaction as Scanlon – that I should think seriously about what I was doing before I got any more involved and consider talking to the cops. When I told him there was client confidentiality and that she had come to me and confided in me what she'd done, he said none of that really washed because she had killed someone. It was as simple as that. I knew everything he was saying was right, but the main reason I didn't want to let Elizabeth go was because of what she had said about knowing my father. That had been the first time anyone had ever really spoken about my father that I remembered since his funeral. Even my steely, miserable Aunt Lily in Sweden, who had become my guardian and with whom I had to live from the age of twelve, only mentioned my father less than a handful of times.

The fact that Elizabeth said her husband had worked with him as a lecturer intrigued me. My memories of my father were fading, as were some of my memories of the early times we had together as a family, and I desperately wanted her to be able to tell me something new, like what he was really like, where he went, what he talked about. Now, on this long journey where Fowler had talked to me about his life and about how much being in Glasgow had lifted him, I felt I was close enough to him to share the fact that Elizabeth had mentioned

my father. It felt something like a betrayal by telling Fowler
and not having told Scanlon. But Fowler would have to know
about it if he was going to be sitting in on any conversation I
had with Elizabeth, so I had to tell him.

'Dave,' I began. 'There's something I haven't told you about
Elizabeth, that's really the driving force for me taking her case.
A personal reason.'

He glanced from the side of his eye, brows knitting.

'What? What do you mean? Did you know this woman
already?'

'No,' I replied. 'Not at all.' I hesitated, and we exchanged
glances as he slowed down a little to listen. 'It's just that when
I spoke to her on the phone for the first time, she said something that intrigued me, and I haven't been able to get it out
of my mind.' I paused. 'She said she knew my father. That her
husband and my father were lecturers together and that they
were good friends.'

Fowler pulled over into a layby and switched off the engine,
turning to me.

'Really? She knew your father? How can that be? Your father
would be . . .' He screwed up his eyes, trying to think. 'He'd be,
what, about seventy years old by now? This Elizabeth woman.
How old is she?'

'I think late forties maybe. But younger looking.'

'Then, she would be early thirties maybe when your father
died?'

'I guess.'

'And if her lecturer husband was around the same age as
your father, that would make him about seventy now.'

I nodded.

'Yes. I thought about that too. But she might have been

much younger than her husband at the time. Maybe he was around fortyish, and she was fifteen or twenty years younger.' I shrugged. 'I suppose that would work.'

'Hmmm. Yes. I suppose. Have you asked her about any of that?'

'No. Not yet.'

'Why?'

I took a breath and pushed it out.

'I don't know. Maybe I'm just apprehensive. Maybe somewhere inside I don't want to go back there, you know, to the pain of losing my dad. Nobody ever spoke about him after he died, except my mother of course, but then she died within the year. I think I just tried to shut most of it out. And now, suddenly Elizabeth walks into my life and tells me she knew my father. To be honest, I'm just trying to process that in my mind before I ask her anything else. I just want to know more about her, about what is going on before I start asking her about my father.' I paused. 'I'm just so shocked that she mentioned it. I mean, what are the chances of someone like that, after what she's done, walking into my life and telling me this? Did she even know who I was? I haven't even asked her what made her come to me and not a private investigator in London or anywhere else. I'm just not sure of her, that's what I'm trying to say.'

Fowler sighed.

'I hear what you're saying, Billie. Maybe you should think twice before you get any more involved with her.'

'I know that too, Dave. But I can't. I have to find out more. I have to know more about my father. I've never thought about looking back before. But she came like a bolt out of the blue, and my instinct is telling me that I need to look further.' I turned to him. 'Does that sound crazy?'

He switched on the engine and pulled out onto the coast road.

'Yes,' he said, glancing at me with an empathetic smile. 'But you know what? I'd feel exactly the same as you. However, I'm glad you told me, as it gives me a fuller picture once we start talking to her.'

We had arranged to go to Elizabeth's cottage at her suggestion, as she wanted to show me the set-up of where it all happened on that fateful night. I'd called her on the way into the sea-side village for directions, and it was only then that I'd told her I was bringing Fowler in on the meeting. She'd sounded suspicious at first, but I put her at ease and said that he was entirely trustworthy and that he works with the agency from time to time. Fowler pulled off the main road up a country lane then turned left into the small dirt track road that led to her cottage. To our right we could see the wooded area where she must have run that night, and to the left as we climbed the road, we could see the sea and the cliffs not too far away. The gravel path scrunched noisily under the weight of the Land Rover, and we parked in what looked like a courtyard next to some outbuildings and what may have been the barn she'd told me about where it all happened.

In the stillness there was something a little eerie about the place. From the front the old cottage looked tired, with old-fashioned windows and a mahogany door, and there was a big weeping willow tree in the garden at the side of the house where a couple of wicker chairs and a table sat in the middle. For a moment I tried to imagine what it must be like to be running for your life so far away from help and with no quick way out, and I gave a little shudder. Through the stained-glass window on the door, we could see the shadow of a figure coming down the hall. The door opened and she gave me as

much of a smile as I suppose she could muster, then glanced
Fowler up and down.

'Elizabeth, this is Dave Fowler who I was telling you about.'

'Elizabeth.' Fowler stretched out his hand and she shook it,
if a little apprehensively.

'As I told you, Dave and I work together a lot on cases, so you
have nothing to worry about with him being here.'

'Are you a policeman?' she asked, looking him in the eye.

'Ex-cop,' Fowler said, half smiling. 'But good spot. I've not
been a cop for a number of years now. But don't let the ex-
policeman worry you. I'm well out of it.'

She nodded, but didn't answer, just bit her lip.

'So, do you want to go somewhere, Elizabeth, to talk?' I
asked, changing the subject.

She looked out at the weather, clouds gathering on the
horizon, and shook her head.

'Don't think so. Best we just go inside, and I'll make some
coffee. I can rustle up some lunch – some sandwiches if you like?'

'Sure, whatever,' I said. 'Don't go to any trouble, though.
Coffee would be fine.'

She stepped back and pulled the door open wide.

'Come on in.'

We followed her down the hallway, Fowler and me
exchanging glances and him giving me a look that said she
wasn't that happy to see him. She led us into the kitchen,
which was neat and tidy, with a big island in the centre with
a black marble worktop. She filled the kettle and gestured to
us to sit at the breakfast bar, where papers were lying and a
brown envelope and I spotted a photograph next to them. She
spread her hands.

'There it is,' she said. 'The blackmailing bastards that they
are.'

'May I?' I asked as I went forward to the island where the documents lay.

'Of course,' she said.

Fowler joined me, and while she took mugs out of the cupboard, we shot each other a glance as I picked up the photograph and examined it. It was dark, a little grainy, but you could clearly make out two figures running. I looked at Fowler as I put it back on the worktop and we both leaned in, examining it closely.

'Looks like a mobile phone pic,' he said. 'Whoever took this is a good distance away – you can see the trees in the darkness.'

'Yes. Whoever it was, they must have been in the stretch of wood I told you about, Billie,' Elizabeth said as the kettle pinged. 'The wooded area is only less than a hundred yards from here, just next to the bottom of my garden. They must have been in there.'

'Elizabeth,' Fowler said as she set down the cafetiere and mugs on the worktop. 'Do you think there could be any connection with whoever was in the woods and the man who was pursuing you? I mean, could it be that it was him they were watching?'

She screwed up her eyes and puffed.

'You know, I've never even thought about that as a possibility. It didn't occur to me at all. I just assumed it was somebody out in the woods for a secret bit of sex or something.'

I hadn't thought it was connected either but given what Elizabeth had told me about her husband being a spy, anything was possible.

'I don't think it can be related, though,' Elizabeth said. 'Because that woman I followed in the car, the one I think delivered the note, and the guy she met in the garage when I followed her . . . they didn't strike me as being involved in the secret squirrel stuff that spooks get up to.'

Fowler nodded.

'Yes. You're probably right. Just wondered.'

I picked up the two notes and looked closely at them. Large bold newsprint meant to look both menacing and also anonymous.

'I checked the reg of the car, her name and address. The woman is local.' I turned to Elizabeth. 'Do you know a lot of people in the village?'

She shrugged.

'Not really. Couple of people I met at a yoga class, but I don't go any more. I've been away a lot of late and my husband hasn't been here for at least three months. Usually when he's home we meet at our place in London. He was supposed to be coming here in the next week or so, but I've put him off. I want to get out of here to be honest.'

There was a long moment when nobody spoke, but I could see from Fowler's expression that he wanted to address the elephant in the room. Finally, he did, and I watched Elizabeth for a reaction.

'Elizabeth, have you seriously considered at this stage that it might not be too late to go to the police?'

'No way. I can't go down that road. No chance.'

'I can see why,' Fowler pressed on. 'But it strikes me that the hole you have dug for yourself is getting bigger all the time.' He paused. 'You know, the police option might not be as bad as it sounds to you.'

'Not a chance in hell. Can you imagine what going to the police would drag up?' she said, the colour rising in her neck. 'Never mind my drunken indiscretion with a complete stranger who I killed while defending myself, and the little fact that I disposed of his body, my husband would be dragged into all this, and I can't afford to let that happen.' She paused, looking from Fowler to me. 'I don't really know the extent of my husband's work and I never will. There is no way in the world I can or would even consider compromising his position.'

We stood, her words hanging in the air, and I was thinking of our next move.

'Elizabeth, I think you should phone that number and arrange a meeting, somewhere that Dave and I could be nearby. Maybe all you need to do to get this couple off your back is to monster them a bit.' I turned to Dave, half smiling. 'He's quite good at that.'

She nodded but didn't answer. I went on.

'It would be good to know just what they have. If they have put two and two together and decided that the man who was chasing you may be the man who was washed up on the beach, you should make the call.'

'Okay, I will.'

'But before you do that, can we have a look at the USB stick?' I asked. 'Have you looked at it yourself?'

'No.'

'Okay. Let's have a look at it.'

She nodded then disappeared out of the kitchen and Fowler and I stood for a moment.

'She's a piece of work that one, I'd say,' Fowler whispered.

I nodded but said nothing. She was indeed a piece of work, and a big part of me didn't want much to do with her. But when the time was right, I wanted to probe her further about what she had said about my father. That was the real reason I was here.

CHAPTER TWELVE

It was going to be a long afternoon. I had no idea if the phone call from Elizabeth to the number on the menacing note would result in a meeting today. But I hoped so. I'd told Lucas this morning that Millie would be picking him up from nursery and I would see him tonight. He looked pleased as he loved being with Millie. But just before he let go of my hand to go through the door, he turned to me and asked, 'You coming back tonight, Mummy?' It wasn't the question, it was the look in his eyes, a little shadow of apprehension. It wasn't fear, but now and again, somewhere in a place I had yet to reach inside him, there were glimpses of a little lost boy and it made me want to scoop him up and take him home and stay with him for ever. But life wasn't like that, so off he went, reassured that I would see him by bedtime, and I was determined to make it happen.

We decided to take a look at the USB stick before we made any phone calls, and I retrieved my laptop from Fowler's car and set it up at the kitchen table where Elizabeth had prepared some chicken sandwiches. Elizabeth hovered behind Fowler and me as I inserted the stick into my laptop and watched as it sprang to life. As the pages came up, I could see there were mostly web links – some of them in a foreign language, Russian or Eastern European, I guessed – that didn't make any sense to me, not that

I expected they would. Then there was a list of contacts: foreign names and phone numbers. Elizabeth watched as I scrolled through them, then put her hand on my shoulder.

'Stop,' she said. 'That number there. That's my husband's phone I was telling you about. It's his regular phone number that I call him on all the time. But look at the name. It's not his name.'

I glanced at Fowler, and he half shrugged with a look that said none of this made any sense to him.

'Have you phoned that number?' I asked.

'No,' Elizabeth said. 'I don't want to go anywhere near it at the moment.'

I kept scrolling through links and names, none of it making any sense. It seemed to be in some sort of code. I sat back. Then I looked at Fowler.

'How about that guy of Brodie's who helped us track down the phantom Bob?' I said. 'He might be able to make some sense of it?'

I looked at Elizabeth.

'I have someone, very discreet, who can maybe give us an idea just what we're looking at here. He has ways of hacking into things. And the information on this USB stick might all have come from someone hacking into a government computer system in the UK or elsewhere.'

'As long as it's quick and not traceable,' she said.

I nodded.

'I'd have to email him one of these links. Just to get some kind of handle on it.'

'Okay,' she said.

Fowler took out his mobile and called Brodie and asked him for the guy's number. Then he dialled it and handed his phone to me. It was answered after three rings.

'It's Billie Carlson, here . . . I've got something I'd like you to have a quick look at if that's possible? It's a web link I have on a USB stick, but I've no idea what it is. Could be anything.'

'Sure,' he said. 'Ping it across to me and I'll see if I can make sense of it.'

I copied the link onto my phone and sent it to him on a WhatsApp message. Then we waited. I was beginning to feel hungry and took one of the sandwiches and Fowler and Elizabeth did the same. I was halfway through the sandwich when my mobile rang. It was the expert.

'Shit, Billie! Where did you get this?' He sounded shocked.

'It's part of an investigation I'm looking at.'

'Well. You'd be smart to get the hell out of it, pronto.'

'What?'

'It's a UK government site. Top secret. Nobody outside of MI6 will have access to this. As soon as I clicked on it, even with my outside untraceable browser, my screen lit up like a Christmas tree. Jesus! I'm not even sure how many alarm bells this set off at the other side. But it just said "Danger: encrypted government code. Highly confidential, illegal. Your email address is being traced." I clicked out of it straight away. Don't click on it at all, Billie. Steer clear of it. Someone is monitoring any foreign body who clicks on it, so I hope I've got away with it.' He paused. 'But hey, thanks for the excitement. It was a slow day!' He chuckled. 'I'm hoping MI6 don't kick in my door in the next hour.'

'Seriously? That's scary. Okay. And sorry. I had no idea. Thanks for your help.'

He hung up. I had no clue where to go with this from here, but it didn't look like there was anything I could do or anything here that would benefit Elizabeth in her predicament. Not right now anyway. And I wasn't comfortable that this device had even been in my laptop. I told them what he said, and we agreed to leave it aside for the moment.

'Let's deal with something we might be able to fix,' I said. 'Can you make that call? And record it on your phone. We'll be right here.'

Elizabeth nodded. She took a breath and a few paces across the kitchen, then pushed in the number. We listened. The phone was on loudspeaker.

'Hello?' A male voice.

'This number was on a note delivered to my home.' She paused but there was no answer. 'Who is this?'

'Never mind who it is.' The man's reply was sharp. 'You saw the photo?'

'Yes. I did.'

'What do you want to do to make this go away? We know who you are. You have a husband. That's not him in the picture.'

'What the hell are you doing taking pictures in the woods? My question is, what were you doing in the woods at that time of night?'

'That's no business of yours.'

'What do you want?'

'What do you think?'

'You tell me.'

'I can make these pictures disappear or I can make sure your husband gets to see them. And by the way, that man running after you, he's the one who turned up dead on the beach, is he not? Cops might want to know that.'

I mouthed to Elizabeth to arrange a meet.

'I want to see you face to face before I say any more.'

'When?'

'Now.'

Silence for a few seconds. Then the voice.

'Twenty minutes. Top of the cliffs. Not far from your home.'
The line went dead.

'Shit!' Elizabeth said, holding out a shaky hand. 'He sounds like a right bastard.'

'We'll soon see,' Fowler said. 'I'm looking forward to meeting this arsehole.'

We walked the short distance along the pathway that eventually led up towards the cliffs. Halfway up there was a car parked in a layby, and Elizabeth turned to us.

'That's the car. Same registration.'

'Yep,' I agreed. 'Maybe the woman will be here too.'

We climbed up the path and finally reached the top where a single dirt track went all along the cliffs and wound its way down the hill to the road below. A solitary walker came towards us and gave us a nod before passing and going back down the road we had come up on. Then on a wooden bench a couple sat looking out to sea.

'That has to be them,' I said, turning to Elizabeth. 'How are you going to handle this?'

'I'm just going to ask them straight out how much.'

'Good. Then we'll take it from there,' I said.

As we approached, the man looked over his shoulder and seemed to stiffen a little, then the woman turned to glance back. They both stood up facing us. He looked at Elizabeth.

'What's with the entourage?' the guy snapped, looking us up and down.

He was wiry and appeared to be in his late thirties or fortyish, wearing jeans and a baggy navy T-shirt that looked as though he'd been wiping his hands on it. The woman seemed a little shellshocked, with short blonde hair, dark eye make-up and red lips. I put her at around late-thirties.

'Never mind that. Just tell me, what are you trying to do here? You're blackmailing me?' Elizabeth's voice was harsh, her eyes fixed on his.

'Whatever.' He shrugged, a smug look on his face. 'Cut to the chase. You want to make this picture disappear?'

'What are you going to do if I say no?'

I was impressed by how in control Elizabeth seemed to be.

He gave her a bored look.

'Maybe I'll just make sure the pictures end up in the hands of the police.'

'Why would you do that?'

The girl piped up.

'Because that guy, that foreigner who washed up on the beach? We think that might have been him that night.'

'Do you now?' Elizabeth retorted. 'And have you any other fanciful theories while you're at it?'

'Shut up, Theresa!' the guy barked at the woman, grabbing her arm. 'Let me deal with this.' He sniffed. 'Right. Here's the deal. You give me five grand cash by tomorrow and that's the last you'll hear from me.'

Elizabeth turned to us, unsure of what to say next. Then, suddenly, Fowler stepped forward, taking up the man's space almost nose to nose.

'Listen, son,' he said. 'You take your bird here and crawl back to whatever stone you crawled out from under. This ends now.'

'Who the fuck are you?'

'I'm your worst nightmare, son. Believe me.'

Suddenly Fowler grabbed hold of the guy, who yelped as he twisted his arm up his back, and in one seamless motion he got hold of the back of his neck with his other hand and pushed him four paces to the edge of the cliff.

'Fuck are you doing, ya prick?'

Fowler pushed him even closer till his feet were almost on the edge.

'I'm seriously thinking of dropping you off here. You're blackmailing this woman.' He gestured to Elizabeth, who was standing beside me, both of us aghast at the scene. 'But what do you think will happen if the cops find out you were a witness to someone being chased in the woods in the middle of the night? And what do you think will happen if they find out you took pictures and tried to blackmail the lady you saw that night?' He leaned him over the cliff. 'And what would your wife say when the cops come knocking on the door and she finds out exactly what you were doing in the woods in the middle of the night?' He looked at the woman, who was ashen-faced. 'The both of you are in big shit. And it might be wise for the pair of you to just take a nosedive off here right now. Because I'm going to make sure that you regret your little blackmailing plan here for a very long time. Do you get my drift, bawbag?'

'Right, right,' the guy croaked. 'Stop. I . . . I'm sorry. It was fucking stupid. It was her idea.'

'And they say chivalry is dead,' Fowler snorted.

'Look,' the guy said. 'I don't know what the hell we were thinking about and that's the truth. It seemed like easy money, because I know this woman.' He pointed at Elizabeth. 'I've seen her around the village, and I know she's married. But . . . but it was a really stupid thing to do. Can we just forget the whole thing? I'll destroy the images.'

Fowler let go of him and dragged him backwards, so he was standing next to the woman, who was looking at him frozen with rage.

'Right,' Fowler said. 'Give me your mobile. Is that where the pictures are?'

'Aye.' He nodded.

'Show me them.'

His hands were trembling as he scrolled down the phone and brought up the images. Then we watched as he deleted each one of them.

'Right. They're gone. That's it.'

'Did you upload them anywhere? The cloud or anything? Copies?'

He shook his head.

'No. I promise.'

Fowler glared at him and stepped forward.

'I don't believe you.'

'I'm telling the truth. No copies.'

'Listen, son. If I find out there are copies, I'll come back down here and I'll throw you right off that cliff. Have you got that?'

The guy nodded vigorously.

'Give me your mobile.'

The guy glanced at the woman then handed over his mobile. Fowler turned towards the sea and the edge of the cliffs, then he reached back the phone in his hand and pitched it as far as he could, and we all watched as it flew through the air and downwards to the sea, lashing onto the rocks below.

'Oh dear,' Fowler said. 'Slipped out of my hand. But I hear you get some great deals these days on Vodafone.' He pushed the back of the guy. 'Now beat it. The pair of you. And make sure I don't have to pay you a visit here any time in the future.'

The guy glanced shamefaced at the woman and walked ahead of her down the path and disappeared. We stood there in silence for a moment, not quite believing what had just happened.

'Bawbag?' I smiled to Fowler as we made our way down the hill.

He shrugged.

'It's a term of endearment.'

'And you don't know if the guy was married, do you?'

Fowler grinned.

'I just chanced my arm there. Worked, though, didn't it?'

By the time we got back to Elizabeth's house it was after three, and I knew Millie would be picking up Lucas by now, and hoped he had remembered that it was her and not me who would be at the gates. We drank coffee with Elizabeth in her conservatory at the back and she went over again what had happened that night and how she had disposed of the body.

'So, what are your plans now, Elizbeth?' I asked her.

She took a long breath and sighed.

'I just want to get out of here. I'm going to pack up a few things and head down to London tomorrow. By the time I travel to Glasgow it'll be the afternoon train I catch. But I'll be glad to be away. Put this behind me, I hope.'

I wondered how she could be taking in her stride everything that had happened. I got that she'd killed a man in self-defence and knew how that felt. But disposing of the body, then getting on with life was a bit of a stretch. I wasn't certain that Elizabeth had told us everything about her past life, but I didn't expect her to be telling me about it now. She'd told me earlier to keep the USB stick, that she didn't want any more of it, and if someone came looking in her house for it, then it wouldn't be there. I was intrigued to know what was on it, but I didn't think I'd ever get to find out. But I took it anyway and put it safely in my bag.

Fowler said he was going out for a walk around the grounds and the woods to stretch his legs before the journey back. So I decided that now that things were wrapped up with Elizabeth and I had her alone, this was my opportunity to ask her what had been on my mind since the first time she made contact with me.

'Elizabeth,' I said. 'Can you talk to me about my father?'

She put down her coffee mug on the table and met my eyes but didn't speak for several moments.

'You don't know, do you?' she said softly.

I looked at her, surprised.

'Know what?' I replied. 'I knew very little or really nothing about my father apart from that I loved him very much, and that he was the centre of mine and my mother's lives. She just went to pieces after he died – especially the way he died.' I paused, swallowed, because I tried not to go back to those dark days, the sadness, the sense of loss. 'I knew he was a lecturer, but I do remember some of his friends – my mum would have them round for dinner and she would cook and they would chat for hours drinking wine and eating. I just remember it as being a very happy home. And my father was really happy, or so it seemed.' I bit my lip. 'That's why it hurt so much that he died the way he did – taking his own life, leaving us like that, with no answers. I . . . I never understood it. I suppose I never will.'

Elizabeth listened, sadness in her eyes, and then she swallowed hard and spoke.

'Billie.' She pushed out a sigh. 'I have something to tell you. I wasn't going to, but I think you need to know the truth.'

'Truth?'

'Yes. About your father.' She shook her head, looked me in the eye. 'Your father. He didn't commit suicide.'

Her words hung in the air, and there was an explosion inside my head that made me feel hot and dizzy for a few seconds.

'What?'.

'He didn't kill himself that night. On the bridge in Glasgow. He . . . he was pushed. He was murdered, Billie.' Her eyes filled with tears. 'I'm so sorry to have to tell you that. But you are a good woman, and he would have been so proud of you. He would never have left you and your mother. He was murdered that night.'

My mouth opened to speak but nothing came out. I was in shock. All of my life since the age of twelve I had been trying to deal, or not deal, with my father's death and how he died. It had shaped everything I had become, and still in my darker moments I could see him and think of how awful he must have felt that night to end his life the way he did. And now this. All of it. Everything I was told was untrue. I felt my hands shaking.

'But . . . my mother? Did she know?'

She shook her head.

'No,' she said. 'She couldn't know. Nobody knew. Only the people who were part of the unit.'

I screwed my eyes up, confused.

'Unit? What unit?'

'Your father, my husband and one other, who is also dead, and, well, the security services of course, who ran the unit.'

'What? Elizabeth . . . I don't know what you mean?'

She took a long time to answer and I watched her, the compassion in her eyes. I wondered what was going on.

'Your father, Billie. He was a spy. Like my husband.'

'A spy? But he was a university lecturer.'

'Yes, he was. Same as my husband. But they were spies for the British government. They'd been sought out by MI6 early on in their careers and that's what they were. They had handlers.

They met with Soviet agents who were double agents and passed information. Nobody who knew them knew what they were. It was a tight secret unit.'

'Jesus!' I murmured. 'I can't believe this. It's all too much to take in. My father, a spy? I don't know what to say, to think.' I swallowed back tears because I couldn't break down here now in front of anyone. I had to get home, to think this through, to process this, to try to understand that so much of my life had been built on a lie.

'I know. It's a lot. But your father was murdered that night.'

'How?'

'The man he was to meet. The Soviet agent. He was to pass documents – photographs or documents, I'm not sure what. But that night it wasn't him who turned up as expected. The man who came said he had been sent to deliver the package, because the usual man he met had been called away. But, in fact, this man had been sent to murder your father.'

I couldn't answer. There were no words, only questions and fear and dread swimming around my head. I wanted to go home. But something in my mind switched.

'Who was this man, Elizabeth?'

She seemed a little hesitant, then spoke.

'His name is Dimitry. My husband has always kept tabs on him. He's retired now apparently. Lives in some backwater town in Siberia or somewhere.'

'Do you have any more information?'

'I think I can find out more . . . Dimitry Volkov. It might not be his name now – it might not even have been his real name back then. But I will see what I can find.'

After they'd gone, the house seemed to be empty of energy, and as the rush of adrenalin from the last few hours began to wane, Elizabeth was surprised at how lonely she felt. She padded around the house, half-heartedly packing a small case to take with her tomorrow, barely even thinking of what she was putting in it. She thought of Billie Carlson, and the look on her face when she told her the truth about her father, and part of her wished she hadn't told her. She'd assumed someone over the years, perhaps this aunt in Sweden, would have told her what happened instead of the poor kid having to go through her life impacted by what she believed was her father's suicide. That was cruel, and she should have been told earlier. But typical of the secret service, they moved on, next business. An agent who had died would be remembered as killed in active service, but their secret life would be kept hidden. They should have found some way to tell her. Such a shame. Now she will have to reprocess everything she had known from the age of twelve.

She walked out into the kitchen and gazed out of the window at the garden as the afternoon light began to fade. She was jaded, but she told herself she would have to shake out of it, and have a look to see what she could find on Dimitry Volkov. She owed Billie that much.

She left the kitchen and went to the spare bedroom, where she removed a picture from the wall and opened the slim door of a wall safe. Inside was the leather-bound diary she'd kept for decades. She sat down on a chair and opened it, going back years, finding notes on Billie's father, Anders, social events with her husband, dinners, meetings in Whitehall. And eventually she came across Volkov and the dark pages she hadn't opened for years. She started reading. As she did, she took pictures with her phone of the pages. Then she went to her living room, opened her laptop and scanned them. She would send them to Billie in Glasgow in the morning on her way to the train station.

She wrote to Billie that she knew no more, but that it was very dangerous to keep probing, and she hoped she could walk away and leave it now, and take time to absorb it all. She was sorry she had put her through the agony of breaking this terrible news. She went back to her bedroom, finished packing and left her bag at the front door. She would take an early train in the morning. She didn't feel like eating but was tired with a kind of depressed exhaustion. She went into the bathroom and ran a bath. Outside it was dark, and she decided that an early night would be the best thing. She lay in the bath thinking back, regretting her betrayal of Christopher. She knew he had been unfaithful too, but it was something she had always dealt with, and only once or twice in her life had she felt like straying. But she never had. It had always been more to do with alcohol as it crept up on her over the years. But now she'd been given a second chance. She would wipe the slate clean and tomorrow she would start again.

After her bath, she lay in bed listening as the wind seemed to whip up and rattle against the window. She was familiar with the sounds and groans of this old house and she found herself drifting off to sleep. Elizabeth had always been a light sleeper, and even though noises in the house didn't stir her, the click and the closeness of that click did, and she instinctively knew what it was. Her eyes snapped open. She saw the man standing in front of her and she knew that it was over. She should have been terrified but she wasn't. She was just sad. Sad that she didn't want to leave like this, sad when she thought of her husband, sad that she wouldn't have the chance to change things for the better, to be honest. The fallout from this would be huge. They would find her shot in the head in a pool of blood in her bed, but they would never find the truth.

The man didn't speak, his dead eyes fixing on her, the pistol in his outstretched arm. His face wasn't covered and she knew it didn't have to be. The last thing she saw was his lips pulled back almost in a sneer and his finger pulling the trigger.

CHAPTER THIRTEEN

More than anything, I wanted to pour it all out, everything that Elizabeth had told me about my father. I wanted to confide in someone the bombshell that had just been dropped on me, as though by repeating it out loud it somehow wouldn't seem so red raw, so devastating as it did now. But I've learned over the years, and many years ago as a child, that letting all my mixed-up emotions spill out never helped anything. I learned to clam up, to put fears and worries in a box and push them away to be dealt with another time. I don't know how I managed it then, and I don't know how I managed it now during the two-hour drive all the way back from Portpatrick. But I kept it buttoned up inside me, made sure I showed nothing.

It's not that I didn't want to tell Fowler because I knew he would be supportive and sympathetic and he would help me contain the fallout until I could find a way to manage it. But this was all too much for me to take in and far too much for me to try and express by telling anyone. So all the way back, it was as though I switched to being another person. We talked about the couple, about Elizabeth and a million other things during the drive to Glasgow, and I didn't think he noticed anything untoward in my behaviour. At least that's what I thought. Until we got to Glasgow, and he pulled up outside my flat. I didn't want to linger in the car for a second more than was necessary and I clicked off my seat belt and turned to push open the door of the passenger seat. But then I felt Fowler's hand gently on my upper arm, and I turned to face him, at first not making eye contact.

'Billie,' he said. 'You okay?'

'Yes.' I shrugged, giving him a sideways glance. 'Sure.'

'It's just that I feel since we left that house, there's something not right about you. Did you get on okay with Elizabeth? I think she's a bit of a hard case myself.' He paused, let go of my arm, his eyes searching my face. 'Did she say anything that upset you?'

I sat for a long moment, my eyes focused on the windscreen. A teenager on a bike cycled past. I didn't know what to say, where to begin. And even if I did, it wasn't for today. I turned to him.

'I'm okay, Dave. Honest,' I said. 'Bit tired maybe.'

He nodded, but his face told me he didn't believe me.

'Okay,' he said. 'But look, Billie. I want you to know that if there is anything you feel like talking about, I'm a good listener. That's all I'm saying.'

I managed a smile.

'Sure,' I said. 'That you are, Dave.' I patted his arm, and opened the door. 'I'd best get in to see what this boy's been up to.' I managed a thin smile as I got out of the car and gave him a wave as I climbed the stairs to my front door.

I spotted Lucas briefly at the front window of my living room. His face lit up when he saw me, then he disappeared and I knew he'd be running down the hall to greet me. In that moment, everything that had torn to shreds the background of my life disappeared. I opened the door and Lucas leapt into my open arms. I was home, and right now that was all that mattered.

'He's been at that window for the past twenty minutes watching every car,' Millie said, smiling as we walked down the hall and into the flat.

'I know. Sorry. Traffic was crazy coming over the Kingston Bridge.'

The aroma of cooking filled the air as we went into the living room.

'Smells divine in here.'

'I've roasted a chicken. Lucas had a snack when he came in from nursery, as I thought you'd want to eat together.'

'Thanks, Millie. You're worth your weight in gold.'

'That's a lot of gold,' she chuckled, going into the kitchen and opening the oven door. 'Chicken's ready. Hope you're hungry. I've enough spuds in the oven to feed six.'

Over dinner, I managed to push the thought of my father to the back of my mind and concentrate on just listening to the chatter of Lucas and Millie, with him telling me of his day at nursery and how he and Millie had played together and he had helped her with the vegetables for the meal. I must have been convincing because eagle-eyed Millie never spotted anything. She was so insightful that if she'd suspected any flicker of change in my demeanour, she'd have asked. I was glad I was able to relay the story to her of how Dave put the blackmailers right in their place and left them quaking and scurrying away with their tails between their legs.

'He's some guy, the big man, isn't he?' she said, impressed. 'I wouldn't like to get on the wrong side of him.'

'Yep,' I said. 'He's a tough cookie all right, but from what I know of him he's deep and sensitive. A good man. I'm glad he's staying in Glasgow, as he's a great hand on cases, and good to have around if it looks like getting a bit rough.'

I wondered if Millie might have a bit of a twinkle in her eye as we talked of Dave, but I wouldn't dare suggest it to her. I had no idea if she'd ever had any other relationships over the years after her marriage fell apart in the wake of losing her children to a hit and run driver. And she'd never mentioned any boyfriends. I suppose it took so long for her to try and deal with the trauma of losing her kids that being in any kind of relationship had been the last thing on her mind most of the time. But she was only human and was bound to get lonely from time to time. I'd seen her involved in banter with Brodie when he came into the office to work, but that's as far as it went. I got the impression she just wanted to manage her life by herself without a man, and that was good enough for me.

After she left, and I got Lucas settled into bed and read to him until he fell asleep, I sat in the living room watching the darkness fall across the square, transforming it into a twilight world of secrets and shame and desperation. I tried to recall the evenings so many years ago when I had sat in here with my mother and father, safe, innocent and secure and – now I realise – totally unaware of what was really going on. Could I really have known nothing of the life my father had? But how would a little girl have any inkling that the world as she saw it laid out in front of her wasn't, in fact, reality?

As I'd got older, it was harder to try to picture actual scenes and faces and days or nights in the flat with my parents, or recall specific times when my father would kiss me on the forehead before he went off on a lecture tour somewhere. I tried to remember my mother's face, her eyes shining with tears as she hugged him in the hallway before he disappeared for a few days, a week, or even longer sometimes. Did she know what he was doing? Did she know anything about him really? I knew if I sat here much longer, I would be awake half the night trying to piece together fragments of our lives, trying to pinpoint if there was any time I ever saw a shadow across my father's eyes that all was not well. And ultimately I would wonder if anything Elizabeth had said was true, and why she had taken so long to even get in touch and tell me about my father. She'd said she assumed I'd been told. I could go around in circles. Eventually I got up, ran a bath and sank into the bubbles, listening to an audio book that took me to a land far away and a story that was nothing like mine.

My dreams were vivid images of shadowy figures hiding in doorways and someone hurrying down a rain-lashed street in the dark, constantly glancing over their shoulder as though they were being followed. I couldn't make out the face or see for sure who it was, but somehow in my dream I knew it was my father. Then the dream switched to a bridge in the city and I could see myself gazing over it into the inky black River Clyde, and every now and then from the darkness of the raging water a hand shot up and a voice called for help.

I woke up with a start as my mobile began to ring and I blinked my eyes open, swallowing hard because the final image had left me with a heaviness in my chest. I rubbed at my eyes and picked up the phone from my bedside table. The number was a mobile but no name.

'Billie? Is that you?'

'Yeah. Who is it?'

'It's Jane . . . Jane McAllister.'

I sat upright.

'Hello, Jane. You okay?'

'Billie, I need to talk to you. I . . . There's things I need to tell you. But I'm scared.'

I was on my feet now, and could hear the tension in her voice.

'Sure, Jane. I can see you any time. This morning all right for you? You want to come into my office?'

'Yes. I'm just worried even about talking to you.'

'Has something happened since we talked a couple of days ago, Jane?'

'Yes. That's what I'm scared about. I don't want to say on the phone.'

'No problem. I can see you in my office at half nine, if that's okay?' I reeled off the address in Mitchell Lane. 'Do you know the street?'

'Yes. I know it. I'll be there.' She paused. 'I need your help, Billie.'

'Okay. Just try to stay calm. I'll see you soon.'

She'd already hung up.

CHAPTER FOURTEEN

I called Dave Fowler on my mobile on my way into the office and asked him to come in. I was intrigued by Jane McAllister's edgy phone call and my mind was firing off all sorts of scenarios as to why she was suddenly sounding so terrified. When I'd spoken to her in the park I hadn't got the impression she was hiding anything sinister, but something had spooked her and I was getting the distinct feeling she hadn't been telling me the whole truth about Cathy Evans and her life in Spain. I called Dave because he was good to bounce things off, and I'd come to value his experience and insight into people when I'd brought him in on cases. I explained to him that I wasn't sure if Jane would want to say anything in front of him, so we'd very much play it by ear when she came in.

When I got into the office, I filled Millie in on the phone call from Jane and she was as intrigued as I was. She made coffee just as Fowler came in the door with his collie, Jess, bounding straight across to Millie, who handed her a digestive biscuit. I watched the clock as we drank coffee and chatted about the Cathy Evans case, and Jane was already five minutes late. Then the doorbell buzzed and Millie pushed the security intercom and we heard Jane's voice. Millie buzzed her through and she stood in the main reception looking frightened, totally different from the woman I'd talked to before. I got up and crossed towards her.

'Hello, Jane. You want a coffee or tea?' I gestured to my office where the door was open. 'We can have a chat in my office.'

She flicked a nervous glance around the room and then at Fowler, looking back at me.

'This is Dave Fowler, Jane,' I said. 'He works with me on some cases.'

There was a trace of distrust in her eye, and I gave Fowler a nod, knowing he would understand.

'Why don't you and I go into my office for a chat first, then we can all talk later if you want?'

She didn't speak and we walked across to my office.

'Sit down, Jane,' I said, going behind my desk and gesturing to the seat opposite. 'Take off your coat, and just take your time. I can see you're worried.'

She blew out a breath.

'I passed worried weeks ago,' she said. 'That's why I left Spain. I thought I could get away, but I'm frantic now. They're after me.'

I looked at her for a long moment before I said anything. She hadn't been totally straight with me from the start, and I wanted to convey that I knew this. But at the same time, whatever she was about to tell me could build up the pieces in the Cathy Evans case so I had to play it by ear. I picked up my mug of coffee and sipped from it, then put it back down.

'Okay, Jane. How about we go back over your life in Spain, and this time, tell me everything.'

She glanced down at the back of her hands then gave me a sheepish look. From the dark smudges under her eyes she looked as though she hadn't slept much.

'Listen, Billie. I'm sorry about the other day. I . . . I wasn't a hundred per cent honest with you. I couldn't be. Not right then. I was going to get back to you and tell you more. I was going to tell you everything. But then the shit hit the fan.'

'How?' I asked. 'What's changed?'

She took a breath and rubbed her face, shaking her head as though she was trying to make sense of it all.

'That couple. That Marilyn and Steve I told you about. I don't know who they're involved with but it must be some heavy people. Drug dealers. Has to be. I got a phone call. Then a text message.' She took off her coat and put her hand inside the pocket, fished out her mobile and held it up.

'When did you get the call?'

'Last night. Then the text.'

'A call from Steve or Marilyn?'

She nodded.

'Marilyn. She called me. I don't even know how she got my phone number. I've never talked to her on the phone. It was always Cathy they phoned. Never me.' She paused for a breath. 'So that means they must have her phone or something.'

I raised my eyebrows.

'It could do. Or maybe Cathy passed them your mobile number some time.'

'She wouldn't have done that. No reason to.'

'So what did she say?'

'She came on the phone quite nice in the beginning. The usual. All concerned, asking how I was, and saying her and Steve had been looking for me after poor Cathy was found. That's what she said – "poor Cathy". Like she was all sincere and stuff, but I'm not buying any of it. She said they'd been worried about me, that I just seemed to disappear off the face of the earth after Cathy was found dead on the beach, and that they were worried in case something had happened to me.' She shook her head. 'Bullshit. They were just letting me know that they could find me, even if I wasn't in the country. She asked me if I'd talked to the police. I told her I hadn't. That the police hadn't contacted me at all, and that maybe they didn't even know I was Cathy's friend.'

'Why do you think they would want you to know that they could find you?' I asked, sitting back in my chair, glancing out of the window then back at her. 'Look, Jane. I need you to tell me the truth. Everything. Otherwise you're just wasting my time. What was really going on with you and Cathy and this couple?' I paused. 'Are you in some sort of trouble with them? Have they got some kind of hold over you? And Cathy?'

I needed to cut through the bullshit, and it worked. For a few seconds she didn't answer, then I saw the colour rise in her neck and her lip tremble as her face began to crumple. She nodded vigorously.

'Oh shit, Billie! I'll never forgive myself. I abandoned Cathy. I feel like I left her to the wolves.'

I wasn't here to dish out absolution but she was clearly in a state of panic. Whatever trauma had gone on in Spain, this was a woman full of fear and regret. I pulled a couple of tissues from the box on my desk and handed them to her, and sat sipping my coffee until she stopped sobbing and got a hold of herself.

'Okay.' She sniffed. 'Sorry. I'll tell you everything. The last time I saw Cathy was the night before she was found on the beach the following morning. We'd been out for dinner with Marilyn and Steve. We all had a lot to drink – Cathy especially. She was being a bit silly and talking maybe out of turn to Marilyn and Steve. They'd all just come back from a trip to Dubai and suddenly Cathy starts talking about stuff, saying about the money they took over in the suitcases and laughing, but half serious, saying that she should be getting a good cut of that because after all she was part of their gang now.' She paused. 'I was horrified. She'd never mentioned any of this before, and as soon as she said it, Steve's face just fell and he looked at Marilyn and they were both raging. The whole atmosphere just changed in that moment. He suddenly snapped at her to shut the fuck up, or she'd be in trouble. He was like a totally different guy from the way I'd known him. But Cathy was drunk and just making a fool of him, trying to laugh it off.

'I just wanted out of the place. I knew this was not good and I wanted to get off my mark. I said to Cathy that we should go home, that it was getting late, but she was in no mood to listen. She suddenly started mouthing off that she'd done a good few trips now and she deserved a bigger cut, that just getting a free holiday and a few quid was not enough. She actually said that. I couldn't believe my ears. Then she suddenly said she knew so much about their deals that she could stick the two of them in it if she wanted. Everything went totally silent. Steam was coming out of Steve's ears, and Marilyn was also fuming, and told Cathy she was just an ungrateful little bitch, and that she was talking a load of rubbish. Steve and Marilyn were looking at me because I'd heard all this, and the way they looked at me made my blood run cold. I said to Cathy we should get a taxi, and Steve said that was a good idea, and to get this bitch out of his way before she got a slap. That's what he said. So I got up and told Cathy we were leaving and she reluctantly came with me, but was still mouthing off at them as we left, saying that this wasn't over. As we left the restaurant I glanced over my shoulder and could see Steve on the phone and Marilyn just sitting there raging. I managed to get Cathy into a taxi and we went back to our apartment block.'

We were getting somewhere now, and Jane looked as though she was glad to get this off her chest.

'So that night,' I said, 'did you leave Cathy at her apartment? What kind of state was she in? Was she still talking about the trips?'

She nodded.

'Yes. She was. She was saying that she knew so much stuff that could blow the whole thing sky high. I wasn't sure what she meant, and asked her, and she said that every single trip they went on, they were either carrying money or bringing in drugs. She told me that on one cruise she'd carried a whole suitcase full of cocaine hidden in presents and trinkets and had been paid two grand for doing it, as well as being given the free holiday. I honestly didn't want to hear it, but she kept going on about how she was always just in the background but that Steve was hooking up with all sorts of people in Morocco and in Dubai and other places, and she said they told her that she would be well paid. But she could see just how much they were doing, and that's when she stupidly and drunkenly asked for more money. I told her to calm down, that she had made a big mistake and that she needed to get out of Spain pronto. I told her we would look at flights in the morning and that she should just go back to Scotland. But she didn't seem to understand the danger she was in. It's not as if she could go to the cops, because she was part of it. And it's not as if I could go to the police either, because I would be dragged into it. Anyway, she was getting tired and said she wanted to go to bed, so I got her settled in and then went to my apartment. To be honest, I looked on the internet for a flight to get out of there the following day, and that's what I did. I booked us both a flight.'

'And what about Cathy? Did you call her in the morning?'

Again, her mouth tightened and she seemed to fight back tears, shaking her head.

'No,' she said. 'Well. Yes. I did, but her phone just went to voicemail. I didn't leave a message.' She looked at me. 'But at one point during the night, I got up to go to the bathroom. I couldn't get to sleep and I happened to look out of the window. It was about two or three in the morning, I think. My apartment faces the front street and Cathy's is on the floor below facing the same direction.' She paused, swallowed, then went on. 'That's when I saw the men coming out of the apartment block. They were carrying something wrapped in a big throwover. I recognised the throwover as the one that had been over Cathy's sofa. One man was at the top of it and another at the bottom. I'm sure they were carrying a body.'

She shook her head.

'Christ, Billie! I'm sure it was Cathy. It must have been. I just know it. They'd done something to her and they were taking her out of the apartment. God knows, I should have called the police there and then, but I was just so frantic and terrified. I was scared Marilyn and Steve would get someone to come to my apartment and I'd be next. I was up all night, pacing the floor until it was morning, then I crept out of my apartment and used the key Cathy had given me for emergencies, and went into her place.' She paused again, biting her lip. 'She was gone, Billie. Gone. Not a trace of her. No sign of a struggle or anything. She was just not there. They must have taken her. I was so scared, I called a taxi and headed for the airport.' She sniffed. 'I'll never forgive myself. I abandoned Cathy. A couple of days after I got home I saw the story in the newspaper that a British woman had been found dead on the beach at Fuengirola. I knew even before they gave the name that it was her.'

I let her sit for a while as she sobbed softly into the tissue, dabbing her eyes, glancing up at me maybe for forgiveness or understanding. And I could see why she'd done what she did. Who knows what any of us would do in a situation like that? Are we going to put ourselves up to the police for scrutiny where we might be held for questioning in a foreign prison cell while they slowly tried to unravel and check out our story? Or are we going to get the hell out of Dodge in case whoever did this came for us before the day was out? I like to think I might take my chances with the cops, but I wouldn't bank on it. It was all about survival for Jane McAllister, and so far she'd managed it. So what had changed? After what felt like a long wait, I spoke.

'You said you got a text, Jane, after the phone call last night. Was that straight after or some time later?'

'About an hour later.' She scrolled through her phone.

'Was it from the same phone number as Marilyn and Steve?'

'I don't know, because their number didn't come up when they called.'

'What did the text say?'

She reached across and handed me the phone.

'See for yourself.'

I took the phone and looked at the message. It read:

Keep your mouth shut if you know what's good for you.

I looked up from the phone at Jane, who was nibbling the inside of her jaw, fear all over her eyes.

'You think it's from the couple?'

'I don't know. They weren't aggressive during our phone conversation, kind of plausible saying how sad they were, and that Cathy had got out of hand and was saying things which weren't true.'

'And what did you say when they were saying things like that?'

'Nothing. I was scared to say anything in case it was the wrong thing.'

'That was wise,' I said. 'Did you answer the text?'

'No. I didn't want to engage with it at all. But if you scroll down, you'll see there's another text.'

I scrolled to the next message.

We know where you live. And where you work. Might pop in for a coffee, just to make sure you keep your mouth shut.

I raised my eyebrows and blew out a sigh.

'Someone is definitely trying to put the frighteners on you.'

'And they're succeeding,' she said. 'Billie, I don't know what to do. I mean, how the hell do they know where I live and work? Are they watching me?'

I didn't want to make her any more alarmed by telling her that if this couple were involved with gangsters, then they weren't confined to the Costa del Sol. There would be a network from Spain to Glasgow and various places in between, from the people who bought the drugs to cut for the streets, to the money launderers who washed money in shopfronts such as barbers' and tanning salons, bars and restaurants across the UK. It would be easy for someone from Spain to throw her name to a contact in Glasgow and track her down.

'You could go to the police,' I said, fairly sure of how she would react.

'And then what?' she replied. 'Suddenly I'm dragged into a murder investigation and maybe an international drugs ring?' She shook her head. 'No way. I'd end up the same as Cathy. Found dead in my house or I'd suddenly go missing, my body washing up some place. I'm terrified.'

'I know.' I nodded, not really sure what to say next. My instinct was to go to the cops and lay it all out and let them take it from here. But I sensed that would terrify her.

'I feel like running away but I've nowhere to go. I can't go back to Spain. My apartment is lying empty and that's not a good thing either as you could end up with squatters. That happens a lot. I've got someone who looks in on it but I can't get hold of them. I don't know what I can do. But if someone knows where I live and where I work, that means someone in Glasgow has seen me. It gives me the shivers.'

As she touched her face, I noticed the diamond ring on her finger, and couldn't remember seeing it the first time we met. I assumed she didn't wear it working in the kitchen of the café. It looked expensive, if it was real.

'That's a lovely ring, Jane,' I said. 'Did you get it in Spain?'

She gazed down at her hand, fiddling with the ring, turning it round and round on her finger, then she looked up at me, perplexed.

'Cathy gave me this,' she said, sniffing. 'She bought it in Dubai and gave it to me when she came home. She was like that. So generous. '

She glanced at her watch.

'I have to go to work now, Billie. But do you think you can help me?'

I spread my hands.

'I can make some enquiries for you,' I said. 'Discreetly. The case I'm investigating is Cathy Evans' death, and for sure you fit into that from what you've told me. But in terms of making things safe for you right now, Jane? I'll be honest with you. I can't do that. You need to think about talking to the police and telling them everything. They have the resources to look at this, and of course maybe offer some protection for you. But that will involve you being all in with them. So you have to consider that.'

She stood up and picked up her mobile from my desk.

'I understand. I have to think if that's the best thing for me. I'll talk to you tonight or tomorrow once I decide. It might be best to go to the police as you say. I'm just scared of everything.'

'I know,' I said. 'Call me and let me know, and I'll also put some feelers out to contacts in the police.'

She nodded, trying to put a brave face on, then turned and left.

CHAPTER FIFTEEN

Dave Fowler was of the same mind as me when I told him everything that Jane had spilled about Cathy. There was nothing really we could do to protect her. It was a job for the police, not us, even though her information did shine a light on what might have happened to Cathy Evans that night. Fowler said there was no time to lose and that if Jane was telling the truth, then she was definitely in danger.

I was mulling this over while we sat in my office, and also thinking of giving Paddy Harper a call to see if he'd heard anything on the ground about this couple on the Costa del Sol. If anyone could find out, then Paddy could. I was about to phone him when my mobile rang on my desk and I picked it up. DCI Harry Wilson, my ex-boss with whom I had a love–hate relationship. Surprised to hear from him, I arched an eyebrow across at Fowler, showing him the name on the screen.

'Harry!' I said. 'This is a surprise. How you doing?'

'Carlson, it's not a social call.'

'Oh,' I said, genuinely puzzled. 'Actually, I was thinking about phoning you for a chat about something.'

'Really, Carlson? Well, it's a bit fucking late.'

'What?' I was wondering how the hell he could know about Jane McAllister or Cathy Evans.

'Aye. Have you been at the capers again?'

'What? You've lost me there, Harry.'

'Elizabeth Fletcher.'

The name hit me like a punch in the gut. If Wilson was phoning me about Elizabeth Fletcher, it had to be bad news.

'Yes, Harry. She's a client.'

'Was.'

'What?'

'She *was* a client. She's dead. Shot at point-blank range in her cottage in Portpatrick. And guess whose number was the last one she called on her mobile?'

I didn't answer for a moment, while I worked out what I was going to say. I had done nothing wrong, so I didn't owe Wilson any explanation even if he did always speak to me as though I was still one of his detectives.

'Yes, Harry,' I said. 'I saw her the other day. I was investigating a case for her.' I paused. 'But how come you're involved? It's a long way from Glasgow.'

'Listen, Carlson. Where are you? I'm coming to see you. The security forces are all over this. I *mean* MI6.' He sniffed. 'But I suppose you'll know that, whatever the hell you were doing with Elizabeth Fletcher. She's a spook. Did you know that?'

I took a moment.

'Well, no, actually I didn't.' It was true, but the way I said it sounded cagey, so I added, 'I think it's best to meet, Harry, as it's not a good idea to talk on the phone.'

'Aye. Yours will be getting tapped as we talk. You in the office?'

'Yes.'

'I'll call round now. Don't go anywhere.'

'You can't order me, Harry,' I said, but he'd already hung up.

I turned to Fowler.

'Christ, Dave! Elizabeth Fletcher has been shot dead in her cottage.'

'Holy fuck!'

'Wilson says MI6 are all over it – and my number is on her mobile.'

'Shit. So he's coming down here?'

'Yes. What a shitshow this has turned into.' He shook his head. 'I think I'll make myself scarce before he gets here.' He looked at me. 'Unless you want me to stay? Moral support? Are you going to tell him everything now?'

I puffed out my cheeks but didn't answer, then he went on.

'I don't think you've got much option, Billie. You have to tell him everything. I've not got a problem being here if you want.'

I glanced at him, bit my lip.

'No, Dave. I don't want to drag you into it. I can handle Wilson – or anything else that comes with it.'

He stood up.

'You sure?'

'Yes. I shouldn't have told you anything about what she did. It was wrong to involve you in the first place.'

He didn't say anything, but I knew he was thinking I told you so and that I should have listened when he told me to go to the cops in the first place. But he was too much of a good guy to say it.

'Give me a shout when it's over, if you need to talk,' he said, beckoning Jess to his side, then they left.

I sat for a long moment looking at the back of my hands as though they had all the answers. Then I stood up and walked across to the big window, looking down at the street, wondering if the lives of the people down there were as complicated as mine had just got.

I was in the main office telling a stunned Millie about Wilson's phone call when the intercom buzzed and she answered it.

'DCI Harry Wilson for Billie Carlson,' came the gruff voice.

'In you come, Chief Inspector,' Millie said, a breeziness about her voice as she made a here-it-comes face to me.

The door opened and Wilson came in, his face like thunder. He looked straight at me, shaking his head. I said nothing but motioned him into my office as I walked ahead of him, feeling his eyes like daggers on my back. Inside we stood for a moment looking at each other.

'What the actual fuck, Carlson?'

I put my hands up in surrender.

'Harry, listen. It's . . . it's . . . a long—' I was about to say story when he interrupted.

'No. Wait. Before you say a word, Carlson. I rushed down here to get the first of you, because the fucking secret service are in HQ right now and they want to talk to you pronto. I told them we'd worked together and to let me talk to you first, but they are in no mood to be fobbed off. So I hope you've got a good explanation as to what the hell you were doing with this Fletcher woman.'

I took a breath and gestured for him to sit on the sofa as I went to the door.

'Okay, Harry. I'll tell you. But you're going to need a strong coffee at least for this.'

'Aye, black,' he mumbled, throwing himself onto the sofa, his legs wide apart, his stomach straining against his shirt. 'But you need to tell me what's going on. You could be in big trouble if you don't.'

I stuck my head around the door and asked Millie to bring us in two coffees, then I sat down on the chair, glancing at my watch.

'Okay, Harry. Just hear me out.'

He didn't reply but sat forward, his eyes searching my face for whatever truth I was about to spill to him.

I took a deep breath.

'It's a mess all right,' I said. 'But here goes . . .'

He listened, engrossed, as I told him everything – from the initial phone call from Elizabeth Fletcher, to our first meeting in the Glasgow hotel where I'd sat dumbfounded as she told me what she'd done. To his credit, he didn't interrupt me once, and I wasn't sure if he was in shock from what I was telling him or he was trying to work out what he was going to say when I finished. Eventually I got to the part about the blackmail and the last time I saw Elizabeth when she gave me the USB stick. The only thing I didn't tell him was about the connection between her and my father. That was not for anyone but me right now.

When I stopped he took a long drink of his coffee and sniffed then rubbed his face and we sat not saying anything for what seemed like an age. Then he looked at me.

'Jesus wept, Carlson! You know how to get yourself mixed up in shit more than anyone else I've ever come across.' He ran a hand through his hair and looked at me. 'You could be in bother here, you know, keeping all this to yourself and not doing the right thing. But I've told you these things before and you never fucking listen.' He paused, shaking his head. 'You might be in danger, Carlson. Somebody might be watching you. Whoever shot Fletcher might have been at her house to get that USB stick and silence her.'

'Cheers for the frightener, Harry,' I said sarcastically. 'I know that. But everything happened so quickly between her telling me about killing the guy then the blackmail that I didn't want to just drop her into the police. She was a client. I was trying to work out how or if I could actually help her. Then this.'

He gave me a look that was almost understanding, that suggested he could see my point. Then he waited a few moments before he spoke.

'Look, Carlson,' he said. 'The MI6 guys who are creeping about my office are not in the mood to sympathise with anyone. Whatever has gone on here and whoever this guy was who somehow found himself in Portpatrick and picked Fletcher up in a bar, I think it's fairly obvious that he was there to get to her. Who knows, maybe even to kill her. So whoever he is – was – I don't think the spooks in Whitehall will be weeping over his loss. But they'll need to talk to you to get the bigger picture – and to get this USB stick. Where is it by the way?'

'Here. In my safe.'

'Oh, that's handy,' he almost chuckled. 'Because a spy who shoots people in their beds would never think of looking in your safe if he thinks you might have it.'

I sighed.

'I didn't know what else to do with it. I was going to talk to the police. Honestly. I'd have phoned you in the next day or so,' I said. 'I was going to phone you anyway about this Scottish woman found dead on the beach in Spain – Cathy Evans. You know the case?'

'Yeah. From what the Spanish cops say she was just another pissed Brit. Collapsed on the beach.'

I shook my head.

'But she wasn't, Harry. That's the point. Her daughter came to me to look into it, and there's a lot to this. Drugs smuggling and money laundering it seems. I was going to talk to you about that.'

He nodded.

'Okay. I'm intrigued. But it'll have to wait. You need to talk to the London spooks before we go any further.'

'And tell them what? Everything I told you?'

He grimaced.

'I think you have to.'

'Harry, I can't risk getting arrested. I mean, I haven't done anything really wrong – well, apart from not repeating to the police what Elizabeth told me about the guy who tried to kill her. And I have no evidence that she was telling the truth at the time. Only her word. She might have been stark raving mad for all I knew.'

He nodded slowly.

'Then that's the position you take,' he said. 'Look, I'll talk to them when I get back to the office and tell them what you told me, and that you were still investigating if she was telling the truth and that's why you didn't go to the cops.'

I sat back and looked at Harry. This big arrogant cop who had given me a hard time as a young detective but who had seen something in me that somehow made him seem to care what happened to me. He'd shown his caring side when Fowler – in self-defence – shot a lowlife thug who was guarding trafficked girls in a stinking basement flat in Glasgow that we happened on not long ago. Wilson was first on the scene and disposed of the handgun before the rest of the police arrived to find Fowler bleeding on the floor and the thug with a bullet in his chest. He didn't have to do that. And he didn't have to talk to the spooks from Whitehall to attempt to defend me in some way so that I wouldn't end up getting huckled out of my office in handcuffs for withholding information.

'You'll do that, Harry?' I asked, not knowing what else to say.

'Aye.' He put a hand up. 'But don't go throwing your arms around me in thanks, because I honestly don't know how this is going to pan out for you. These guys are not cops as we know it. They're secretive bastards who wouldn't show you a bird's nest, so who knows what's on their agenda. But the guy who seems to be running the show might be all right, so I'll talk to him and give him the lowdown.'

He saw me glancing at my watch and stood up.

'Right.' His eyes narrowed, and he looked at me. 'Do you want me to get someone to hang around and keep an eye on you?'

I was beginning to feel a little paranoid that someone might be out there watching me.

'I don't know,' was all I could manage to say. 'What do you think?'

He hesitated a moment then looked at me.

'I'll get a squad car to follow you and make sure you get home, then cruise around for the night. I'm going to speak to the head spook and tell him you are not able to see him until tomorrow.'

I tightened my lips.

'Thanks, Harry.'

He nodded.

'Don't thank me yet.'

Then he left.

CHAPTER SIXTEEN

Within ten minutes of Wilson leaving my office he was back on the phone to say that the MI6 agents wanted to talk to me today. He suggested that I come to his office at police HQ. From the polite, reasoned way he was talking I gathered that whoever the shadowy figures were who wanted to interview me were standing beside him. There was no way I was going to HQ to be grilled by any of them, to be somewhere out of my comfort zone where they were the guys in charge and who knew where it could end up. I told him I would be willing to talk to them – I had no choice – but explained in the most co-operative way I could that it would be more convenient for me if we met in my office. He was silent for a moment – probably consulting the spooks standing over him – then he agreed. They would be here within the hour.

When I came off the phone, I asked Millie if she would take Lucas out to a café for a little while when I brought him to the office after nursery, so that I could speak to the Whitehall people alone. I felt a knot in my stomach, anxious as to how I would handle these guys. Wilson was one thing, but I'd never really encountered the forces of British intelligence before, and anything I knew was based on spy movies. I had no idea that my own father – according to Elizabeth Fletcher – was one of them, and that single factor seemed to give me a bit of strength inside. If what she told me was true – that my father did not commit suicide but was pushed off that bridge into the River Clyde – then for all I knew these very men coming to pick away at my story might well already know all about my family history. My head was full of the possibilities, but I knew that no matter what happened in the next couple of hours, I would never let on about what I'd been told about my father's past. Anyhow, it was a long time ago, and these guys might not know a thing about it.

As soon as the nursery doors opened my thoughts were banished as Lucas came racing towards me as though he was seeing me for the first time. I knew I'd never tire of that. Ever.

I fiddled around my desk with papers, making it look neat and orderly for no apparent reason as these guys weren't coming to assess the tidiness of my office. I checked my watch. Millie had just left with Lucas bouncing that they were going out for a walk and to the café in the sunshine, and I waited for the spooks to arrive. Even though I was anticipating it at any moment, I still jumped when the intercom buzzed.

'We're here, Billie.' It was Wilson's voice.

I buzzed them in and went out into the reception front of house to meet them as they came through the doorway. Wilson was first in, his expression deadpan as he turned to the two men behind him. He gestured to the man at his side, tall, navy pinstriped suit, wavy silver hair. Forties, I'd have said.

'Billie, this is Major Colin Palmer, British Covert Intelligence commander.' He turned to the major. 'Billie Carlson, Major. Former Glasgow detective – of some note.'

Wilson's breezy introduction surprised me a little, as it appeared that however secretive and shadowy he'd said these figures were, he wanted to let them know that he was a supporter of mine. I gave a half-smile, shook the major's out-stretched hand but said nothing.

'Ms Carlson,' the major said, fixing me with steely blue eyes. Then he turned to his sidekick, a tall, willowy thirtysomething pasty guy with horn-rimmed glasses and an intense tight-lipped look. 'This is officer James Thomson-Smith.'

He didn't give any more details, not that I expected a brief biography, and I waited for the next line from the major to start the grilling.

'Can I get you some coffee? Tea?' I asked, gesturing to them to follow me into my office.

'No thank you,' the major answered for everyone. 'I'd like to get down to the business of why we're here, Ms Carlson.'

I moved across to behind my desk for some protection, a little irritated by the 'Ms Carlson'. I looked at the major.

'Do call me Billie,' I said to Palmer.

Again, he fixed his steely eyes on me for a few seconds, then he nodded.

'Billie.'

I waited. He took a breath and sat forward, clasping his hands together as though ready for a speech.

'Billie,' he repeated. 'Elizabeth Fletcher.' He turned a fraction towards Wilson. 'DCI Wilson has given us what you told him, and while we are grateful for that, it doesn't detract from the fact that you withheld this information for, what was it, a week, two weeks? Not sure.'

I swallowed. Right in with the first punch. There was not going to be any gentle chat here, and I sensed that he had started this way to put me on the back foot. I was for a second, but I kept my face straight, and put my hand up in protest.

'Yes, Major,' I said, looking him in the eye. 'I absolutely do appreciate that and understand.' I leaned forward, pushing my hair back. 'But what you have to understand, and hopefully respect, is that this was a client who had come to me seeking help. Someone I knew nothing of, someone who could have been stark raving mad but who told a very fascinating and convincing story, if a little far-fetched. But to tell you the truth, I had no idea if she was making all that stuff up. I absolutely didn't. So up until a day or so ago, I was still trying to investigate this woman to find out if she was authentic.'

He looked at me, his blue eyes softening to something like a smile, but not a smile. It was a look that said yeah, pull the other one, matey – I see you've got your story right. He nodded.

'Yes, er, Billie. I do understand and respect that. But there actually was a genuine dead body of a male fished out of the sea a few weeks ago. So perhaps you may have thought there was something to her story.'

'Sure,' I said, glancing at Wilson, whose expression was flat. 'But how did I even know that she wasn't one of these people who had latched on to some story in a newspaper about a dead body and then begun to create her own fantasy?'

'Hmm,' he said, not looking convinced, but aware I was no pushover. He pushed out a breath. 'Okay. But what we are here today to do is get a full statement from you as to every little thing she said on your encounters and absolutely everything she told you about this man, and what else she said, well, about anything really. Are we clear on that?'

'Yes,' I said. 'I am.'

The major turned to his sidekick, who reached into his briefcase and brought out a small recording device.

'Officer Thomson-Smith here will record your interview. You're okay with that?'

I glanced at Wilson.

'Hold on, though, Major,' I said. 'I'm not under arrest, am I?'

'No,' he assured me. But from his expression, I could see that he was dying to say 'not yet'. He waited a moment before he went on. 'No. We are recording it because it is easier and more convenient to have it in a recorded form as well as a written document statement.'

'Okay,' I said.

Thomson-Smith shifted around in his seat, then set up the tape on my desk with the microphone close to me, voice-tested himself on it a couple of times, then said into it that this was a statement from Billie Carlson, private investigator, taken from her at her office in Billie Carlson Investigations, Mitchell Lane, Glasgow. Then he nodded to me.

After a long pause, with me glancing at the microphone, then from Palmer to Wilson, the major began.

'Billie, can you talk us through your first encounter with the now deceased Elizabeth Fletcher – date, time, all of that, how she introduced herself? What did she say exactly? In your own words, please. In your own time. Just that first encounter – the phone call.'

I took a breath, glad that Millie had given me a prepared log of the dates and times of the first phone call from Fletcher. I began. And so it went on. From the first phone call, everything I could remember. But I kept to myself Fletcher's parting comment that day when she'd told me she'd known my father. That was for me. I didn't want to involve any of them in that because it felt too raw and personal to be shared with some people who were cold and distant, who may or may not have known anything about my family.

'Thank you,' he said. 'Do you need a break before we go to the next part, where you actually met her?'

'No,' I said. 'I can go on.'

I told him about our meeting at the Hilton, my shock when

Elizabeth unfolded her story like a terrifying scene from a horror movie. I knew that all of what I was telling him was the truth, but missing was the crucial part of why I even took on this case in the first place. Because if he knew anything about what Fletcher had told me about my father's background, then they would know all about me – they would have made it their business to know that before they even met me. I wasn't entirely comfortable with it, but it was private. I told him everything about what she said. Then about the blackmail, the phone calls, and then what happened on that day with the USB stick. When I got to the end, I stopped and took a breath.

'The USB stick,' he said, giving me a long look. 'Where is it?'

'It's in my safe,' I said.

'Did you look at it?' His expression said that whatever I told him, he wouldn't believe me.

I held his gaze.

'Not personally,' I said.

'What?'

'I didn't look at it myself. I had one of my associates look at it.'

He was trying his best to control his shock.

'Who? What associate? Why would you do that?'

'Well, because I was investigating a client's story, as I told you, and this was part of it. I'm not good with tech things. Of course I was going to look into the contents of the USB stick. Wouldn't you?' I didn't wait for an answer. 'I mean, it could have been anything, holiday snaps, an elaborate hoax for all I knew.'

'So, who looked at it?'

I glanced at Wilson.

'It doesn't matter who looked at it, but all I can say is that as soon as it was put into the computer there were warning lights everywhere and it was immediately taken out.'

He breathed in a controlled way out of his nostrils as though trying to stay calm. He probably knew exactly who looked at it but wouldn't want me to know that.

'What kind of lights?'

'I don't know. The expert said it was like government warning lights saying it was top secret, all that stuff, so he immediately removed it.'

'Can you give me the USB stick now?'

'Yes. Of course.'

I got up and went across the room to my safe on the wall, opened it with the combination, and took out the box with the USB stick. I handed it to him and sat back down. He handed it to Thomson-Smith and nodded to him to put it into his laptop. I waited with bated breath, wondering if we would get to know what was on this. Silence for an age, then Thomson-Smith looked at his boss and turned the laptop screen so he could see, and the major got up and stood looking over his shoulder as they scrolled down whatever was on the screen. If there was anything on there that moved the earth for the major, then his expression never changed. He read through it, impassive, then took a sharp breath through flared nostrils before snapping the laptop shut. After a long moment he turned to me.

'I think we have got everything you have told us, Billie, unless there is anything you have neglected to tell us? Anything at all?'

He looked right through me and I felt the colour rising in my neck. I shook my head.

'No,' I said. 'That's it.'

His eyes narrowed and I had the chilling sense he knew that I wasn't telling the whole truth.

CHAPTER SEVENTEEN

It had felt like a long day by the time I left the office and headed home with Lucas chattering in the back because he was excited that Scanlon was coming for dinner. I'd called him earlier and told him about Elizabeth Fletcher being murdered and my grilling by the spooks, and he was fascinated to hear the full story. I was making a chicken pasta dish with vegetables that I could knock up in a few minutes when I got into the flat so it would be cooking away by the time he arrived. He was coming straight from work and asked if he could shower at my place. I loved that about Scanlon, the way he never took me for granted even though in recent weeks he'd stayed over at my flat and slept in my bed and we'd made love. He never assumed he could just swan in and use my flat as his own, and that level of respect went both ways. I had never stayed over at his flat because every time we were together Lucas was always with us, and I would not have been comfortable asking anyone to babysit him while I spent the night elsewhere just for the fun of it.

Lucas had his cars and a fire station all laid out on the living room floor by the time Scanlon buzzed the intercom, and he was off like a shot to greet him at the door. Scanlon came in with Lucas on one arm, and a brown paper bag on the other.

'Dessert!' he declared, planting a kiss on my cheek as he set the bag down on the kitchen worktop. 'Apple pie and ice cream. The healthy option.' He smiled. 'Well . . . healthy-ish. I mean, it is one of your five a day.'

'Perfect,' I said, moving across to the pan where the chicken, with peppers and tomatoes, was gently cooking and the pasta was simmering in another pot. 'This is even healthier, so we can indulge ourselves in a bit of ice cream later.'

'So did the spooks rough you up?' Scanlon smiled, coming across and stroking my hair. 'At least they didn't put you in handcuffs.'

'Not yet anyway,' I said. 'They were okay, actually. Not exactly the best bedside manner, but I told them everything that had happened and that I couldn't come to the police because I was investigating whether Elizabeth was telling the truth.'

'They bought that?' he said, eyebrows raised.

I shrugged. 'They seemed to.'

Scanlon backed away as Lucas pulled his hand, declaring, 'Emergency! Emergency! Fire! Fire! Come on, Danny! Let's go.'

Scanlon laughed as he was dragged away and I watched with a surge of happiness in my stomach at the pair of them interacting together.

I opened a bottle of wine with dinner as we sat at the table, where most of the chat was about Lucas and nursery and new friends he'd met and television shows, and how soon it would be summertime and holidays and could we go somewhere, all of it spilling out, and we chatted and said let's see and promised we would go somewhere together. Once the ice cream and apple pie had been scoffed, Lucas watched a bit of television before he got ready for bed. Scanlon took him in, and I went in afterwards to tuck him in, and watched as his eyes got heavier and he drifted off.

'Another glass?' Scanlon asked as I came back into the living room.

'Small one,' I said. 'It's a school night.'

'Me too,' he said. 'I'm on at eight in the morning.'

We settled down on the couch and sipped our wine, Scanlon surfing the channels on TV to see what was on Netflix, and we decided on an old Jack Nicholson movie that we'd seen a few times but still made us laugh.

'So,' he said. 'How you feeling about it all?'

'What?' I said, suddenly wondering what he meant because I knew I was harbouring a secret. 'Oh, you mean the Fletcher murder? Yes, it was all so sudden.'

'Obviously some heavy-duty foreign spy capers going on. I mean, MI6 coming straight up like that and grilling you.'

'Yes,' I said. 'It was all a bit overwhelming.'

We sat for a long moment and the urge to tell him everything just completely took over. My mouth suddenly felt dry, and my throat tightened.

'You all right, Carlson? You've gone a bit quiet.'

I nodded. Then he sat forward so he could turn and face me.

'You're not telling me everything, are you?' Scanlon said. 'It's written all over your face.'

I grimaced, took a breath and sighed.

'No,' I said. 'I haven't told you everything, Danny. It's . . . well, it's just where to start. I haven't told you because I was still trying to get my head around it.'

'Around what?' he asked, taking my hand in his. 'You know you can tell me anything, Billie. Totally in confidence.'

'I know.' I swallowed. 'Danny. That woman. Elizabeth.' I paused, looking at him, then away, then back at him. 'The first time she phoned me, when she asked for a meeting, at the very end of the phone call, she suddenly said, "I knew your father."'

His eyes widened.

'What? She said that?'

I nodded.

'Yes. Took my feet from under me.'

'No wonder.'

'After all these years ... I was only twelve when I lost my father, and you know what? Hardly anyone has ever mentioned his name since. I was completely stunned when she said that. And to tell you the truth, that's really the only reason I took the case. It's the only reason I went to see her in the first place.'

He puffed, nodded, but didn't say anything.

'That's not the half of it, Danny,' I said.

'What? Did she tell you more?'

'Yes. But not until the day of our last meeting. The day somebody shot her after I left.'

'What did she say?'

'She said my father had been a spy for the British security services.' I felt my face burning, and my hands suddenly felt shaky. 'And . . . and she said he was murdered that night. That he was pushed off the bridge.' I bit my lip and blinked back tears. 'My father, Danny. She said he was murdered.'

'Oh, Christ, Billie!'

He wrapped his arms around me and held me close. Then the tears came, taking me by surprise. The floodgates opened. They were tears that had been kept back for years, for the father I'd loved and needed so much but who had left us, and now the tears were of frustration, confusion and rage that someone had killed him when I was a little girl and nobody ever told me the truth.

'I'm sorry,' I said. 'It's suddenly kind of hit me.' I sniffed, eased myself out of his arms and we sat facing each other.

'Most of my life, I have never looked back. It was too painful to look back, so I put it all away somewhere in my mind and didn't look at it as my life took over – studies, work, police, Lucas, all of that. There was no time, and no need to dwell on the past. I had dealt with it, or so I thought. But as you can see, I haven't.' I shook my head.

'It's all understandable, Billie. Everything you're feeling right now. You should just let all of those thoughts come to the surface.'

'I don't think I can deal with them.'

'You don't have to deal with them. Not yet. You just have to allow yourself to feel bad about it, to feel sad and angry and everything you're feeling right now. You've shut it all away for such a long time.'

'I know. I just didn't expect to have to look back and find that everything was all a lie.'

'Not so much a lie, Billie. You were twelve years old. What could your father possibly tell you about his work that you would understand? Nothing. He was protecting you from it all. And who knows, maybe your mother didn't even know about his other work while he was travelling abroad, apparently lecturing.'

I nodded, sighing.

'I'll never know. Thanks, Danny.' I took his hand. 'I don't know where I'd be without you. Honestly. From the time Lucas was stolen to everything that has happened since. I'm so grateful to have you in my life.'

We looked at each other for a long time then he reached across and pushed my hair behind my ear.

'I love you, Billie. No matter what.'

It took me a long time to truly realise it, but I said it out loud.

'I love you too, Danny.' I sniffed. 'But I'm still a bit of a mess.'

He ruffled my hair.

'I know. I love that about you.'

CHAPTER EIGHTEEN

I was doing my best to put into some perspective everything that I'd been told about my father, and I knew I would have to find a way to deal with all the emotions. Scanlon might be right, that I should not push it all away as I seem to have done from an early age. There was nothing to be afraid of here. And there was nothing I could do to change what happened all those years ago. So it was up to me to find a way through it.

My life was different now, I told myself. I hadn't had my parents since I was twelve years old, and I'd grown up without them and faced the hardest time in my life in recent years when I lost Lucas. I hope I'm stronger for all of that. I could face the memories of my childhood, and I promised myself that over the next few days I would take a step towards that by going into the place in my flat where I knew my father and mother had kept so many things. I had never even ventured into the walk-in cupboard since I was a little girl, and the door had been locked from the day I left for Sweden as a child. Who knew what I would find when I went in there. I'd never even had an inclination to look inside it until now. So, I had to make up my mind if I wanted to go ahead and look at the past, or if I kept the cupboard door firmly shut and moved on. It was up to me. I would mull over it in my mind until I was ready to make a decision.

I was daydreaming a little about this and about how gentle and supportive Scanlon had been last night as we lay in bed after we'd made love. He held me until I fell asleep, and I was surprised that I hadn't even woken up until the morning when he'd gone and I'd found the bed empty.

My reverie was broken by the ringing of my mobile on the passenger seat. I could see Jane McAllister's name on the screen and pushed the hands-free answer on my dashboard.

'Jane. You okay?'

'Billie. No. I'm not.' Panic in her voice. 'Some guy came into the café yesterday and sat for ages. He was staring at me for a while. Then at one stage when I was clearing the table next to him, he spoke to me.'

'What? What did he say?'

'He asked me to sit down. I knew exactly what this was, that he was someone sent to scare me. My legs were like jelly. But I couldn't sit. I'm not allowed to sit with customers. So I told him I was busy.'

'What did he say?'

'He sat for a second then stood up, and grabbed my arm as I turned away. He told me, "I've got a message from Steve and Marilyn. They want to help you out a bit after losing your friend."' She paused. 'I didn't answer.'

'What happened then?'

'He just said to me they could make it worth my while if I made sure I kept my mouth shut about that night. I told him I didn't know what he was talking about but I was busy. Then he stood for a second, let go of my arm and gave me a sneering look as he walked away. Before he went he said, "I'll be in touch." I felt physically sick. I had to go to the toilet and sit for a minute to compose myself. Once I came out he was gone. But I know he's out there. I'm terrified.'

'I talked to the police about you. They want to speak to you.'

'Yes. I'm ready to do that now. I think I'm in danger. Can I talk to the police today?'

She sounded desperate.

'Okay. Let me make a couple of calls and get back to you. Where are you?'

'Just about to leave for work. But I feel as if someone is watching me.'

She was probably right, but I didn't want to tell her that.

'I'll get back to you as soon as I can, Jane. I'm at the other end of the phone if you need me.'

'Thanks.'

She hung up, and despite me reassuring her that she could call me, I knew there wasn't much I could do to help this woman right now. She needed protection; to be away from here where she couldn't be found by whoever was pulling the strings of this dodgy couple on the Costa del Sol. The police could do that, or a level of that for sure, once she told them the full story. But the way Jane was talking, and especially considering the random frightener visit by the guy to the café, they were already all over her. There was only one man I knew who could find out the strength of the threat, or what kind of power, if any, this Steve and Marilyn had, and who they worked for. And that was Paddy Harper, an old-school Glasgow gangster allegedly now retired, but who I'd turned to recently when I needed help and action urgently, without going through the stages of opening up a police investigation.

I pulled my car into a parking space outside my office and climbed up the stairs rather than use the clanky ancient lift with the wrought-iron sliding gate. It gave me the creeps. Millie was by the coffee machine and greeted me with her usual smile as I swept through the door. Before I pushed the key to call Harper, Millie handed me a mug of coffee.

'Billie, I just took a call before you arrived from Elizabeth Fletcher's husband. He's looking for you.'

I stopped in my tracks, putting the mug on a desk while I hung up my jacket on the stand.

'Really?'

'Yep. I told him you'd call him back. He said he was eager to talk with you.'

'Did he say anything else?'

'Only introduced himself as Christopher Fletcher, husband of Elizabeth Fletcher, client of yours. Plummy accent. Not Scottish, I think. English, educated. Said he was in Scotland assisting police with the investigation but wanted to speak with you.'

'Sure,' I said.

'The number is on your desk.'

I thanked her and headed into my office with the coffee. At my desk I saw the mobile phone number but put it to the side to call Paddy Harper first. I pushed the key, and it was picked up after two rings.

'Billie. You all right?'

'Yes, Paddy. All okay here. Yourself?'

'Aye, enjoying life. Just back from my house in Spain. I was there for three weeks just enjoying the good life in the sun.'

'Good for you, Paddy,' I said, wondering if he was really relaxing and retired as he said he was, or if he was over there making sure the wheels of his organisation were still turning. Whatever else he was these days, Harper was a good guy who had looked after some people I had been helping and he knew where to go when the doors were closed to them.

'What can I do for you, Billie? Or is this just a social call?'

I could hear the chuckle in his voice. He knew I never called him socially.

'Well, truth is, Paddy, I'm looking to pick your brains,' I said. 'About a couple in the Costa del Sol who I think are involved in the death of a Glasgow woman out there.'

'What Glasgow woman?'

'A woman called Cathy Evans. She was found on the beach, head wound, soaking wet. Couple of months ago.'

He paused a moment, then spoke.

'Oh, aye. I do remember seeing a line about that in the newspaper. Seems to have been some drunk Brit who ended up on the beach. I don't think it's a big police investigation.'

'No. It isn't.'

I told him about her daughter coming to see me and her suspicions, then about Jane McAllister, and gave him everything she'd told me about the Dubai trips and cruises and money being brought in and taken out, drugs smuggled, and the ugly scene that unravelled that night. He was silent for what seemed like a long time, then he spoke.

'Well, I don't know this couple personally to be honest, but put it this way, I know a man who will know them. He knows everyone and has his ear to the ground all the time. The couple will be working for someone, that's for sure. There are only about two guys out there who use people like that, so I'll be able to throw their names in and see what comes out. Where is this Jane woman now?'

I told him the café she worked at and that she wanted to talk to the police and tell the whole story.

'She probably should, Billie. But if they are on to her in

Glasgow, then time is not on her side. She needs to be moved. Taken out of the way. What do you think?'

'I agree. I told her I would talk to the cops and maybe she could meet them today, but I'm not sure how quickly that will all happen. I know what these things are like.'

'If you want, I can have someone go to the café and make contact with her. Tell her that you asked us to do it. Is she likely to freak out if we do that?'

'I don't think so, if you mention my name. But I'll try to get her on the phone now and tell her one of your guys will be down in a while.'

'We will be there in the next half hour. Not me, though. I'll get Jimmy and one of the guys to go and pick her up.'

'What about the cops, though, Paddy?' I asked. 'She wants to tell the cops everything. I think she needs to.'

'Of course. No problem. I'll just get her out of the way until the plods are ready to talk to her. Meanwhile I'll make some enquiries out there and see what's going on and find out who sent the guy to the café to monster her.'

When I came off the phone, I called Jane's mobile. I looked at my watch as it rang out. She was either parking her car or had just got to the café to start work and couldn't get to the phone. I gave it a few more minutes, picked up the piece of paper with Christopher Fletcher's number on it, and pushed it into my mobile. But I didn't ring it, instead phoning Jane's number again, which still rang out. I checked the name of the café on my laptop and phoned the number.

'I'm looking for Jane McAllister,' I said. 'Is she there?'

'Hold on, please,' the voice said.

Then a few seconds later I heard the phone being picked up.

'Sorry. Jane hasn't arrived yet. Can I ask who this is?'

'I'm a friend of Jane's,' I said. 'She's not answering her mobile and I just wanted to make sure she was at work.'

'She's not here yet. She's already a half hour late, which isn't like her.'

My stomach knotted. She'd been leaving the house when she spoke to me, and the journey to work is only around ten minutes. I rang her number again, and still it was ringing out. I scrolled down for Harry Wilson's number. The police had more immediate resources to search for someone who may be missing, who may have been kidnapped. Wilson's number was on divert. Shit. I called Harper.

'Paddy. I can't get an answer on Jane's mobile, and she hasn't turned up at work.' I told him she was leaving the house when I'd spoken to her earlier.

'That doesn't sound good, Billie. Was she driving to work? What kind of car?'

'Yes, I assume she was driving. It's only just over ten minutes' drive away.' I paused, trying to remember the car I saw in her driveway that day we first met. 'I think it's a Citroën, yellow. That's all I can remember. I didn't really pay any attention to the car when I met her outside her house.'

He asked me for her address, and I gave it to him.

'I'll get someone to her house and ask around. She lives on her own, right?'

'Yes.'

'Maybe neighbours saw something. I'll get back to you.'

He hung up.

I got up from behind my desk and paced across to the window, a niggling feeling that something bad had happened to Jane. Whatever it was, it must have happened without warning, otherwise I was sure she would have called me.

My mobile ringing made me jump and I swiftly went to the

desk and picked it up, surprised to see the number of Lucas's nursery on the screen.

'Is that Billie Carlson?'

'Yes, it is.'

'This is Mrs Reynolds, head of the nursery.'

'Is Lucas okay?' I asked, alarm in my voice.

'Oh, yes. Of course. He's fine. He's here. It's a security issue, Billie. Did you ask someone to pick Lucas up today? To pick him up early?'

'What?' My stomach dropped. 'Absolutely not. Has someone been up there?'

'Yes. There was a man who arrived at the reception and said he had been sent by you to bring Lucas to your office. He said Lucas had a dental appointment. But we only have two names, yours and Millie's, and would obviously never allow anyone else to pick him up without contacting you.'

'Jesus! Who was this? Did he give a name?'

'Yes. Gordon Smith he said his name was, said he was a friend of yours. He's just gone. We told him we would have to contact you.'

I swallowed the panic in my throat, trying to compose myself, then spoke.

'Mrs Reynolds. I'm coming up to the nursery now to talk to you. It's almost time to bring Lucas home so I'll collect him a little early. Have you any more information on the man who came to the reception?'

'No. Sorry. He left quite quickly after we told him we would not allow Lucas to be taken without speaking to his mother. My next call is going to be to the police. We have to report this.'

'Of course. I'm on my way.'

My heart was pounding, and I could hear the blood in my ears. I came out of my office and told Millie, then grabbed my jacket. I headed up there, calling Scanlon on the way to tell him, and then Wilson.

CHAPTER NINETEEN

By the time I arrived at the nursery, there were already two police patrol cars and officers on the gate, as well as one of the nursery teachers. I'd also put a call in to Harper to tell him what had happened. He was convinced it was something to do with Jane McAllister, and said he would send a couple of guys up to be in the background and keep an eye out. I introduced myself to the uniformed sergeant at the gate and the nursery teacher vouched for me, and they waved me through. Mrs Reynolds was at the door when I buzzed and she let me in.

'If you come into my office, Billie. Sorry to give you such a fright.'

'Not at all. Thanks for being so vigilant. I can't believe it. Have the police spoken to you directly?'

'Not yet. They sent officers to the gate, but there is someone coming up to take a statement. It's very serious. The idea that someone comes up and lies to staff to get a child. It really doesn't bear thinking about. It's never happened before.'

I shook my head.

'I nearly collapsed when you told me. Are you able to describe the man? Age, or anything else at all?'

'He was in his thirties – late thirties, I'd say. Not very well dressed. In fact, a bit dishevelled. To be honest, from the get-go it just didn't feel right. I know with Lucas's background that anything untoward like this – in fact, for any child – does set off alarm bells all over the place. There was no question at all of anyone allowing Lucas to leave the building with a stranger, no chance at all. But as soon as something like this happens, it makes everyone feel uneasy.' She paused. 'Have you any idea who this stranger might be?'

'No.' I shook my head. 'None at all.'

The old haunting thought that we have never been a hundred per cent sure forensically that Lucas's father perished in the fire in that US trailer park came back. But I brushed it away. This visit was a message to me. This was something to do with Jane. Maybe they had seen me with her, or maybe they had her phone and she had told them she met with me.

'It's very worrying. But security here is of the utmost importance,' she said. 'Obviously we will have to inform other parents of the incident as the police are involved.'

'Of course. Anything I can do to help, I'd be glad.'

'Billie, do you think this is something to do with the work you do? I mean, your private investigator work, or being an ex-police officer?'

I pushed out a sigh.

'I don't know,' I said, not entirely telling the truth. 'It could be. But I deal with a lot of clients and cases. I just don't know.'

There was a knock at the door, then it opened, and DCI Harry Wilson came in along with a female detective.

'Mrs Reynolds.' He nodded in her direction, then at me. 'Billie. You all right?'

I puffed.

'I am now. It was some fright to get, though.'

'Any ideas who this might be?'

I gave him a look and he glared back as though to say there's probably a list as long as my arm of people I've noised up over the years. I shrugged.

'I had a missed call from you, Billie. Actually, not long before the call came in about this incident at the nursery.'

'Yes,' I said. 'I was trying to call you. Not about this. That woman. The one I told you about – she wants to talk to the police now. But she seems to have vanished on her way to work.'

'Jesus,' he muttered. 'Can we step outside for a chat?'

He looked at Mrs Reynolds.

'Officer Clinton will take a statement from you, Mrs Reynolds. I'll be back in a minute.'

Out in the corridor, Wilson ushered me to the small cloakroom, rows of little jackets and bags hanging up, and it sent a chill through me that one of them was Lucas's and that it might have been gone by now if the nursery wasn't so on the ball.

'What the fuck, Carlson? What's happened here?'

'I've no idea. But it has to be something to do with this woman, Jane. She called me this morning to say she wanted to talk to the police and tell them everything about what happened in Spain. Then she didn't turn up at work. Someone's grabbed her, Harry. And I'm sure they got someone to come here and try to get Lucas too, maybe to get a message to me. This is really fucked up.'

'I know. Thank Christ the nursery is heavy on security.'

'They all are these days, thankfully. Doesn't bear thinking about what might have happened.'

My mobile rang and I pulled it out of my jacket pocket. No name on the screen. I glanced at Wilson and put the mobile on loudspeaker but didn't talk.

'You was lucky today, Billie Carlson.' The voice sounded as though it belonged to someone from Liverpool or Manchester. 'You might not be so lucky next time.' Then silence.

'Who is this?'

He didn't answer. But suddenly there came a woman's pan-icked voice. It was Jane.

'Billie! Billie! Please help me!'

Then an agonising scream as though she'd been struck. The line went dead.

Wilson was on the phone telling someone he needed a phone checked to see if there was any way of tracing the location of the call. He needed it now.

'Can you come back to HQ with me? They need to look at your mobile.'

I looked at my watch.

'I'll need to bring Lucas with me.'

'Fine. Let's move it.'

I followed Wilson's car as he was driven up to police HQ, with Lucas piping up from his seat in the back, asking, 'Where are we going, Mummy?' He was such a smart kid. He sussed as we were driving away from nursery that we were going in the wrong direction to be going home. I told him we were going to see the police station and that it was an adventure. He was asking questions all the way, like 'Will I get a hat, Mummy? Can I sit in a police car?' Of course, I told him, hoping I'd find a friendly uniformed cop. I called Scanlon and explained that I had Lucas in the car and couldn't talk but that someone had come to the nursery. I didn't want to say any more in case Lucas was listening. I told him I was going to HQ with Wilson and would meet him there if he was around. We drove into the car park behind the building and Wilson got out of his car as I parked beside him.

'Let's go straight upstairs,' he said, walking ahead of me. 'I'll get someone to amuse the wee man.'

In the lift Wilson pushed the button for the fourth floor, then Lucas swiftly pushed one, two and three, thrilled that the buttons lit up and causing the lift to stop at the first floor.

'Sorry,' I said, then turned to Lucas. 'You've not to touch the buttons, Lucas.'

Wilson shook his head and rolled his eyes upwards, tongue in cheek.

'The apple doesn't fall far from the tree, I see,' he said, nodding at Lucas. 'Determined to do it his way.'

The lift stopped at the second, third and finally the fourth floor, and we headed out and along the corridor to Wilson's office, where two officers with laptops stood up when he entered the room.

'All right, boys,' he said, then turned to me. 'Billie, can you give them your phone?'

'Sure,' I said, handing it over.

They immediately crossed to a long mahogany table at the other side of the room, opened laptops and mobiles and got to work.

'You want a cup of tea or anything?' Wilson said.

'No thanks,' I replied. 'I'm honestly traumatised about what happened at the nursery, Harry. If . . . It doesn't bear thinking about. After all Lucas has been through.' I swallowed the sudden lump in my throat and shook my head. I couldn't speak any more.

Wilson shot me a long look as though he could really see the agony in my eyes. He didn't speak for a moment, then he looked away, walked across to the window, and spoke over his shoulder.

'Well, don't think about what might have happened, Billie. Because it didn't. So, get a grip.'

Despite everything, I felt my face smiling and almost laughed.

'Cheers for the pep talk. You should become a therapist when you chuck it in here.'

From the side of my eye, I could see the two officers exchanging glances and trying to keep their faces straight. Wilson turned around to face me.

'Always the last word, Carlson.' He shook his head.

'Sir,' one of the officers piped up. 'We've got a hit on the phone. It's a burner, obviously, but there's something we can scramble from it. Location. The call was made from the Partick area. We can still see the phone, going somewhere headed out of the city.'

Wilson went across to them, looking at the screen.

'Good work, lads. It could be going anywhere, though.'

He went to his desk, picked up the phone and called to get a squad car in the area, then looked at me.

'That's about as much as we can do now. I've put a few bodies on it, so we'll see.'

'Do you need my mobile any more?'

'Lads?' He looked towards them. 'You clear with the mobile?'

'Yes, boss.' The officer who had answered glanced up at me. 'Thanks.' Then their heads were back in the laptop.

'Okay,' I said. 'Harry, I'll get Lucas home and fed. Will you keep me posted?'

He looked at me.

'No. I won't. You know that.'

I nodded.

'Didn't think so.'

He walked me to the door.

'Take this wee boy downstairs for a glass of juice and I'll get someone to show him the police cars.'

Outside in the corridor, Wilson stopped.

'I'll be honest with you, Carlson. It's a bit of a long shot chasing a mobile phone in a moving car. These bastards could just chuck it out of the window and we're snookered.'

'Yep,' I said.

'I'll let you know what's happening – if I get any news,' he said. Then he added, 'But knowing you, there will be some dodgy bastards with their own rules who will also be trying to find her.'

I didn't answer, because I genuinely didn't know what to say.

CHAPTER TWENTY

Once I got to the police car park and strapped Lucas into his car seat, I called Paddy Harper. As it rang, I glanced up at the HQ building, feeling a niggle of guilt that I was calling a known criminal, and thinking how Wilson would not be happy with any of that. But he would know that if it was criminals who had snatched Jane McAllister, then there was probably a better chance of criminals catching them. They had their own rules. And their network of informants was much broader than anything the police could come up with. Harper answered after three rings.

'Billie. Everything all right? After that stuff at the nursery?'

'With me it is, Paddy, thanks. But it's Jane McAllister. Someone's grabbed her. I got a phone call. She was freaked out. She's been kidnapped.'

'When? Just now?'

'No. Just after it was all over at the nursery. The cops were there in the nursery when I got the call, so they took me to HQ to get someone to look at my phone. This is the first chance I've had to give you a call. I'm just out of the police station and on my way to my flat. But the cops got a hit on the phone the call was made on. It was somewhere in the Partick area, mobile on the road. God knows where it is now.'

He was silent for a bit then spoke.

'Okay, Billie. That's good to know. We've got a handle on who it was in the café the other day intimidating Jane. I've got someone on the way out to talk to him. We'll get some answers very soon.'

I imagined how his men would 'talk' to the guy and thought how I wouldn't like to be in his shoes when they came knocking on his door.

'Is he working for someone up here or down south?' I asked.

'He's one of Vinnie Martin's boys – East End. It will be them who've got her. Vinnie's a psychopath, and he does a bit of enforcing for some of the London mob who have a lot of stuff going on in Marbella. They're probably the people that Steve and Marilyn are muling for.'

'Sounds heavy, Paddy.'

'It is, Billie. Big business bringing in a lot of drugs from across Europe and beyond to the UK. That dodgy couple are only bit-part players, but the London mob will want that all nailed down pronto.'

'Do you think you'll be able to find Jane before they do anything?'

He took a moment to answer, then pushed out a sigh.

'Don't know. I'll get a better picture once we've talked to this big bastard.'

He told me he would keep me posted then hung up.

Back at my flat, Scanlon came over with a pizza and we sat around the table chatting and eating as if we were in a scene from anyone's ordinary life. Except that behind the scenes, this picture was far from normal. Once Lucas had finished and was setting up his toys on the floor, I told Scanlon about Jane. He agreed that even though the police had a trace on the phone, it was unlikely to get them very far. I was going to tell him about Harper, but decided not to, and again I felt a bit guilty about not telling him the whole truth.

Scanlon was working the early shift in the morning, so he only stayed long enough to play with Lucas for a bit then he left. After he was gone, once I'd got Lucas bathed and settled into bed, I sat in the living room and looked for Christopher Fletcher's mobile. I rang it and he answered after several rings.

'Christopher Fletcher?' I asked.

'Who is it?'

'It's Billie Carlson. Sorry I couldn't get back to you sooner. I was caught up in things today.'

'That's all right. I understand.'

'Christopher, I'm very sorry about what happened to Elizabeth. It was such a shock. We'd only just been with her hours earlier.'

He took a moment before answering.

'Yes, I know. The police told me.' He paused. 'It's awful. I'm not sure it's hit me yet if I'm honest.'

I didn't answer because I didn't really know what to say. I knew nothing about this man really, and I wondered if the police or secret service had told him what his wife had done. I didn't want to have that discussion. It was him who'd called to speak to me initially, so I was waiting for him to say something.

'Billie, I don't want to talk on the phone. I'm in Glasgow for a few days sorting things out. Could we possibly meet tomorrow? I wanted to talk to you.' Another pause. 'About your father.'

Just the word 'father' hit me like a punch in the gut and for a moment I didn't answer.

'Are you okay with that, Billie?'

'Yes,' I replied eventually. 'Tomorrow. Where?'

'I'm staying at the Grosvenor Hotel. When would suit you?'

'Mid-morning,' I said. 'Around eleven?'

'Okay. I look forward to that.'

The line went dead. I didn't know if I was looking forward to it. It felt weird and surreal somehow that I was going to see someone who could talk about my father in a way that I would never know him, about a life I never knew, because I assumed, as children do, that my father and mother were just that, not people with lives and problems of their own. How wrong we always are.

I was beginning to get tired, the tension and stress of the past few hours catching up with me. But I wasn't ready to switch off yet and knew sleep wouldn't come. I stood up and crossed the living room and walked softly towards the walk-in cupboard down the hall, and the door I had never opened in all the time I'd been here since I came back from Sweden. I'd never wanted to, not out of fear or dread or anything like that. I just had no reason ever to look back, and it always felt better to drive myself forward. A shrink would have a field day with that.

I took the small key from a little box inside the drawer of an old sideboard that had stood against the wall all my life and went to the door. Now, after all these years, I stood looking at it with a mixture of dread and morbid curiosity. What good would it do to go in here and rake around the remnants of another life? Of my parents' lives? What if I found they were not the people I had always remembered in the images that were fading in my mind? The loving people who made my world safe, who walked me to and from school, who soothed me when I had nightmares and who told me they would always be there? I swallowed. It didn't matter what I found, I told myself. I knew that they loved me with all of their hearts, and maybe somehow in spirit they were on my shoulder now, urging me on, telling me to be brave, be strong, as they'd always done.

I pushed the key into the lock and pulled open the door. Before I stepped in, my hand automatically went to the left of the cupboard where, somehow, I had managed to remember the light switch was. I clicked it on, and the room came to life, bathed in the harsh light of the bare bulb on the ceiling. I took a step inside, quickly scanning the room as though expecting something to suddenly leap out in front of me. I stood for a moment. The room looked smaller than I'd remembered it, but that was probably because I had been small then, and it had looked big with boxes and books spread out on shelves and stacked in corners along the wall.

I didn't know where to start. The first thing I saw was a cardboard box with a soft toy hanging out of it and, as I looked closer, I could see it was filled with toys. I knelt down on the floor, my hands brushing along the contents, and was surprised that with everything I touched I could see myself and remember distinctly having these things in my hands, playing games with them. Why did they not give me these when I was shipped to Sweden where I had nothing to remind me of home? I turned around. There was a box of framed photographs, some small, others larger. I lifted one out – my father and mother at a dinner party, each with a cigarette and a drink in their hands. My mother had her hair pushed behind her ears the way it used to be, her face glowing. She was dressed in a black dress that glittered and clung to her slim body, and was throwing her head back in laughter, and my father was next to her, his eyes crinkled in the laughing expression I remembered so well, his arm around her shoulder. Others at the table laughing at something that must have amused them, perhaps a funny story. The whole scene looked quite glitzy, and I wondered where they'd been and who the people around the table were. I sifted through some other pictures: me as a child on holiday in Sweden, hiking with my backpack; one of me when I was younger, on my father's back climbing a hill, my mother already at the top, waving. I closed my eyes, trying to picture and remember, but I couldn't. Maybe it would come. Then I turned to an old music player – a record player from years ago. I remembered it being in our house long after people had stopped using them and were using stereos and tapes. I went across and lifted the lid. There was a record on the deck. I picked it up and read it. 'La Vie en Rose'.

I looked at the flex with the plug attached and wondered if it would still work. I pulled the flex and pushed it into the nearby socket on the wall, and to my surprise the record player lit up. For some reason that made me happy, as though something was alive after all these years. I put the record back on the deck and lifted the arm with the needle and placed it on the spinning disc. Then came the strains of 'La Vie en Rose' through the tiny speaker at the front and I was suddenly transported back as far as I could remember.

Suddenly, I saw them in my mind, in the living room, a black and white image of them dancing, and remembered I'd peeped through the corner of the door long after I'd gone to bed and the dinner guests had left, to watch them sharing this time with each other. I distinctly remembered creeping out of bed when I heard the music because I knew they would be dancing and it had filled me with joy just to see them like that because my father was always so busy and away. But here he was with the woman he so loved, and they were so very happy, and that always made me feel safe. My eyes stung with tears, a mix of sadness and joy that I could actually vividly revisit this memory after all these years, a moment in time like that, which could just open up with the sound of a song. And as I listened, I saw them clearly for the first time in all those years I'd been without them.

'La Vie en Rose'. Over the years, I had probably heard this song from time to time but somehow I didn't seem to know why I knew it. Perhaps I had closed my mind to it. Who knew. But tonight, I was in the room with an old record player, and I could see it all so clearly as though I was watching it now. I let the record run until the song was finished and the needle hissed as it came to the end of the music, and I placed it back on its rest and turned off the record player.

I stood for a moment, glancing around at the boxes and folders, and had no idea where to start with any of this. I knelt beside the bookshelves and looked along at the books, of faraway places in the Middle East, Russia, Asia. Then at the back of the books, one hardback leather-bound book poking up caught my eye, the band pulled over it to close it. I reached across and pulled it out. Then I tentatively turned to the first page, my heart stopping as I read.

My darling Billie, my beautiful bright, unbreakable Billie. I am writing this for you and one day I will give it to you to help you understand . . .

My father's unmistakable exquisite handwriting. I immediately snapped it shut. I couldn't read any more. I was afraid. Afraid that this beautiful moment I'd just had listening to the music and remembering would be ruined by something I read that would take me to a place I didn't want to go. But deep down, I knew I did want to know. Why was my father writing this? When would he have given it to me? I would never know, because whatever this was, perhaps he didn't get a chance to finish it.

CHAPTER TWENTY-ONE

I had been awake since six a.m., and was standing at my living room window sipping from a mug of coffee, gazing out at the stillness of the morning. The city was already gently moving to its regular beat, with cars beginning to head past Blythswood Square on the way to Charing Cross and the M8 or the west end and beyond. It was still quiet, though, and despite not having slept well, I was glad to be up and have this time to try to make sense of and process what may lie ahead today.

I'd received a text from Fletcher last night confirming our plan to meet at the Grosvenor Hotel where he was staying while he liaised with police, who were still investigating the murder of his wife. I was wondering where to start with this man who knew more about my father than I did; would he be telling me the truth about everything? And why, after all this time, was he even seeing me? Part of me felt anger that he must have known where I was and yet he didn't in all the time I was growing up see fit to come to me and tell me the truth. Why not? I supposed the answer to that was that he worked for the secret service. That was the part I was finding most difficult to get my head around. I knew nothing of that world other than what I'd watched in films or read in books.

I didn't know where to start with my questions, or even if I could believe anything he told me.

My mind was already confused and full of questions after reading the opening lines last night of some kind of journal or letter my father had been writing to me. I wasn't even sure what opening all this up would do to me, how it would benefit me, yet I felt compelled to carry it through.

The picture of my mother and father dancing in the living room made me smile as I watched the thin grey morning, and fleeting images came to me of life here so long ago, of watching my father as he'd turn to wave to my mother and me standing at the window as he was off on his travels to who knew where. It had never seemed mysterious or dark or dangerous to me back then. It was just my father going to work, to lecture in physics to students across the length and breadth of Europe. I had no way of preparing myself for anything I'd be told today that would dispel that.

I parked my car on a side street off Byres Road and walked to the hotel. The Grosvenor, with its striking Venetian terraced townhouses converted into a luxury hotel back in the 1930s, had become a magnificent, historic landmark in the city, and would not look out of place in Paris, Berlin or any exotic city in Europe. I'd dropped Lucas off earlier at nursery and called Millie to say what I was doing, and she asked if I was sure I wanted to do this alone, not take Fowler along with me. I hadn't even thought about that. She asked if I thought the MI6 men who'd come to see me at my office would also be there. I hadn't even thought about that either. I'd been so immersed in what Fletcher might tell me about my father that I hadn't considered anything else. Now as I walked through the brass and stained-glass doors into the sumptuous marbled foyer, I found myself glancing around me, over my shoulder, across the large room and into the wider areas. But all I saw were the uniformed concierge, waiters, guests and nothing any different from any ordinary hotel in any city.

I stood for a moment at the foot of the staircase area as Fletcher hadn't said in his text where we would meet. Then after a minute I noticed an older man with wispy, balding grey hair standing at the entrance to a lounge and we exchanged eye contact. He walked towards me, a tall figure in a grey suit that matched his complexion. He looked at me from tired, dark eyes and his lip flickered into a thin half-smile.

'Billie,' he said, reaching out a hand. Then his eyes softened as I took his hand. 'I knew straight away. You are the image of your mother, Billie.'

I didn't answer but felt a catch in my throat as I looked back at him, his hand still holding mine. I hadn't ever considered if I looked like my mother as I grew up. There was no time somehow, no point in wondering who I resembled. My parents were gone. I was alone. He let go of my hand and turned towards a lounge area.

'Do you want to come into the lounge over there?' he said. 'It's very quiet and secluded.'

I shrugged.

'Sure.' I bit the inside of my jaw as I followed him, chastising myself for suddenly feeling led. But I didn't know how to do this. This wasn't like a normal client who had pitched up to my office or met me outside, asking for help. This was raw, uncharted territory.

We went into the lounge, dimly lit with wall lights behind the gantry and amber leather seating that was cosy and warm – a place where secret trysts could happen, promises could be made, deals struck. Only two other people were there, at the far side, heads in laptops. We sat in one of the areas of semi-circular wall seating, far enough away from each other but close enough to talk. A waiter came across and I ordered tea and he coffee. Then we sat in a silence that was long enough to make me feel awkward.

'So, Billie,' he finally said.

I looked at him for a long moment not knowing what to say.

'So,' I said back. 'Tell me.' It came out harsher than I'd wanted, and he flashed me a look. I back-pedalled. 'I mean . . . Look, I'm sorry for your loss . . . But where do I start to ask questions?' I looked at the table then back at him. 'I'll be honest with you, I don't know what to say here.'

The waiter arrived and set down the tea and coffee on the table. Fletcher sat forward.

'I know, Billie,' he said, taking a breath and letting it out slowly. 'I'm sorry. I understand how you must feel.'

'Do you?' I said, looking straight into his eyes. 'I'm all over the place with this. Have been since your wife – since Elizabeth – called me and dropped the bombshell that she knew my father.' I shook my head, confused. 'Why? After all this time?'

His face was a mask of regret, dark shadows beneath his eyes, and we sat in prolonged silence.

'It's complicated, Billie,' he said finally. 'But I will try to tell you some things.'

'Where do you begin?' I asked, lifting the cup to my lips. 'With my father's death, with his murder? He was murdered, wasn't he? That's what Elizabeth told me the final day I met her.' I shook my head. 'My father was murdered. Is it true?'

I don't know why, but right at that moment that seemed more important to me than anything. Was my father really murdered? His death had cast a long shadow throughout my life, because his suicide had always been part of who I was.

It had always been there, the sadness that he perhaps wanted to leave my mother and me and I never knew why. If he was murdered, would that feel better? I had no idea.

He scanned my face and his lips tightened, then he finally nodded.

'Yes.'

I sat for a moment, trying to take a breath and feeling an ache in my chest and the urge to run to the bathroom and weep. But I managed to hold it together. Then when I could trust my voice, I spoke.

'Tell me,' I said. 'Everything. Can you do that?'

He nodded. Then he began. I listened. The story taking me to a world that to me was alien and dark and mysterious, a world I never considered that my father was part of. But I listened, because I had to hear this.

CHAPTER TWENTY-TWO

'I'm telling you this,' Fletcher said, 'but no one must ever know that I have. Do you understand, Billie?' His eyebrows went up for emphasis and his face was stern. 'For me to tell you this is against everything I have ever done in my work for the government.' He paused, inhaled and held it for a moment, then exhaled. 'But you deserve to know the truth.'

I put my hand up to pause him. I couldn't stop myself.

'But why now?' I shook my head. 'Why not years ago, when I became old enough to understand? Though I will never understand fully. But please. Tell me. Did my mother know the truth about my father? What he did? How he died?'

He shook his head.

'No. Sadly.'

'But she was heartbroken,' I said, choking. 'I was so young, but I remember how crushed she was, bewildered that he had taken his own life without warning. How could you not tell her the truth?'

'Because we couldn't. We were protecting her. Protecting you. Because it was impossible,' he said. 'There was too much at stake. And, after she died, we knew your life was in Sweden.'

I looked at him, surprised.

'You knew my life? You knew all about me?'

He nodded slowly.

'Of course. All the time. In Sweden with your aunt. And when you returned home. We have always known where you were. We had to.' He paused. 'To protect you.'

'Protect me? From what? From whom?'

He took a while to answer, and I watched him as though he was trying to find the words.

'The people who wouldn't stop at your father. We had to make sure you were safe.'

I couldn't get my head around the idea that all this time I was in Sweden, in Glasgow, at university, when my son was missing, these people knew.

'You knew about my son?'

He nodded, blinking.

'Yes.'

'Could you not have tracked him down? Found him?'

He lifted the coffee cup to his lips, took a sip.

'We tried. We tried everything. But we lost the trail.'

'Jesus!' was all I could mutter.

All this time, the agony of feeling so alone searching for my son, and the most powerful force in the country was looking for him and couldn't track him.

'Well, I found him,' I said, looking blankly at him. 'By my own means.'

He pursed his lips, accepting the dig.

'Yes, you did, Billie. Your father would have been proud of you.'

We sat in the empty silence, me taking this in, another snippet of information about the life that had been going on around me that I knew nothing about. More stuff to keep me awake at night. I could scarcely believe it. Eventually, Fletcher spoke.

'But let me tell you about your father.'

I looked him in the eye and nodded. He glanced at the couple on the other side of the room, and lowered his voice to a whisper, even though they were well out of earshot.

'I was the one who recruited your father into MI6.'

He paused as though waiting for me to say something, but I didn't, and he went on.

'He was lecturing in physics, and toured universities in Europe and sometimes beyond. I first met him when we were both at a conference in Berlin, back in the days of the Soviet Union. I had known Anders Carlson by reputation as someone with a brilliant mind, who was renowned for his meticulous research and work in the area of nuclear physics. We were at a dinner one evening, and afterwards in the bar we had drinks and got talking. Your father had a moral compass, and he had a big heart. The more he moved around the Eastern bloc working, the more frustrated he felt that the people he was lecturing to and working with were not able to realise their full potential, because of life in the Soviet Union and the satellite states. Everyone was so oppressed by the regime. We were on the same wavelength in that respect and met again at a lunch the day before he left, where we said we would keep in touch. I liked him. I told my bosses at the Foreign Office he might be someone we could use, and they said to watch him in the coming weeks and look at it again. I met him weeks later in Prague on the lecture tour, and we talked more. I told him there was more he could achieve by coming to work under cover with the security forces. He baulked in the beginning – a spy? I'm no James Bond, he said. But then he came back from a tour of a Soviet Union border country where he'd seen some bad things there and contacted me. Someone he'd been working closely with had disappeared and he wanted to see if he could do anything. That is how it began.'

He paused and we sat for a long time not saying anything. Eventually I spoke.

'So, did he carry on as a lecturer? All those times he was away from me and my mother he was a spy?'

'Yes and no. He was always lecturing, but certain places he was able to pick up intelligence to pass to MI6. The university bosses in these countries would take him to research sites – obviously not showing him all of their secrets, but enough for him to glean information. His reputation went before him and he was able to pick up information about communication and, most importantly it also transpired, about evidence of their nuclear capability development. When I look back at the naivety of the Soviets, how they had no clue. But then they always talked the game and were eager to show the West how clever they were. Also, I think your father's personality and easy way is one of the reasons they trusted him. All the time he was picking up and passing information on, and over the years he became more and more crucial to the service. It was a period covering about five years and he became invaluable. He was able to recruit and turn one of their own agents and that was a triumph. So, he and this agent he handled would meet in various places and the agent would pass on information, documents, details we would never have been able to get a sniff of if it was not for your father. I would meet him sometimes in Scotland and come here with my wife Elizabeth – much younger than me – and we had dinners in the city and got to know each other. I never met you, but he talked of you, as your mother did, all the time, showed us photographs – their little Billie.'

He fell silent. While he'd spoken, I imagined my father in his role across Europe, the secret clandestine meets with shadowy figures. It was so much to take in.

'Then it happened.' He shook his head. 'There was no warning, no suspicion. If only we'd had an inkling, we could have done something. But it happened so quickly. We were involved immediately after we learned of Anders' death.'

'How did you know he was murdered?'

'Almost straight away, through our connections, we learned the man he was to meet – the man he'd handled who was passing secrets – had been replaced that night. By an assassin. He had no way of knowing until he turned up on the bridge. We don't know what happened during the encounter, but your father ended up in the river. From what we gathered from forensics there had been a struggle, and he was pushed. The security services took over as soon as the body was recovered, so there were no details released, hence the reason it was regarded as suicide.' He swallowed. 'But it wasn't.'

I had no memory of my father going out of the house that night, but he sometimes did go for a drink in one of the local pubs or to see friends at the university. I only remembered the chaos and the heartache after he didn't come home. Listening to this now took me back and filled and me with an ache I hadn't felt so deeply for a long time. My eyes filled with tears, and I blinked them away.

'Sorry,' I said. 'It's all just a bit overwhelming. Even after all this time.'

He leaned across and took my hand.

'I'm so sorry,' he said. 'So very sorry, Billie, for your loss, for your mother's loss. I also lost someone who had become my greatest friend, and always I will ask myself could I have done more, why had I not seen what would happen? I was the head of the small prestigious unit that we worked for, and I should have seen this. But I didn't.'

He looked genuinely sad.

'Why are you telling me this now?'

After a long moment he said, 'Because . . . I am dying.'

I looked at him, his face impassive. I didn't know what to say. He was the man with all the answers, the man who could tell me about the secret life in the shadows my father kept from my mother and me. I wanted to ask him how long he had left, but it didn't feel right. He looked at me as though reading my mind.

'I have six, maybe eight months, they say. Who knows.'

'I'm sorry,' I said, and part of me meant it, but I didn't know this man enough to feel genuine sadness for him.

'Do you have family?'

'No,' he said. 'Elizabeth and I couldn't have children. And to tell you the truth, our marriage hadn't been good for a long time. The way we lived – me always away from home. But I still loved her very much. We had been so happy for such a long time together, but we drifted in recent years.' His mouth tightened.

'Are you still working for MI6?'

He took a breath.

'Not for much longer. I'm an old man now. I'm sixty-two. I've seen it all. I've had enough.' He looked at me and then away.

The silence hung heavy in the air for a while, then I had to ask.

'The man who killed my father,' I said, looking him in the eye. 'Did you ever find out who he was?'

He nodded slowly.

'Yes.' He paused. 'He was a Russian agent. Though to our knowledge he hadn't come up on our radar before. It seems he was used when people had to be made to disappear, if you get my meaning.'

I blinked in acknowledgement.

'Is he still alive?'

'Yes. He's old now too. Retired by all accounts. But in the service, you are never really retired. I've kept tabs on him over the years. My instinct was to chase him down and make him vanish. But I was told not to go near it. Relations were improving and I had to behave.'

'Do you know his name? Where he lives?'

He sighed.

'Yes. His name is Dimitry Volkov. At least, that's the name he goes by now, but it might not be his real name. I heard a while ago that he has moved to Poland. In a place near Krakow.'

'How do you know that?'

He shrugged, looked straight at me.

'I just know.'

CHAPTER TWENTY-THREE

How do you go back to who you were when everything you thought you knew has just crashed around you? I asked myself that as I got into my car and drove away from the Grosvenor Hotel, away from the man and the story he'd just told me that changed everything I knew about who my father actually was. All the time I had been his little girl and he was my absolute hero, he'd been living a double life, one that my mother had no knowledge of. Now I was wondering if she secretly did know, because every time he went away on his lecture tours abroad, I remember the sadness that seemed to engulf her, and I couldn't quite understand it. I knew she loved him, and we both would miss him until he returned, but she was always weepy and distant every time he left. Perhaps she knew there was more to his lecturing, and maybe she knew the truth and always agonised that one day he wouldn't come home. And he didn't.

I didn't go straight back to the office after my meeting with Fletcher. I wanted to be alone to process what he'd just told me. When he walked me through the foyer and out of the hotel we'd stood for a moment, saying nothing. Then he took my hand and told me again that he was sorry, but if I wanted to know any more about my father's life, then maybe we could keep in touch and meet again. He seemed to want to. He said that he would be retiring very soon and would have all the time in the world, until, well, he had no time left. He looked sad then, as though now that the end of his life was in sight, he was asking himself if it had all been worth it, if he had done enough. I felt sorry for him, and told him we could meet any time, though I didn't expect he would ever contact me again, nor I him. I wasn't sure if I wanted to know all the details of my father's life and work at this late stage. But the name Dimitry Volkov was etched in my psyche, and I knew that would chip away at me in my nightmares.

Eventually I got to the nursery and sat outside in my car, closing my eyes for a minute to shake off the darkness, to rationalise what I'd been told, and to try to put it somewhere out of the way for the moment. I would deal with the fallout in my head another time. I got out of the car and crossed to the nursery where the doors were opening, and I could see Lucas skipping through the crowd of children and parents when he spotted me. *This is who I am*, I thought. As I picked him up and he hugged me tight, my heart hurt at how much my father would have loved to feel this little boy's arms around him.

I was taking Lucas to my office for a couple of hours to try to get some normality into the day, after Fletcher's revelations. As I parked outside my mobile rang on the passenger seat and I picked it up. It was Wilson.

'Billie. There's a woman's body being fished out of the Clyde.'

'Shit, Harry! You think it's Jane?'

'Don't know yet. Going down there now – over at the Kinning Park side, near the Sheriff Court. A woman maybe in her forties or fifties we've been told. Hard to say. And it's fresh.'

So, whoever it is hasn't been in there long.' He paused. 'Do you know any relatives? We'll need her ID'd.'

I blew out a breath.

'I don't know anyone except her.' I turned to see Lucas trying to unstrap his seat belt, having sussed we were getting out. 'You want me to come down? I'd be able to say straight away if it's her or not.'

'Are you okay with that?'

'Sure,' I said without hesitation. 'I'm just taking Lucas into my office then I'll be right there.'

'Good. You'll see the commotion. Mortuary vehicle on its way.'

I quickly unstrapped Lucas and got him out of the car, then we went into the building and used the ancient lift for quickness. I was somewhere between shock and disbelief that this woman might be Jane. I don't know how I'd expected this to end after she'd been kidnapped, but I hadn't even considered it would be like this, so sudden. What shit kind of people were they? In the office, Millie's eyes lit up when she saw Lucas, and Fowler's dog came bounding across and jumped up, licking his face, making him giggle.

'How's it going, Billie?'

I sighed, pacing.

'Getting more surreal by the minute, Dave,' I replied. I had no time to go into detail about Fletcher's revelations and wasn't ready to tell anyone yet anyway. 'Listen, guys. I just took a call from Wilson. A woman's body has been fished out of the Clyde. He thinks it might be Jane McAllister.'

'Oh, Christ!' Millie said. 'That's awful.'

I shook my head.

'I know. But he's asked me to go down and see if I can identify her before they start trawling around looking for relatives.'

I turned to Millie. 'Can you amuse him for half an hour? I'll be straight back.' I sighed. 'Not looking forward to this.'

'You want me to come?' Fowler asked.

'That'd be good.'

'We'll take my car.'

Lucas was so interested in rolling around on the floor with Jess that he didn't even notice me leaving. We took the stairs and climbed into Fowler's car a couple of yards from mine, and he headed down towards Argyle Street and into Clyde Street. Fowler drove fast and we didn't say much as he turned to cross the Jamaica Bridge to the other side of the river. I couldn't help myself having a little moment as we crossed the bridge, thinking of my conversation earlier with Fletcher, and the images he described of there having been a struggle before my father was pushed into the river all those years ago. I closed my eyes, blinking it away. Once we'd crossed, further down we could see the police cars and flashing emergency vehicles.

'This is some shit, Billie, if these bastards have just disposed of Jane like that. It must be heavy stuff.'

'I know,' I said. 'I just thought we'd have more time. Harper was trying to put the squeeze on the guys who were behind it, but this has all happened so fast.' I braced myself as we turned into the street and pulled up in front of the taped-off area where an officer stood. 'Maybe it's not her,' I said, more in hope than belief.

'Road's closed,' a fresh-faced, young uniformed cop said, putting his hand up as we approached.

'I've been asked to meet DCI Harry Wilson,' I said. 'Look. He's over there.'

He looked at me then over his shoulder, just as Wilson saw me and waved me on. The officer lifted up the tape and let us pass. There were several police cars and an ambulance, as well as the long low hearse mortuary vehicle that had just pulled up. A few uniformed officers stood around in silence, watching as the covered body on the stretcher was eased onto the trolley to be transferred to the mortuary car. Wilson put his hand up.

'Hold on a minute, lads,' he said. 'I've got someone here who may be able to do a preliminary identification of the body.'

Everyone turned to look at me as Wilson waved me forward, and I took a few steps towards the trolley. I felt a sudden knot in my gut and a sense of dread as I approached.

'You all right with this, Billie?'

I nodded.

'Okay,' he said. 'Come forward.'

We took steps right up to the trolley and I looked down at the dark green tarpaulin tucked over her. I could see the slim outline of the body.

'You ready?' Wilson said.

I nodded.

He blinked a gesture to the officer next to the trolley, signalling to him to pull back the cover. When he did, I stood rooted, feeling shock and fear and nausea all at once as I looked down at the pale, soaked face and hair plastered across her forehead, her slim neck and shoulders bare and bruised as though there had been a struggle. Her fleece was pulled up and her torso was naked. Her hands were pale and covered in cuts and bruises. Her eyes were half closed and her mouth slightly open, lips turning blue. She didn't look like the woman I had talked to in the park so recently, where I could see the stress and worry in her eyes and the panic. The diamond ring on her finger was missing, and there was a bruise where it should be. Then I saw the necklace that I'd remembered – a silver Celtic cross on a chain. There was no mistake. This was Jane McAllister. I looked around to Wilson and nodded.

'Is it her?'

'Yes.'

'You sure?'

'Yes. Her face is a bit bloated with being in the water, but it's her all right. The chain on her neck. The little Celtic cross. I remember seeing it on her.' I paused. 'But she had a diamond ring on her finger, Harry. It's not there any more. Once you get a closer look with forensics, you'll see the mark where it was.'

'Good spot, Billie. We'll get on that. Thanks.'

I swallowed hard as I took one last glance at Jane before they pulled the tarpaulin across and pushed the trolley towards the hearse. My heart broke for her there and then. She was just a woman alone, someone who had worked all her life and then enjoyed the good life as an ex-pat, living the dream in the sunshine, where every day she could make her own mind up how she wanted to live. She had asked for nothing but the peace to get on with her life, enjoying making new sets of friends and getting away from the rat race. Because here it's cold and you're limited in what you can do, and sometimes you become invisible as you grow older. In the sunshine your life feels plentiful somehow. But how different lives can be for so many ex-pats who go there to live the dream only to find it dies for one reason or another. Jane had done nothing wrong – she'd only been the witness to an angry, drunken conversation by her friend. She knew nothing of the drug smuggling or the money laundering that Cathy had been caught up in. For her to meet her death like this, alone, frightened – innocent really – was too hard to witness. I sniffed back tears as I turned away.

'These fuckers!' Wilson said. 'It's so quick. We haven't even got a handle on it yet.'

I looked at him.

'Word on the street is that it's Vinnie Martin's boys who snatched her. You know him?'

'Lowlife toerag.'

'Word is he works for some of the mobsters in Spain. So that'll be what he's been doing.' I shook my head. 'Why the fuck did they have to kill her, though, Harry? She'd done nothing.'

'If she saw what she said she saw that night when they took Cathy Evans' body out of the apartment, then they weren't taking any chances.'

I nodded.

'They'll get away with it, the bastards,' I said.

'Not if I can help it. I'm putting a team on this. And the Cathy Evans death.'

I was glad to hear that. But it was too late for Jane and Cathy.

We stood in silence as the trolley was carefully pushed to the hearse and eased into the back, then the doors were closed, and Jane McAllister would be a statistic, a body pulled out of the river, a brutal, senseless murder of an innocent woman who'd been living the dream. Someone had to be called to account for this.

As we headed to the car, I let Wilson walk on while I rang Paddy Harper.

'It's me,' I said when he answered after two rings. 'Jane McAllister has just been pulled out of the Clyde.'

'Aw, Jesus, Billie. When? They are sure it's her?'

'Yeah. Big detective called me, and I went down to identify her – unofficially of course. But it's definitely her. She'd not been in the water long so not a lot of erosion and stuff. I recognised her, plus I could tell from the trinket round her neck she was wearing. But they took her diamond ring. It's missing. I told cops that too. She told me Cathy Evans gave it to her after she'd been on a trip to Dubai. Bastards.' I paused. 'It's so sad, Paddy. She had nothing to do with any of this shit.'

'Someone will pay for this, Billie.'

I hoped so. And maybe the rough justice that Harper was used to dishing out was what was needed here. But I didn't want to say that out loud.

CHAPTER TWENTY-FOUR

It didn't take Harper long to begin the retribution.

In the morning, half awake, I flicked on the television news as I got into the kitchen to prepare for Lucas getting out of bed. The headline item snapped me wide awake. A car dealership was blazing, an inferno of flash cars on the forecourt exploding into the night sky, and the showroom in flames. The on-the-scene reporter told how the fire started in the small hours of the morning, and neighbours had heard what sounded like fireworks and when they looked out across to the garage cars were exploding and the showroom was up in flames. The footage had four fire engines hosing water to douse the flames but already there were burned-out wrecks across the area. The garage, which sold top of the range cars including BMWs, Land Rovers and Porsches, was in the east end close to the motorway, which had to be closed at one point because of the flames. The reporter wasn't able to say exactly who owned the showroom, only that it was a limited company and there were several directors. He reported that speculation so far was that some feud had broken out, resulting in an arson attack, but police were remaining tight-lipped, and their investigation was ongoing.

I switched on my mobile to hear the ping of messages that

must have arrived while I had finally fallen asleep after the harrowing day yesterday. One was from Harper. I opened it.

Wee message sent to that prick Vinnie Martin last night. As cops would say, enquiries are ongoing. 😠

Shit. Another was from Wilson.

Call me.

I shook some cereal into a bowl for Lucas and poured fresh orange juice into a glass before setting it out on the breakfast bar. Then I pushed Wilson's number.

'Harry,' I said. 'Sorry. I was asleep and had my phone off.'

'You seen the news?'

'I just put it on. Fire in garage in east end. Big one.'

'That's Vinnie Martin's place. Or he's got a lot of money in it.'

'Really?' I said, as convincingly as I could. 'I don't know what he's into.'

'Looks to me like payback, Billie.'

'What? For Jane McAllister?' I tried to sound surprised.

'Yep. Do you know anything about this? Not that I expect you to tell me if you do.'

'I just watched the news, Harry. Too early for me. I didn't think some woman being thrown into the river would spark something like this. But if I'm honest, hell mend the bastards. If Vinnie Martin is involved, and he killed Jane, stuff him. I hope he has more coming to him.'

'I get that, Billie. But I'm trying to get the bigger picture here. There's more to this than Vinnie Martin and his mob. It's who he's working for, and what's going on in Spain that I want to nail down. And burning his business down isn't going to help me.'

I didn't answer. I could see where he was coming from and I half agreed, but I was glad Harper had put out a message. Wilson went on.

'I want to nail this down, get these bastards in the pokey. I've got people looking into fences who'll be moving that diamond ring on and stuff like that. Snitches will talk. It'll just take time.'

'I know, Harry,' I said. 'It will take time, though. That's because you can't beat the information out of them. It would be much quicker if you could.'

'You're talking like a criminal, Carlson.'

'Well, maybe it's the only way to deal with these people. When I saw Jane McAllister lying on that trolley yesterday, it made me want retribution. I don't know what the hell went on last night, but no matter what, you'll not find me complaining about it, if it was payback for the guys who beat and murdered an innocent middle-aged woman.'

'Aye. You've got a point. But rest assured we will be looking for the people who set fire to this garage too, Carlson. We're not living in Deadwood. It's not a fucking free for all, even if it seems like it sometimes. Call me if you hear anything.'

He hung up, knowing I wouldn't call him. I turned to see Lucas padding into the kitchen rubbing his eyes.

'I'm hungry, Mummy.'

I called Harper as I drove to the office.

'Billie. You all right? After your ordeal yesterday identifying the body?'

'I'm okay,' I said. 'Poor woman. I wish I hadn't asked her to help me. Maybe she'd still be alive.'

'Don't beat yourself up, Billie. This is not on you. This is on the pricks in Spain who wanted to make sure she kept her mouth shut after what she saw that night. It's not your fault. They would have tracked her down anyway.'

'I suppose you're right, but I just feel bad.'

'Well, don't. Because we'll find out who did this to her here and who's behind it in Spain, and every one of them will get what they deserve. What kind of pricks murder two women?'

'The cops are all over it,' I said.

'Aye, well, I wouldn't hold my breath waiting for justice from them,' he replied sarcastically.

'I talked to the DCI this morning after the fire in the garage. Apparently, Vinnie Martin has a lot of money in the place.'

'Aye,' he said. 'That's why it's up in smoke. And it's only the beginning.'

'Do you think Martin will disappear to Spain, if he's not already there?'

'He'll try. But he's not there yet. We're looking for him. Hopefully we can dig him out today.' Harper paused. 'Billie, do you remember anything about that diamond ring Jane had? I mean, how big or stuff like that?'

I hesitated, remembering the ring, large enough to assume it was fake, but Jane had told me when she saw me looking at it that it was genuine. That she'd been given it by Cathy, and had it valued in Spain at something like twenty grand. I told this to Harper.

'Okay. Great. That will turn up somewhere in the next couple of days, I'd say. Whoever took it off her finger will be trying to shift it pronto.'

I shuddered at the image of some thug ripping the ring off Jane's finger in the struggle, terrified, as it would be dawning on her she was never getting out of this.

'I've got an old jeweller friend in the city,' I said. 'I'll ask him to put some feelers out.'

After I came off the phone I drove to the office and took the steps upstairs to the second floor. Inside Millie was chatting to Fowler and they both looked up at me when I entered. I'd told

Fowler about the missing ring when I'd come back to the office yesterday after identifying Jane's body and asked him to come into the office to see if we could find out more.

'Did you see the huge fire in the garage last night?' I asked both of them. 'Word is that it belongs to Vinnie Martin – the guy who Harper says is behind Jane's murder.'

Fowler raised his eyebrows.

'I wouldn't mind a ringside seat when Harper gets a hold of them.'

'Me too,' I said.

Millie handed me a coffee as I sat down.

'Cops are all over it, Dave,' I told him. 'Wilson says they're putting a team on it and trying to find more on Cathy Evans' death in Spain. So that's a positive.' I turned to Millie. 'Millie, can you get me Gina Evans' phone number? I need to talk to her and let her know what's going on. Cops haven't released Jane's name yet as they were tracking down a brother who can do the formal identification today. But I want to give Gina a heads up.'

Millie went across to her desk and looked at her screen then wrote down a number on a piece of paper and handed it to me. I stood up and turned to Fowler as I headed for my office.

'I'm going to call her,' I said. 'Looks like she was right all along that someone had dumped her mother's body on the beach that night. She'll be distraught when she hears what's happened to Jane McAllister.'

I went into my office and closed the door, then sat behind my desk for a moment gazing out of the window at the patches of blue sky now that the sun was beginning to come through. Then I picked up my office phone and keyed in the number for Gina Evans. It rang several times, and I was about to hang up when a voice broke in.

'Hello?'

'Gina Evans?' I said. 'It's Billie Carlson.'

'Yes. I was going to call you again when I hadn't heard from you. Is there any news?'

I took a long breath and tried to pick my words carefully, but there was no easy way to say this.

'Gina, you mentioned your mother's friend Jane McAllister?'

'Yes. But I've never met her. Have you spoken to her?' She sounded enthused.

'Er. Yes. I have.' I paused for a moment. 'Gina, there's no easy way to tell you this, but Jane McAllister is dead.'

'What? You serious? When? Where? In Spain?'

'No. Here. In Glasgow. Her body was recovered from the River Clyde yesterday.'

'Oh my God! What happened to her?' She was agitated.

'Gina,' I said. 'Listen. I'd been in touch with Jane since I decided to take your case. I've met her a couple of times and we talked. She told me an alarming story about your mother and some people in Spain who were apparently her friends.'

'What alarming story? Why did you not get in touch and tell me this?'

I cleared my throat.

'Gina, I was working on the investigation as promised. There were lines to be pursued, and meeting and talking to Jane McAllister was one of them. I had no reason to call you back. I hope you understand that.'

A long silence, and then her voice was soft.

'Yes. Sorry. I understand. I'm just shocked, that's all. I don't know what I'm doing here. This has to be something to do with Mum, Billie. It has to.'

'Yes,' I said. 'It has. Look, I can't go into all the details right now, but basically Jane told me of a row your mum had with this couple, Steve and Marilyn, who were her friends. English couple. I'm still working on who they are, but it is looking like they were drug smugglers.'

'What? Drug smugglers? What the hell! My mum wasn't the kind of woman to mix with drug smugglers.'

I didn't answer for a few moments because she was going to go over the top if I told her everything.

'Well, I'm still looking at it, but Jane told me about an argument. Everyone had a lot to drink, and that she went home with your mum – they lived in the same apartment block.'

'That's right,' Gina interrupted.

I went on.

'Jane said that your mother had told them she could go to the police and tell them everything they had been doing. About trips abroad and cruises, and how it was all about money laundering.'

'Aw, hold on a minute. This is my mother you're talking about, Billie. Money laundering? My mum wouldn't even know what that meant.'

'I understand that. But she may have been used unwittingly by these people.'

'Oh, Jesus!'

Silence. I could hear Gina's breathing. Then sniffing.

'And you think some harm came to my mum after the argument?'

I sighed.

'Yes, I do.'

I didn't have the heart to tell her that Jane had seen what she believed was her mother's body being carted out of the apartment in the middle of the night, and that was why she bolted for the airport the next morning. There was no point in telling her everything while she was trying to let some of it sink in.

'So,' I said, 'I'd met with Jane, and she was telling me everything she knew and about that night, and then she called me a few days ago frantic because she'd got a call from Spain threatening her.'

'Jesus!'

'Then the next call I got was that she had been kidnapped.'

I waited to let that sink in.

'I told the police, and they had a search out for her, but then yesterday a body was fished out of the Clyde and I was contacted. Because I had met her a couple of times, cops asked me to ID her unofficially and I did.'

'My God. You saw her? Dead? Are you sure it was her?'

'Positive. It was awful, Gina.'

'It must have been.'

I waited a few moments.

'Gina, do you have any photographs of your mum and Jane together?'

'Yes. She sent some to my phone. She was always sending pictures. They were in a restaurant in Spain and she sent me some pictures of that.'

'Can you look at them for me? See if Jane had a ring on? She was wearing an expensive diamond ring when I met her, and she told me your mother brought it back from Dubai for her.'

'I can look them out and see,' she said. 'If there are any, I'll send them to you. But what's the interest in the ring?'

I took a breath.

'It wasn't on her finger when she was pulled out of the water.'

'Shit. They took it. My God, Billie. This is terrible. I knew something bad had happened to my mother. I just knew it, and now poor Jane. What are the police doing?'

'They told me they have launched a big investigation, here and in Spain.'

'About bloody time,' she said.

I couldn't argue with that.

'Will you look out the photos as soon as you can?'

'Yes. I'll do it now and get back to you.'

I gave her my mobile number and we hung up.

CHAPTER TWENTY-FIVE

My mobile pinged with messages within half an hour of my conversation with Gina. The first one was to apologise if she sounded a bit hysterical, but she was still in shock as she now realised something bad had definitely happened to her mother. She said she trusted me to do everything to help. I opened the picture she sent next. It was Cathy Evans and Jane McAllister together in some beach bar, raised glasses of cocktails and big smiles on their faces. Two women having the time of their lives far away from everything they'd been back in Glasgow. Another snapshot was of them sitting on a low wall on a boardwalk with the sea and beach in the background and the pair of them linking arms. When I pulled the photograph up, I could see Jane's right hand and on her third finger was the diamond ring I'd seen on her. The next snap was Jane on her own sitting with her hands clasped in her lap at a restaurant and the ring was clearer here when I made it bigger. This is what I needed.

I opened one last picture, and it was Cathy at a dinner table with a few other people. There were two younger guys and a well-dressed good-looking woman, and beside her with his arm around her shoulder was a man who looked to be in his forties or fifties, flash jewellery and a set of five grand veneers.

I pulled the picture up to look at them, and the young guys. They both looked British, well-groomed, hair gelled, expensive-looking designer shirts. The backdrop was not Spain, though, and Jane wasn't in it. It looked more like the opulence of Dubai with garish waterfall-coloured lights. The whole party looked glowing in their surroundings, like an ordinary dinner party on a night out in the glamour of the Arab sandpit. I put the phone down, then picked it up again, staring at the couple. Could this be Marilyn and Steve?

I sent a text to Gina asking her if her mother had ever told her who was in the photograph in what looked like Dubai. She texted back saying she didn't know their names, but they were English living in Spain, and they had gone together on the trip to Dubai. I thanked her but told her no more. It had to be them. I drained my coffee mug and sat back, my hands clasped across my stomach. Who should I share the pictures with first, Wilson or Harper? My conscience said Wilson, but my gut said Harper. It would be Harper who could ping these to connections across on the Costa del Sol and could probably get them identified quickly. Wilson would have to go through the motions of contacting Spain, and I knew this would take an age by the time he got everyone over there on board. But I had to be fair about this. I sent the pictures of the couple to Harper along with a text, asking if he could see if he could find out if this was Marilyn and Steve. Then I called Wilson, who answered immediately.

'Hi, Harry. Listen. I'm about to send you a couple of pictures here.'

I told him I'd contacted Gina and she'd sent the snaps and I explained what my suspicions were.

'Good shout, Carlson,' he said. 'You should be in here working, you know that.'

'No thanks. I'm good where I am.' I paused. 'But Harry, I know the ropes, how it will have to be done officially and stuff over there, with you working with the Spanish cops, and I know from experience how notoriously slow they are to get things moving. So, here's the deal, and I'm being honest with you. I'm giving the photos to someone I know who has big interests in the Costa del Sol and he knows plenty of people who will be able to ID these people. If they are this Marilyn and Steve, then he will find out very quickly.'

'Fuck's sake, Carlson. That's a bit underhand.'

'It's not underhand, Harry. It would be underhand if I wasn't telling you.'

'But you're bringing in some gangster.'

'I'm just trying to move things a little quicker for you, Harry. Do you really care who can dig out who these people are? Come on. As long as you can establish if that's who they are, then you're ahead of the game.'

I knew that he knew that, but he would protest because he had to. It wouldn't be the first time he'd worked with crooks to get to where he wanted to be.

'Aye, whatever. When do you think your buddy will come up with the information?'

'Quicker than the police anyway – here or over there. I'll let you know as soon as I know.'

'Make it soon then. I'm going over there with a few officers in the next day or so. Just doing the protocol now, making arrangements with the Guardia Civil.'

'Sure,' I said. 'It's that stuff that keeps you back.'

'I'm taking your boyfriend – Scanlon,' he said.

'He's not my boyfriend,' I said, feeling a little punch in my gut that Scanlon was going away on an investigation that could turn out to be dangerous.

'Aye, fine.'

He hung up.

I had a couple of hours before I picked up Lucas from nursery, so I walked from the office down to the London Road, where I knew an old jeweller who had a shop. Some might say it was the wrong end of town to buy quality jewellery, and young couples looking to get engaged were more likely to seek out the traditional jewellery shops that glistened the length of the Argyle Arcade. But they'd be wrong. Whatever Avi Berg sold you would be a lot cheaper than the arcade or any of the high-end stores. And you got the same guarantee.

But Avi was also a fence. You might not be able to guarantee that the ring you purchased hadn't been on anyone's finger before, but nobody could ever prove it. And all of his customers left his shop happy. Avi had worked in the shop learning the jewellery trade from his father, Nat, a Polish Jew who'd come to Scotland as a child after the Second World War. Over the years Nat had built up contacts and connections from Glasgow to Hatton Garden to Amsterdam. He knew everyone in the trade and had made a fortune starting out repairing watches and clocks and then graduating to buying gold and gems second hand and selling them on or creating new pieces of jewellery. He was also the go-to guy if a villain had some dodgy jewellery to shift.

When he died, Avi took over the business with the same set of principles as his father. He didn't ask questions if someone walked in the door looking to move a top of the range Rolex watch or a diamond necklace – unless it smelled mega shady. He would do the same haggling as his father did, because it was clear the goods were the proceeds of a robbery, but he always gave a good enough price – at least half of what he would sell it on for. Everybody was happy. The cops tried to turn Avi over a few times, but nothing ever stuck, and his business seemed to thrive, as he drove a Rolls Royce to and from his comfortable home in a luxury old housing estate Newton Mearns on the south side of the city.

I'd encountered him as a young detective investigating a robbery at a wealthy elderly couple's house and the theft of diamond rings and a haul of gold jewellery. He seemed to take to me for some reason, and told me he'd seen the goods, but when he'd read in the papers about how the old couple were beaten and left for dead, he'd knocked them back. There were lines he didn't cross. And he was good enough to give me the name of the guy who'd tried to sell them. That was Avi. He was a crook. But a decent one, and I'd been friends with him after that, often dropping by his shop for a coffee or going out to one of the greasy spoon cafés on London Road and listening to the raft of stories he told.

There was nobody at the shop counter when I walked through the door and the bell at the top of it tinkled loudly, heralding my arrival. Avi put his head around from the back room, an eye glass in, then he took it out and came around, all smiles.

'Ah, the lovely Billie,' he said, both hands outstretched. 'Been too long. How are you?'

I smiled back as we held hands briefly.

'Long story, Avi. Long story.'

He raised his eyebrows, concerned.

'You are all right? Still a cop? I remember the shit about the shooting.' He put his hands out in surrender. 'You did good.'

I smiled at him.

'Well,' I said. 'Was a bit of a turning point for me. I left the force a few months later.' I paused, looked at him. 'A lot has happened since then, Avi – bad stuff – and I'll tell you one time over a coffee. But not today.'

He looked at me, frowning.

'You are okay, though?'

'Yes. I'm brand new. Honestly. I'm a private eye now.'

'Really? Like the movies?' He chuckled.

'Yeah. Sometimes I'm in the wrong movie, Avi.'

We stood for a moment, and I could see he was waiting for me to speak.

'So, what can I do for you, Billie?'

'Avi, I'm trying to track down a diamond ring. It was pulled off the finger of a middle-aged woman who was fished out of the River Clyde yesterday She'd been helping me in an investigation.'

He looked at me, shocked.

'Shit, Billie.' He shook his head. 'Bad people out there these days. Ruthless. They killed this woman?'

'Yes,' I said. 'Part of a bigger investigation.'

I gave him the shortened version behind Jane's murder. He shook his head when I told him about her and Cathy Evans and the drug smuggling and money laundering racket in Spain.

'My God,' he said, sighing. 'What a terrible thing to happen.'

I pulled up the photograph on my phone and held it out to him, pulling up the picture of the diamond ring on Jane's finger.

'This is the woman who died, Avi. She told me the ring came from Dubai. I saw it myself on her. It was a big rock, big enough to look fake, but she said it was valued at around twenty thousand pounds.'

He kept his eye on the photograph, examining it.

'It's big all right. Few carats there.'

'Would it be real?'

He shrugged.

'Sure. If she bought it from a legitimate dealer in Dubai. They can sell diamond rings for half what we do here. They have access to more diamonds easier. Smuggled into their country.'

After a few moments I asked, 'So, you haven't seen it in here?'

His mouth downturned.

'Nope. Not yet anyway. When did the body come out of the water?'

'Yesterday.'

'It's a bit early. But nobody will want to hang on to that. There are a few people they can go to.' He looked at me. 'If it comes here, I will knock it back for sure.'

'Cops are on this too, Avi. And I've got someone I know trying to find out a bit more of who is behind this. But any help you can get if you hear anything at all would be good.'

He nodded slowly.

'Of course. I will put out some feelers quietly. It's a big rock. Someone will want to move it quickly. If I hear, you'll hear. You can trust me on that.'

'Thanks, Avi.'

'You want a coffee?'

'No, thanks. I have to get back. There's a lot on the go. But soon, Avi. Soon. Would be great to have a good talk.'

'I'll phone you if I hear anything at all.'

CHAPTER TWENTY-SIX

Driving to nursery to pick up Lucas, my mobile pinged and I was glad to see Scanlon's name on the screen.

'I hear you're off to the sunshine,' I said.

'Yeah. Who told you?'

'Who do you think?' I joked. 'He said to me, "I'm taking your boyfriend with me." Big Wilson.'

'What did you say to that?'

'I told him you're not my boyfriend,' I said, immediately hoping he would take it in good humour.

'I want to be your boyfriend,' he said, his voice cheery. 'But you won't let me. I'm just your friend with benefits, Carlson.'

'Nah,' I said. 'You're much more than that, Scanlon. You know that.'

There was a moment's silence between us and although we'd been joking and bantering, I knew that Scanlon was always so sensitive to our relationship. I knew he wanted more, and I think I did too, but I was happy the way it was going along.

'What's the sketch then, Scanlon?' I changed the subject. 'Are a few of you going?'

'Four. Wilson and me, two women detectives.'

'Cosy,' I said, joking.

'I don't think so,' he said. 'Wish it was you who was going.'

I thought for a moment, and he was absolutely right. Before Lucas and before my life had gone into meltdown, I'd have been thrilled at the chance to go abroad on an investigation. I'd done it before and loved it as a cop when it was mixed with danger and a collar at the end of it. Of course, I could go now if I wanted to, as a private investigator. But not now I had Lucas. I wouldn't leave him. I knew that restricted me in so many ways, but that's the way it was now. And I was happy.

'Yeah,' I agreed. 'A part of me would love that too, Scanlon. On a big job like this with you and the troops. But it's all different now. I'm working away here on stuff.' I paused. 'I sent Wilson pictures of the diamond ring that was missing from Jane's finger. And I've just been to see Avi Berg down in the east end. He said he'll keep his eyes open and tell me if he hears who is trying to shift it.' I parked at the nursery. 'When you off?'

'Flying out in the morning. I'm at my flat now, packing.'

'Your budgie smugglers?'

He laughed.

'Aye. Wilson said he was taking his.'

'Oh, please,' I said. 'You'll put me off my dinner.'

'How about going out for a pasta early doors when you're finished?'

'Great idea,' I said. 'Just picking up Lucas now. Come round to the flat and we can walk down to the restaurant. About six?'

'Perfect.'

In the restaurant, the waiter sat us at a booth near the back and close to the kitchen and serving area, and Lucas was fascinated by what he could see of the buzz inside the kitchen and by the bell ringing every time a dish was put up on the counter for serving. As the waiter took our order, Lucas asked if he could see inside the kitchen, and we laughed and told him it was very dangerous. The waiter knew us well as we came here for pizza a lot, and he whispered to Lucas that he would ask the chef if he could have a special ice cream treat later. Lucas's eyes lit up, and he continued to watch the goings-on while we settled down with crayons and colouring paper, and waited for our order of pizza and pasta with chicken. We didn't drink alcohol as it was going to be an early start for Scanlon, and I had too much going on with the investigation.

Just before the food arrived, my mobile shuddered on the table, and I could see it was Harper. I caught Scanlon glancing quickly as the name came up on the screen. I took the call.

'How're things?' I said, without saying Harper's name.

'Not bad,' he said. 'Still trying to dig up Vinnie Martin. He's not left the country, though. We know that for sure.'

'Wonder where he can be,' I said.

'We'll find out tonight. I've got a couple of the lads out seeing his driver. So he'll know.'

'I went along to see Avi Berg today. To see if the ring had popped up yet. But nothing.'

'I'd be surprised if Avi touched it anyway. He's a good man.'

I agreed, conscious that Scanlon was watching me, and I told Harper that Avi would let me know if he heard anything.

'By the way,' Harper said. 'I've got people on the Costa trying to dig out that couple you sent in the picture. They'll be lying low just now, as they'll have been told the heat is on over here.' He paused. 'But if they find them, then they'll talk all right.'

I didn't want to say to him that the cops were about to be on their way, but I'm sure Harper's connections would know soon enough. He hung up after telling me to be careful.

'You deal with Harper a lot?' Scanlon looked straight at me.

'Now and again, Danny,' I said. 'Remember he helped on that

Jackie girl whose kid got stolen from the car. He's not all bad. He gets things done.'

'He kills people,' he said in a whisper, glancing at Lucas who was busy drawing.

I shrugged. I didn't really want to have this conversation.

'I know. But he's not the worst of them,' I said.

'You'll be telling me he has a moral compass next.' Scanlon half smiled.

I smiled back.

'Well, he's got people in Spain trying to find that couple who might be behind Cathy Evans' murder. No matter what, Scanlon, that would be good.'

'Yeah. As long as we're not caught in the crossfire.'

'Wilson will know what he's doing,' I said. 'And the cops in the Guardia Civil are good once they get going and are onto something.' I paused, changing the subject. 'I'll be worried about you, though,' I said, then smiled. 'Even if you're not my boyfriend.'

Scanlon smiled and reached across the table and our fingers interlaced.

'I'll miss you, Billie.' He ruffled Lucas's hair. 'This.' He paused. 'When I get back why don't we look at going somewhere sunny over the Easter holidays? You fancy it?'

My eyebrows were up.

'All three of us?'

'Of course.' He put his arm around Lucas's shoulder. 'No show without Punch.'

I felt my face smile, imagining how amazing it would be if we could pitch up somewhere sunny, a beach, a hotel, have some fun in the sun.

'I'd love that, Danny. I really would.'

'Great,' he said, as the food arrived. 'Okay. You have a search around and see what we can sort while I'm away. I don't imagine I'll be away very long.'

I looked at him and smiled.

'With Wilson as your companion, you'll be desperate to get home after a few days.'

'Especially if he insists on wearing his budgie smugglers to the poolside.'

'Oh, stop!' I said, as the waiter set down the food.

After dinner we walked back up to my flat, with Lucas between us clutching our hands. We'd taken pictures of his face when the chef came out of the kitchen with an ice cream for him, topped with a wafer, and he even let him wear his hat for a few seconds. It was a perfect end to a cosy dinner, but as we walked back, I sensed we were both conscious that we didn't know what the next few days would bring. As a cop, you never really did know what could happen in any given shift, but travelling abroad to investigate the deaths of two women gave things a real edge.

Back at the flat, Scanlon came in and played with Lucas for a little while until I called time on it as it was bath time for the wee guy and Scanlon needed to get some sleep before his early flight. I wasn't sure whether to tell Lucas that Scanlon was going away for a few days as I didn't want him to have someone he clearly loved disappearing, even if it was for a short time. Scanlon gave him a huge hug before I walked him to the hall and the front door.

'You be careful out there,' I said to him. 'And do what you're told.'

'I'm not like you,' Scanlon said, pushing my hair back behind my ear. 'I always do what the boss tells me.'

He opened his arms, and I stepped in and we held each other

tight for a long moment, then he eased himself back, his eyes scanning my face. He kissed me softly on the lips, and it stirred feelings inside me, having him this close and the taste of his mouth on mine. As we stopped, feeling the heat of our breath on each other, he kissed me on the cheek.

'I'd better get out of here or I'll be awake all night,' he said, brushing the back of his hand on my cheek.

'Yeah. Get going, Scanlon. I've got a boy to put in the bath and get into his bed.'

We parted.

'Will you call me?' I asked.

'Of course. When I can.' He turned to go, then looked over his shoulder. 'And get looking for a trip for us when I get back. I'd love that.'

'I will.'

I threw him a kiss as he opened the door and stepped out into the night. Then I went into the living room and watched from the window as he walked down the street, turning his head for a final look and waving before he disappeared over the hill.

CHAPTER TWENTY-SEVEN

Once Lucas was in bed, I should have been able to settle down for the evening, maybe even have an early night. But I felt a little wired, with everything that had been unfolding in the past few days, and knew I was far from tired enough to go to sleep. I sat flicking through TV channels for a few minutes, but nothing stirred my interest.

I found myself walking down the hall towards the cupboard at the end. I wasn't sure I was ready to rake over anything else that was in there from my past, from my parents' past, but there was this morbid curiosity that I had to find out more. I opened the door and flicked on the light. It was just a room full of junk, I told myself. Like any other storeroom where people threw in everything they had not quite wanted to part with but had no use for either. There was nothing to be afraid of. I sat down cross-legged on the wooden floor and sighed as I gazed at all the stuff, the boxes, old suitcases, an old clothes rail with coats of my father's still hanging there, blazers, jackets of my mothers, and as I looked at them, I could remember seeing them. I had no idea if this was good for me, delving into past memories like this, but I couldn't help myself.

I sat for a few moments, then turned to the shelf where the bound book had been, the journal or whatever it was. I reached across and pulled it out, holding it, letting my hands run across it, trying to picture my father with the book in front of him somewhere, thinking, planning what to write, or did he just open it and start writing in an impulsive way? I would never know now.

Instead of opening the first page as I'd done before, I skimmed over the pages, watching them fall as I held the book, my father's handwriting a blur, and I couldn't make out any of the contents. Then I started at the beginning again. Moved to later pages. They seemed to be written with dates and sometimes places: Warsaw, Moscow, Leningrad, Belgrade, Dubrovnik. Why was he writing to me from all of these places? I couldn't have been any more than ten or eleven judging from the dates and would have been too young for him to tell me anything about them. Perhaps he meant to give this book to me when I reached an age where I could read and understand it. But my father never got the chance to explain. I began again at the first entry.

My darling Billie. I write to you here because one day these pages will help you to understand more about the world and about me. You see, I work in the universities, but my work is much more than that, although I cannot say what it is. But I am working for the greater good, so that the powers who seek to oppress and to punish ordinary people who hanker after the kind of freedoms we take for granted cannot prevail. I know we cannot win all of these things and we will never defeat the forces of the Soviets and the threat they pose to all of us, but my work involves limiting their power in some way, with their research, so that we can put a halt to them. I will give you some examples of my travels in these pages. In Warsaw I see people queuing for everything in the bitter, cold winter. Children and women working like slaves, living in hovels, while in the city there are palaces and the KGB live in splendour and want for nothing. And in the universities, students keep their heads down knowing that to question is to end their careers, and academics know that if they open their mouths and speak out, they will disappear. That is what I see as I tour the universities and lecture to all of these people who are just like us, but whose children will never be free, unlike you. In my work, I find things out and I try to help by discovering ways in which we can thwart their progress in communications and in nuclear capabilities. All of these things . . .

I turned the pages as there was more of this and it sounded a little like the rantings of some politician who had seen things abroad in regimes he didn't like. It was the kind of writing you see in newspapers when people speak out. I suppose he must have been writing it to me to make me understand why he was away such a lot and how important his work was. I only know that I missed him whenever he went on these trips and our house felt empty and sad until he came home to us. I turned more pages and my eyes scanned quickly some of what he'd written, but there was so much here and I would need to spend more time going through it if I wanted to learn anything. I decided to call it a day and put the journal away, then came out of the cupboard, switching off the light and locking the door. It was for another day.

I had a restless night, and my dreams were full of the usual garish scenes. I was glad when I woke up and checked my watch. It was already seven a.m. and I liked to get up and showered and organised before Lucas got out of bed.

When I came out of the shower my mobile was ringing on the bedside table and I snatched it up in case it would wake Lucas. I saw Fletcher's name on the screen.

'Hello,' I said in a whisper.

'Are you all right, Billie? I can hardly hear you.'

'Yes. I'm speaking quietly as my son is still asleep.'

'Oh, sorry for calling at this time.'

'It's okay.'

A moment's silence. I wondered why he had called.

'I'm going back down to London this evening, Billie, and I wondered if you could meet me before I go. Are you free for a coffee any time today?'

I took a moment to answer. I could hardly say no.

'Sure,' I said. 'Maybe early afternoon, before I pick my son up from nursery.'

'Thanks.' He hung up.

I checked my text messages and saw one from Scanlon. On board. Thinking of you. I texted him back. Take care, with a couple of kisses.

On the way to the office my mobile rang. It was Avi Berg.

'Avi. How are you doing?'

'All fine here, Billie,' he replied cheerily. 'I've got some news for you on that ring.'

'Great.'

'I put some feelers out as I told you I would and got some information late last night. Someone is trying to shift a diamond ring like the one you showed me and has been to a guy who works out of a pawn shop off Argyle Street. Apparently, he wouldn't touch it. Too big for him. He could see it was genuine and he was too scared to handle it in case it would cause trouble for him. It was two guys who came into the shop.'

'Do you think they're not going to regular jewellers because the ring is valuable and looks too hot?'

'Yes, probably. But my wee pal told them to try going down south to move it.'

'Does he have any idea who the guys are?'

'Yes. Well, kind of. One of them he knows is called Johnny. He's been in there before. Wee guy with a limp and tattoos on his knuckles – you know, like the kind of tattoos that get done in jail.'

'Yeah. Johnny,' I said. 'No second name?'

'No. Sorry. He didn't know who the other one was. Big curly-haired bulky figure. Youngish. Johnny, he says, is in his late thirties. He knows him from coming into his place before. But my mate wouldn't go near a ring like that with a barge pole. Apparently, Johnny was well pissed off when he left. He told him to make sure he keeps his trap shut about him being in there.'

'I should be able to find out who he is,' I said. 'Did he ask for an idea of how much it would be worth?'

'Yeah. He was told upwards of twenty grand. And my mate told him that it was way beyond anything he would buy.'

I thanked Avi for his help, and he said if he heard any more, he would be in touch.

'And remember, we need to have that coffee, Billie. I like your chat.'

'Thanks.' I smiled. 'We will. Soon, Avi.' I hung up.

I scrolled down and pushed the key for Harper's mobile.

'Paddy,' I said when he answered. 'I've got some information. How did you do?'

'Good. We know where Vinnie Martin is, so we will get the squeeze on the wee prick today. What you hearing?'

'I spoke to a jeweller friend and he tells me that someone called Johnny was at the pawn shop down off Argyle Street trying to move a diamond ring. You know a guy called Johnny with a bad limp?'

'Aye. I sure do. Johnny Morton. He's only got four toes on his right foot after somebody shot off his big toe a few years ago.'

'Jesus,' I said, trying to picture how that was even possible.

'He stiffed a prick called Tommy Burnside on a five-grand coke drop, and when they found him, he ran like the clappers. But they caught him. He doesn't run much these days. But he's a nasty wee bastard. What did Manny at the pawn shop tell him?'

'Apparently, he said it was too big a rock for him to handle and to shift it down south. He wasn't happy. He was with a big guy with curly hair.'

'That's Irish Jim the Tim. He's a bit of a handful. IRA man. But I'll get the boys to dig them out.'

'Do you think they're the guys who took Jane and dumped her in the water?' I asked.

'Yep. They'd be doing it on Vinnie Martin's instruction, because he wouldn't want to get his hands dirty. And he'd have been doing it for whoever instructed him. But between them all, we'll get some answers before the day is out.'

That level of confidence, I thought. I suppose it comes from years of having a survival of the fittest mentality, backed up by ruthless brutality and a bottom line that if you lose, you die.

CHAPTER TWENTY-EIGHT

I agreed to meet Christopher Fletcher in the Starbucks café in the Buchanan Street precinct, as he said it was handy for him catching the train to London in the late afternoon from Central station.

'The city is full of so many memories for me,' Fletcher told me as we sat on the leather sofas in Starbucks. 'It has changed so much from when I used to come here with Elizabeth back in the day. We sometimes met your mother and father and had dinner in a great Italian restaurant close to here.' He stopped, looked beyond me. 'I don't suppose I'll come back here again.'

There was no answer to that, so I watched and wondered if he regretted how he had lived his life, much of it in the shadows, and also the danger of it. Now it was too late. I wondered how much time he had left. He said six months, maybe a year, but you never really knew with cancer.

'Will you be alone in London when you go back? Or do you have family?' I asked, thinking what a sorry end to life to be heading home with your murdered wife's body to follow you.

He looked at me and his lips stretched into a grimace.

'I'll be all right. I don't mind being alone.' He paused. 'To be honest, Elizabeth and I had become so estranged in the past couple of years that I was used to living on my own – that's whenever I actually came home. For me, it was often better just to stay on wherever I was – Paris, Berlin or Switzerland. I just stayed there a few days or a week. I had no desire to come home.'

I wondered why he was telling me this. I assumed he'd been told by the police that Elizabeth had killed the man she'd picked up in the bar. I'd been curious from the start who this was and why he was chasing her, presumably to get the USB stick. I couldn't help myself asking.

'The man who died,' I ventured, 'he was looking for some USB stick.'

'I know, Billie. I know you gave it to the agents who came up after Elizabeth died.' He sipped his coffee and looked at me. 'But you must know that I cannot talk about that.'

'I'm sure you can't. But I was curious. What was worth so much that someone was prepared to kill for it? Would they have killed you if you were in the house and wouldn't hand it over?'

'He wouldn't have been in the house if I was there.'

'Yes. I know.' He looked mildly disgusted at what Elizabeth had done. 'But I can't help thinking what was so important.'

'All I will say to you is that it was proof. It was the testimony of someone who can prove that . . .' He stopped. 'Do you remember the poisoning of the man in the hotel in London? Poisoned by a nerve agent? It was all over the news at the time.'

'Yes,' I said, fascinated. 'I remember it.'

'The USB stick contained evidence. There was testimony and documents to prove what happened.'

'I see. What will it mean now that it is with the secret service?'

He sighed.

'They will be able to pursue it through the diplomatic

channels, you know, pull some strings, get some breakthrough, release some prisoner, that kind of thing. It will be a bargaining chip.'

'But nobody will ever be brought to justice for the poisoning, or for what happened to Elizabeth?'

He looked down at the table.

'No. Unfortunately, nobody will stand trial or be punished in the way we would expect.'

We were silent for a long time, then I spoke.

'Was it all worth it?' I felt a niggle of guilt at the question.

He looked at me for a long time before he finally answered.

'I think, Billie, you are asking that question as much for yourself . . . because you lost your father.'

I nodded.

'Yes, I suppose,' I replied. 'But I wonder if there was ever a time over the years that my father asked himself if any of it was worth it. And you.'

Again, the silence.

'I know that for your father it was more than work, more than gathering intelligence. He had a genuine wish, a drive, to make things different for the people who he saw being oppressed in the regimes he encountered.'

'He had us,' I said. 'He had us waiting for him all the time. Maybe he should have thought about us.'

He nodded.

'Yes. I think there will always be that feeling of regret, of guilt, in all of us who work like that. And maybe your father too.'

I didn't know where this was going, but before I could stop myself, I asked, 'Did you know my father kept a journal?'

He looked me in the eye.

'No. I didn't. But I'm not surprised. How do you know?'

'Because I was going through some things I found in a storage cupboard in my flat. A place I have never gone into in all the time I was there, because somehow I didn't want to go back. You know, it felt too painful. And anyway, it was all a long time ago and I knew it would be difficult to look back.'

He studied my face.

'But you did.'

'Yes. Just these past few days. Ever since Elizabeth told me about my father being murdered. And then you, talking about him. It made me want to find out more.'

He nodded slowly, a little cautious.

'And did you find anything?'

I sighed.

'I found this journal in his handwriting. It's like, well, letters to me, as though he's writing it to me.' I swallowed. 'It was quite moving, just to read the way he started the diary – saying this was for me, so that I may understand.' I paused. 'But I've only looked a little at it. I've put it to the side for another time. I . . . I'm just not ready to go through it all. But mostly he was writing about the regimes, and the oppression of the people. That kind of thing.'

'It meant so much to him,' he said. 'Your father was a great man. He was respected and revered in the service.'

'And he died doing his work,' I said, feeling the catch in my throat.

Christopher didn't answer, but blinked his acknowledgement. He looked tired.

'What about Dimitry Volkov? Do you know any more about him?'

Our eyes met.

For a long time, we said nothing and he looked at me and waited for me to speak.

'I would like to meet him – this man who took my father away from me.'

He didn't answer, his eyes lingering on my face. Then he glanced at his watch.

'I must go, Billie. My train is in a little while.' He stood up and stretched out his hand. 'It has been so good to meet you. To see the daughter of my best friend, how she has grown up. Your father would be so, so proud of you.' He paused. 'Let that be enough for you, Billie.'

I looked back at him, swallowed hard.

'It will never be enough.'

He didn't look me in the eye as he touched my arm, and went past me, then walked to the door, leaving me standing there watching until he disappeared in the busy precinct.

CHAPTER TWENTY-NINE

Even though I didn't see Scanlon on a daily basis, I felt somehow at a loose end because he wasn't there. It was a weird feeling. We would often go for a few days without talking or getting in touch, but lately he had been more and more in my life, and especially with Lucas it was beginning to feel that we were a close little unit, even if technically we weren't. I seldom entertained these notions in case I would have to make a commitment, but it was unspoken and I was just comfortable being around him. Now, with Scanlon in Spain and me not being able to have any involvement in what he was doing I felt ridiculously lost. I'd taken Lucas shopping for new trainers, and all the time he was in the shop trying different shoes on, he kept asking me if Danny would like them or which ones he would like best. On the way back to the flat he asked if Danny was coming over to see his new trainers, and I told him as gently as I could that he was away for a few days working. Lucas stopped in his tracks and looked up at me, big, sad, bewildered eyes.

'Is Danny never coming back, Mummy?'

'What?' I bent down so I was close to his face. 'Of course he's coming back. Why would you think that, Lucas? Danny is a policeman. Sometimes he has to go away from Glasgow for a few days.'

He stood for a moment, searching my face, then said, 'I don't want Danny to go away.'

I picked him up and hugged him.

'Come on, Lucas. You'll be okay. Danny will be back soon and we can all go out for dinner.'

'What, tonight?' he asked, pleading.

'No,' I said patiently. 'Not tonight. But soon. And you know what? When he comes back, we are going to look at going on a holiday together, on a plane somewhere with a beach and the sea. How do you like that?'

He nodded, smiling.

'I like it,' he said. 'I can pack my case tonight!'

I eased him down and looked at him.

'Well, if you want, then we can do that,' I said. 'But might be a few days yet.'

'Okay,' he said, and we walked to Blythswood Square and up the steps to the entrance to our home.

Once I'd got Lucas settled into bed, after he had packed things into his suitcase, I had to tell the same story over and over of the planned holiday, because he had latched on to it.

'Tell me about the airport again, Mummy.' Lucas pushed himself up on the pillow.

'Okay,' I began, for the third time. 'We will get into the taxi with our bags, and Danny will be with us. Then we will get to the airport to check in.'

'Don't forget our tickets,' he piped up.

'Of course not. And then we'll have some breakfast at the airport and the tannoy will tell us to head to the plane. And we will get strapped into the plane, and then watch out of the window as the pilot says ready for take-off.'

He made his hand flat to look like a plane racing down the runway.

'Like this, Mummy?'

'Yes. Like that. And then we can watch out of the window as the plane gets higher and higher and the ground is further away and suddenly we'll be up above the clouds and the sky will be pure and blue.'

He was in awe of the story as though he was actually there right now.

'And then the plane will land, and it'll be very hot outside, and we'll get into our taxi to the hotel.'

'Will there be a swimming pool, Mummy?'

'Yes. There will be a swimming pool,' I said, puffing up his pillow. 'But right now you must go to sleep and dream about it, because soon we will be there.'

'And Danny too?'

'Of course. Danny too.'

He snuggled down in the pillow and I kissed his cheek and eased the duvet up under his chin. I watched as he closed his eyes and he drifted off quickly, hopefully dreaming of aeroplanes and blue skies and swimming pools and beaches.

Afterwards I sat in the living room flicking through the TV channels. My mobile rang and I picked it up quickly from the coffee table in case it would wake Lucas. It was Harper.

'Paddy.'

'Billie. You all right?' he asked, and I told him I was. Then he spoke quickly. 'Been a busy day all right. But we've got some good work done.' He paused. 'That Johnny Morton, didn't take him long to squeal like a stuck pig.'

I didn't know how to answer that, so I said nothing. Harper went on.

'He spilled about Vinnie and told us where we would find him, so we picked him up early afternoon.'

'Okay,' I said, feeling I had to say something. 'And is Vinnie saying much?'

'Well, not any more he isn't.' There was a brief pause then Harper went on. 'He said he was told to get rid of Jane McAllister by a guy called Billy Brown in Spain. He's from Manchester. I don't know him, but I know people who do, and they told me he's got a vicious crew at his back. He's got two bars out there. It's Brown who runs the mules on the Costa del Sol – people like that Steve and Marilyn couple. It's big business, and a slick operation, because people like middle-aged couples are seldom viewed with suspicion by cops and border control. The guy I know out in Spain says this couple are his best operators, so that'll be why they had to close Cathy Evans down.'

I took in what he said, matter-of-factly reporting on how the system worked, and was thinking how along the line a gullible, lonely woman called Cathy Evans had fallen into the trap and paid for her free holidays with her life. And her friend Jane McAllister, who did nothing except witness a row, had met the same fate.

'You still there, Billie?'

'Yes,' I replied. 'I'm just trying to take it all in, Paddy, how these people operate. Not that I'm surprised, but no matter how many times I come across things like this it still sickens me. They're the scum of the earth.'

'Aye. All about money and greed. Some people will never have enough.'

Harper said it as though he'd been squeaky clean all his life, which he wasn't. But I pushed that thought away. He was digging out good information.

'The cops are out in Spain now working on the investigation,' I told him. 'I can pass this to them.'

'Yep. Feel free. But as long as they're not looking for anyone to talk, because Vinnie and those two pricks won't be talking any more.' He paused, and I could hear him clearing his throat. 'Oh, and Billie, Morton told us about that visit to the nursery trying to get your boy.'

'He did?' I said, surprised.

'Aye. He said it was Vinnie who said to do it, to send a message to you because Jane McAllister had said she'd been talking to you. It wasn't Morton who went – just one of their boys. Anyway, he's been spoken to, for want of a better description, so you won't have any more problems there.'

I didn't know what to say, so I just mumbled, 'Thanks, Paddy.'

It took a moment for it all to sink in. Vinnie, a pawn in the game, had served his purpose for the big boys in Spain, and for Paddy Harper. Whatever reign he had in Glasgow was over. As for Johnny and Jim the Tim, they were history. I should have been at least a little appalled at the swiftness of the justice meted out, but I wasn't.

I scrolled down for Harry Wilson's number and called him. When he answered I could hear the chatter of what sounded like a noisy dinner table.

'Carlson,' Wilson said. 'How're things?'

'Good, Harry,' I said. 'You?'

'Yep. So far, so good. That's as much as I can say.'

'Harry, I've got some information for you. Are you okay to talk?'

'Sure.'

The noise abated and I assumed he had moved away so he could hear me.

'Hi,' he said. 'I'm outside the restaurant now. We're having a bite to eat with the Guardia Civil cops, working things out.' He sniffed. 'What did you hear?'

'My contact here made some calls in Spain and his mate says

the man behind the mules is a guy called Billy Brown. He's an English ex-pat but runs a slick operation. Owns a couple of bars. One in Fuengirola.'

'Where's this coming from?'

'Vinnie Martin,' I said.

'You talked to Vinnie Martin?'

'No. Someone else did.'

'Someone got to him?'

'Yeah. Through a wee guy called Johnny Morton. Morton had tried to shift the diamond ring at a pawn shop in the city, so he got picked up.'

'By whom?'

I didn't answer and Wilson waited a couple of seconds then spoke.

'Aye, okay, Billie. Not that I expected you to tell me anything with some of the dodgy fuckers you talk to.'

'Doesn't matter, Harry. It's good information.'

'It is. And I'm grateful. I'll get someone to pick Vinnie Martin up.'

Silence.

'Er, I'm not sure he's around any more.'

I heard him puff and could imagine him shaking his head.

'Fuck's sake, Carlson. Would be easier to nail him on the witness stand.'

I didn't want to disagree, so I changed the subject.

'Vinnie confessed that he was the one who sent Johnny Morton and some Irish guy called Jim the Tim to get rid of Jane McAllister. He said he was hired by Billy Brown to clean up the loose ends on the Cathy Evans killing.'

'I don't suppose Gimpy Morton and that big Irish fucker are helping police with enquiries either?'

After a moment I answered.

'No. I mean, I don't know. But I'd doubt it.'

He was quiet for a moment, then sighed.

'Okay, Billie. It's good to hear this. I'll talk to the Guardia and see how we get to this Billy Brown character.'

'Good. Glad to be of help, Harry.'

I was dying to ask how Scanlon was, but I knew I didn't dare.

'Watch yourself back there, Carlson.'

'Of course,' I said. 'You too.'

He hung up.

CHAPTER THIRTY

It had been two days since I'd talked to Wilson in Spain, and I'd heard nothing. Not that I was expecting an update from him, but I'd kind of hoped Scanlon might drop me a text or a quick call. I knew it was stupid to think that way, so I did my best to put it out of my mind. I was busy enough anyway, new clients coming to see me to look at their cases. Fowler was working with me most days, especially if I was out of the office meeting a client, which I seldom did these days, and if I did, it was only in a public place. We were in my office trawling through possible cases when Millie put her head around the door.

'Have you seen the news?' she asked, glancing at the TV mounted on the wall.

We both looked up. I'd had the TV on mute and had barely looked at it in the past couple of hours. I could see police activity around the River Clyde and that the area was taped off. I picked up the remote control and turned up the volume. The strapline read *Breaking News. Three bodies discovered across Glasgow. Police are investigating.*

I looked at Millie and Fowler and watched as the presenter spoke.

'The first body was discovered early this morning when a tug on the river reported what looked like a body in the water down past Whiteinch. The Humane Society boat was called in to recover the body of a man in his forties. Police are not giving out his identification as yet, but we can reveal that the corpse had a finger missing from his right hand.'

We all looked at each other. The presenter read on.

'The second body was discovered in his car, and is believed to be that of Vinnie Martin, a notorious Glasgow criminal feared as an enforcer. He was discovered in a layby on the outskirts of the city in a car with the engine running. A hosepipe was attached to the exhaust and passed through the driver's window. Martin was alone in the car and unconscious when a passing motorist stopped and immediately called the police. He was pronounced dead at the scene.'

'Christ!' Fowler said. 'Rough justice right enough.'

I nodded, as the scene moved to a derelict builders' yard in the Maryhill area. The presenter spoke.

'The body of a man in his thirties is thought to be that of Jim O'Brien, an Irishman who'd been living in Glasgow for a number of years and was a hardman who worked for Vinnie Martin. O'Brien, with suspected links to the IRA, was known as "Jim the Tim". He was found tied to a chair with a polythene bag over his head.'

Fowler glanced at me, wide-eyed.

'Well, that's three wastes of space off the face of the earth.'

I nodded.

'Can't disagree with that.'

'It was double quick how they were found, though,' Fowler said. 'Do you think cops were tipped off?'

'Yep. I think they wanted the bodies found to flag a message to someone, maybe in the bigger picture, that they have to watch their step.'

'Probably,' he agreed. 'But the big bosses in Spain with all the connections won't flinch that some low-rent villains in Glasgow got the chop.'

'That might be their first mistake,' I said.

'Harper's handywork?' Fowler asked.

'All I know is he told me he'd had them picked up and they spilled their guts on what happened to Cathy Evans and Jane McAllister. He told me they wouldn't be talking any more.'

'But the missing finger.' Fowler shook his head, half smiling. 'That's rich. It really is.'

'That'll be Johnny Morton. He's the guy who tried to punt Jane's diamond ring in the pawn shop.'

'I wonder if they cut it off before or after he was dead.'

'Forensics will know soon enough. My money is on it being cut off before. That's probably why he spouted on where to find Vinnie.'

'Oh well,' Fowler said. 'I hope it hurt like a bitch.'

Later, driving to the nursery, my mobile buzzed and I glanced across the passenger seat to see Paddy Harper's name on the screen.

'Paddy. I just saw the TV news. Bodies everywhere.'

'Aye. That's what happens. Nobody will miss the bastards who bump off a couple of middle-aged women. Cowards.' He paused. 'And I hear there's been a shoot-out in Spain?'

I felt a punch in my gut.

'Really? When?'

'Sometime yesterday evening from what I hear. Happened around a bar owned by Billy Brown in Fuengirola. Cops and some of Brown's mob. One of them was killed.'

'Jesus! You hear anything else?'

'Not yet. A couple of people injured. Not sure what the score is, but I'm keeping an eye on it. Will give you a shout if I hear.'

Harper hung up. I wanted him to talk more. I wanted to hear details of the shoot-out, exactly who was involved – if it was a joint operation with Spanish and UK cops. My immediate instinct was to call or text Scanlon, but I knew that was not on. Who knew what he and the team with Wilson might be in the middle of. I'd have to wait it out.

Lucas came out of the nursery clutching my hand and we crossed to the car, and I strapped him in. All the way back to the flat the chattering of Lucas from the back was drowning out my anxious thoughts of what was happening in Spain. I really had no idea what the police operation Wilson and the team were undertaking in Spain involved on the ground. I had assumed that when they were going across there, they'd be looking to pick up evidence of the death of Cathy Evans first and foremost as it happened on Spanish soil. It was the murder of Jane McAllister that drove Wilson to widen this across to Spain. No doubt Spanish cops would be glad of the intelligence they could provide, but there was no indication when I spoke to Wilson or to Scanlon before they left that they were going into a gun fight. I knew Scanlon and the rest of the team were trained in firearms and all had been part of the armed response team at various stages, as I was some years ago. But working as armed officers alongside the Guardia Civil wasn't something I'd even considered they'd be doing. Perhaps I was getting it all out of proportion. If there was a shoot-out, I told myself, it would be the Guardia Civil who were on the front line, not the Scottish cops.

Back at the flat, Lucas kept me busy, insisting I played Ghostbusters with him, and I followed him all over the house, throwing open the doors in every room, chasing ghosts along the walls with our Ghostbuster proton guns, then back at the HQ in our living room where he insisted I answer the next call bringing in yet more ghost sightings. It was fun, and a diversion from the reality of what might be happening in Spain with real guns and people getting shot. I cooked fish and chips, and I watched Lucas clear his plate – except for the salad – marvelling at the huge appetite he'd had almost since the day I brought him home from New York. I used to wonder where and what he ate while he was over there, but whatever it had been, he never mentioned it at any time since he came home, and I never asked him.

Later, once he was asleep, I sat on the sofa scrolling through my laptop for any breaking news across social media that there had been a shooting on the Costa del Sol. Then, as if on cue, my mobile rang, sending a jolt through me when I saw it was Wilson.

'Billie. It's me,' he said, then before I could answer, 'Listen. You don't repeat this to anyone, and I mean anyone, okay? I shouldn't be phoning you at all, but I felt I had to, in case you hear it anywhere else.'

My stomach was sinking to the floor as he spoke, because I knew it could only be bad news. I was barely breathing. Then it came.

'Scanlon's been shot.'

'Christ, Harry! Is he . . . I mean, is it serious?' I could hardly get the words out.

'It's serious enough, Billie. He's in the hospital, so he's in good hands. But he lost a lot of blood.'

A raft of questions flooded my mind and I stumbled over my words.

'Wh . . . where? I mean, where is he shot?'

'Just below the shoulder, close to the chest.'

'Oh shit.'

'He's lucky,' Wilson said. 'Though he might not think that

at the moment. He was wearing a Kevlar vest, as we all were. But the bullet was above it. And any closer and it would have severed a main artery, or maybe hit him in his neck, or some shit like that.' He stopped. 'But listen. He's alive, and he's been through an operation to remove the bullet. So, it's a wait and see. I'm phoning you because I know you two are close and he'd have wanted me to.'

'Is he conscious?'

He took a while to answer, and I could feel panic rise in my throat. Then he spoke.

'He is. They took him off life support this afternoon. And he's breathing by himself.'

Life support? Breathing by himself? A bullet in the chest. Jesus wept!

'Harry,' I said, feeling my throat tighten. 'Is he going to be okay?'

I heard him sigh. I sensed it was difficult for him having to deliver news like this. He loved his officers and the fact that he'd chosen Scanlon for his team meant he had trust in his ability, as well as an affection that he would probably never admit to.

'I think so. Lost a lot of blood and been through an operation, but I think he's out of the danger zone now.'

'When did it happen, Harry?'

'Last night.'

So many things I wanted to ask. Had it been during the shoot-out in Fuengirola? But I thought it was best I didn't rile him by letting him know I already knew about that. But I wanted to know.

'Where did it happen? Can you say?'

'Not at the moment, Billie. I need to go now. I'll tell Scanlon I spoke to you when I can.'

'Tell him . . .' I stumbled. 'Tell him I . . .' I stopped because I wanted to say tell him I love him, but I couldn't say that right now in front of Wilson. 'Tell him I'm here. We're here. Me and Lucas. And we're waiting for him to come home.'

'Aye.' Wilson hung up.

CHAPTER THIRTY-ONE

I barely slept. I don't know what I'd expected if I ever heard something bad had happened to Scanlon, but the depth of my shock and panic took me by surprise. I was in no doubt about my feelings for Scanlon and had known for some time that I loved him, and deep down that I was in love with him too. Maybe I'd always been. But as things had developed between us in recent months, we had never made a real declaration or commitment to each other and I was happy the way it was. Now, suddenly faced with the thought that I might lose him, I was distraught.

I tossed and turned the whole night, trying to imagine the scenario when the drama had unfolded over in Spain, picturing him lying in a pool of blood, imagining what must have been going through his mind, because he would know the level of his injury. I found myself wishing I had called him before this happened, just to tell him that I missed him and was thinking about him. But what if it was all too late? What if everything I had felt for him was now too late, and he didn't survive? Or what if he came back a different person? No matter what happened, I resolved, I would be there for him, the way he was there for me at my weakest point. I would help him get back and I would look after him and love him whatever it took.

Lucas came padding into the kitchen rubbing his eyes as I was standing at the breakfast bar pouring some orange juice into a glass for him.

'Is it today Danny comes home, Mummy?' he asked, climbing onto the bar stool.

A surge of emotion ran through me, and I suddenly felt choked, glancing at him then turning away to face the television, trying to compose myself, blinking back tears. I turned back to him.

'Not today, sweetheart. Not yet.' I swallowed hard.

He gave me a quizzical look, his head cocked to the side.

'Mummy. Are you crying?' His brows knitted.

I sniffed.

'No, darling.' I dabbed at the tear that had escaped. 'I think I got something in my eye.'

He looked at me again as though not convinced, then he swirled his cereal around in the bowl and took a spoonful.

'Can we watch *Pip and Posy*, Mummy?' he said.

He turned to the television, having already moved on from the conversation, and I was glad. My mobile rang and I picked it up, walking away from the breakfast bar when I saw it was Harper.

'Paddy. You all right?'

'Aye,' he said. 'I'm hearing that a cop was shot the night before last over there. One of the cops who went from here.'

'Yes,' I said. 'I heard. It's Danny Scanlon. He's a close friend of mine, Paddy.' I paused, took a breath. 'My best friend.' I felt the catch in my throat.

He was silent for a moment, then he spoke.

'Sorry to hear that, Billie. I didn't get the name. Only that it was one of the Scottish boys,' he said. 'Are you all right?'

I sighed.

'I have to be,' I said. 'I've got my wee boy having his breakfast as I speak. He adores Danny. I was told last night that he was shot. He's been through an operation to remove the bullet, so they're hopeful, was all I was told.'

'That's good. One of my mates over there had been told the cop was in a bad way, so I'm glad he's picking up. I'm sure he'll be fine. Did you hear what happened?'

'No. Wilson called me but he wouldn't say.'

'I can tell you. Do you want to hear?'

'Yes. I'd like to know, Paddy.'

I could hear him breathing, then he started to speak.

'Way I heard it was that two of the Scottish cops, along with Guardia Civil officers, were at the home of that couple, Steve and Marilyn. They were being brought in for questioning. Then from nowhere as they got into the car, shots were fired.'

'Christ!'

'It happened about an hour after the shooting at the bar in Fuengirola I told you about. So not sure why the action was moved to down there. But I'm thinking maybe Brown and his mob got wind that the couple were going to get pulled in, and they decided to move in. They wouldn't want them blabbing to the Spanish cops and dropping names in all over the place.'

I thought about what he said.

'So do you think Brown's men had gone to the house to get rid of Steve and Marilyn? But they were too late because cops were already there?'

'Who knows for sure. But it might have been that. Maybe they would have squirrelled them away somewhere and they'd never be heard tell of again. But they were met by armed cops.'

I pictured the scene, thinking of the police taking the couple out of the apartment when suddenly they were ambushed in the street.

'So where is the couple now?'

'As far as I know they got arrested.'

'What about Billy Brown?'

'I'm told police picked him up too, and he's in custody.'

'That's a result,' I said. 'But with a price.'

'Yep.' He was quiet for a moment. 'Keep your chin up, Billie. I'm sure your mate will be okay. We Scots are hardy buggers. I've been shot in the chest twice, and I'm still going.'

I felt myself smiling despite my anguish.

'I hope Danny's as tough as you, Paddy.'

'Listen. If you need anything, let me know.'

I told him I would, and he hung up. I stood in the living room looking out at the rain dripping off the sycamore branches, my heart heavy with worry, my mind a blur of images of what had happened in Spain the night before last, and Scanlon lying in a hospital bed so far away.

'You look like you've been out all night,' Millie declared as I walked through the doorway into the reception.

I puffed.

'I might as well have been,' I replied. 'I've been awake most of the night. Shattered.'

'What's up?'

'Scanlon's been shot in Spain.'

'Oh, Jesus, Billie. Is it bad?'

'It looked that way at first. Lost a lot of blood,' I said, taking off my coat and hanging it on the stand, then turning to her. 'He was shot just above the chest. Wilson called me last night. Apparently, he's had an operation to remove the bullet. But he's survived.' I paused and plonked myself onto an easy chair. 'So far.'

Millie got up and went to the coffee machine.

'That's terrible, Billie. Poor Danny.' She turned to me. 'But he'll be all right, I'm sure. If he's made it through an operation like that, he'll survive.'

'He was on a life support machine, Millie.' I shook my head, feeling choked. 'I can't stop thinking about him. I feel helpless.'

She handed me a mug of coffee.

'I know. But that might be normal after the operation, especially if he had breathing problems and he was being monitored,' she said. 'He's such a good guy. But he's fit and young. Try not to worry. I'm sure he'll be okay.'

'I hope so,' I said. 'I just want to talk to him on the phone, but Wilson said he's conscious but not out of danger.'

'Do you know what happened?'

I told her what Wilson had briefly relayed to me, and then Harper's more detailed information.

'I'm still not sure how it all happened. But hopefully I'll be able to talk to Danny soon.' I sipped from the mug of coffee and placed it on the table. 'All I've heard from Lucas in the past couple of days is when is Danny coming? I can't even think about telling him he's in hospital. I keep saying he'll be back soon.'

'He will be,' Millie said, and she went back behind her desk.

I went into my office and sat scrolling through emails on my computer, sifting through the possible clients who I'd have to arrange to meet in the next few days. But it was all a bit half-hearted. Between the exhaustion from not sleeping and being distracted thinking about Scanlon, I couldn't get myself focused on anything concrete. I heard the office phone ring in reception and Millie answer it with her usual professional tone. Then she popped her head around my door.

'It's Gina Evans,' she said. 'Cathy's daughter. She wants to talk to you. Urgently.'

'Shit!' I said in a whisper.

I'd been meaning to keep in touch, but with everything that had been going on it had slipped my mind.

'Put her through and I'll talk to her now,' I said.

I braced myself, then picked up the phone on my desk.

'Gina,' I said. 'I'm really sorry I haven't been in touch, but it's been full on these past few days.'

'Billie,' she said, her voice shaky. 'What you were telling me about Jane McAllister and my mum, and those foreign holidays, might explain something I've only just discovered.'

'What?' I asked, confused.

'This is going to sound bad, no matter how I say it.'

'Just take your time and tell me,' I said.

'On my mum's last trip here about five months ago, she left a little suitcase here at my house. Like a hand luggage kind of case. She must have forgotten it. It was locked. It's one of those wee solid cases that can withstand travel, and it looked quite new – expensive. I phoned her when she got back to Spain and told her it was here, but she said she forgot to lift it but just to leave it and she would get it next time. So I never attached any importance to it. I didn't open it, because it was locked, like in a code lock where you had to know the number. So I just put it in the back of a cupboard and forgot about it. I would have taken it with me next time, or she could have got it when she came over.'

She paused, and I waited, intrigued by what she was going to say next.

'So,' she said, 'earlier today, I decided to try to open it. But it was locked solid. But I took a knife and a strong drill to it and cut a bit of it open. Don't ask me what was going through my mind because I don't know. But something told me to open it.' She paused, swallowed. 'When I pulled back the part I'd cut through I could see inside. I nearly died of shock, Billie. The case was full of money.'

'Jesus!' I said, staggered by the revelation. 'Did you get it fully open?'

'Yes. I managed to snap the lock and open it completely. Christ, Billie! There's thousands of pounds in Sterling notes in there. And, I mean, maybe tens of thousands! I haven't even checked it, but it's loads.' She paused. 'But not only that. Below the pile of money is a little black velvet pouch, which is full of . . . Christ, I can hardly say it . . . It's full of diamonds, Billie. Diamonds! Jesus almighty! What did my mum get herself into? I still can't believe it. I keep going in and opening it again, then closing it quickly because the truth is, it fucking terrifies me. I mean, whose money is this? Who do these diamonds belong to? They must be worth an absolute fortune. There are seven or eight of them. Big diamonds! What am I going to do, Billie?'

I took a moment to catch my breath before I could answer.

'I don't know, Gina. I honestly don't know. Have you touched the notes or the diamonds?'

'I only looked at the diamonds, shaking them to the top of the pouch. And I only touched the money a bit – one pile – to lift it to see how many piles there were.'

'Good,' I said. 'Give me your address and I'll come out and see you now.'

CHAPTER THIRTY-TWO

I called Dave Fowler, and we were on our way to Gina's flat in Knightswood, close to the west end, within half an hour. Fowler was as shocked as I was when I relayed the story to him. This was the first time there had ever been a mention of money or diamonds, or a suitcase, anywhere in my investigation. Jane McAllister had apparently known nothing about it when she talked to me. So Cathy Evans had kept it to herself when she last visited.

The picture of the middle-aged woman retiring abroad to enjoy sun and sangria was beginning to unravel big time. How did she even manage to get this kind of money and diamonds into the UK in the first place? And if the story Jane had told me – that she'd been going on trips with Steve and Marilyn to bring in drugs and launder money – was true, then how did she end up with this amount of stuff in her own case? There was no way the people she was involved with would not know if suddenly a pot of money and diamonds went missing.

'Do you believe her, Billie?' Fowler shot me a sideways glance as he drove towards Byres Road.

I gazed out of the windscreen. I was still trying to get my head around Gina's phone call.

'I don't know, Dave,' I replied. 'How are we ever going to

know? She seemed really genuine when she came to see me to ask me to investigate her mother's death. And on the phone, she definitely sounded distraught about Jane McAllister. Then she suddenly dropped the line about the case of money. She doesn't strike me as devious. But you never know.'

'It's just that she's had this suitcase in the cupboard for a very long time and she's not even checked inside it. I find that a bit strange.'

'Yeah. She told me she'd just put it there at the time and completely forgotten about it. I suppose that's possible. She didn't expect at any time that her mother would turn up dead. And maybe then everything was all a bit overwhelming recently, so she never even thought about the case.'

'Hmm.' He half smiled. 'We'll see once we look at the whites of her eyes.'

We drove into the council estate in the Knightswood, a new-build estate of terraced houses that looked more like egg boxes than homes. But the area was neat and clean and most of the houses had a car parked outside, which made the narrow street where Gina lived difficult to negotiate.

'That's the number there, Dave. On the left.'

I pointed as he slowed down then pulled across the road and parked half up on the pavement. We got out of the car and walked up the short path to the front door. I noticed the small PVC windows. Everything about the street and the houses was small and compact. Perfect if you wanted a little piece of somewhere to call home. Soulless, though. By the time I pressed the doorbell, Gina was already at the door and opening it. She looked pale and edgy.

'Come in, Billie,' she said before glancing at Fowler.

'Gina, this is Dave Fowler. We do a bit of work together.'

She nodded to him and stepped back so we could enter the

narrow hall before making our way into a cosy living room. Gina went into the kitchen and stuck the kettle on. Then she came back into the living room and gestured to the sofa, asking us to sit. We did, and she sat on the armchair opposite, but only for a second, then she stood back up.

'I'm a nervous wreck, Billie. That's the truth.'

'I understand, Gina. But just take your time.'

The kettle pinged and she backed out and returned a couple of minutes later with mugs of tea on a tray. She set it down on the coffee table and took a seat. I let the few moments of silence hang there as we sipped our tea, then I put mine back down on the table and looked at Gina, who was biting the inside of her mouth.

'So, Gina. It's where to start here,' I began, then took a long breath. 'But let's take it from the very beginning. Okay?'

She nodded. I went on.

'I want you to go back to the last time your mum visited – the time she had the case with her. I take it that was the last time you saw her? You hadn't been over there or anything?'

'No,' she replied. 'I had been over for a week about two months before she came here, but she was going on holiday after I left, and said she would visit after that.'

I could feel Fowler's eyes on me and I shot him a quick glance. A plan was starting to fall into place.

'So why did your mum come over so soon after you'd been visiting, Gina? Was that normal for her?'

She shrugged and puffed, as though trying to remember.

'Not really, I think. Any time I saw her it was mostly over there, because it would give me a break in the sun, and we could enjoy being together. She didn't come back here any more than twice a year.'

'So, it was a bit unusual for her to come over that last time.'

'Yeah.' She paused, her brow suddenly furrowing. 'Oh, now I remember,' she said. 'She told me she was coming over because a guy she knew was driving over from the south of Spain and he told her he would give her a lift if she wanted. I remember now. She said it was a free trip, that she could get a lift and save on the air fare. Then she could fly back. She came over in a car, she told me. A big four-by-four.'

Again, the exchange of glances with Fowler.

'Do you know who the guy was? Did you meet him?'

'No. He dropped Mum in the middle of Glasgow, and I picked her up in my car.'

'And how was she?' I asked. 'I mean, did she seem any different to you?'

Gina shook her head.

'No. Not a bit. She was really happy to be here. She looked great, but I think she was exhausted after the long journey by car.'

'So where was the guy going? Did she say?'

'No. He had some business and drop-offs, he said – luggage for people he knew on the Costa del Sol – then he would head back in a few days via somewhere down south. I don't know. It didn't seem to matter to her.' She narrowed her eyes. 'Why? Do you think it should have mattered? I never even gave it a second thought, because I know that Mum knew a woman once who was going back to England a couple of years ago, and she got a guy to drive her in a van so she could take some bits of furniture. It's quite common for people to get a lift from the south of Spain.'

I nodded in agreement.

'Yes. I suppose so,' I said. 'And did she have a lot of luggage, apart from the small case?'

'No. Just a normal-sized case and the wee case that she left in the cupboard.'

I took a sip of my coffee.

'And when she was leaving, did you not notice that she didn't have both cases?'

She shook her head.

'Well, no,' she said. 'You see, that morning I was working and left her in the house to get organised for her flight. I was at work and she was getting a taxi to the airport. So I didn't notice the case was left behind until I got home. In fact, I didn't notice it at all, because it was in the back of the cupboard, and I didn't even know it was there until a few days later.'

'And did you call her about it?'

'Of course! I called her as soon as I saw it. But she was not even worried about it. She said she'd get it when she came over next time, that she'd forgotten to lift it. But just to put it away until she visited.'

I nodded.

'And you didn't do anything about it or even think about it until the last couple of days?'

'Exactly, Billie. Honest to God, I nearly died when I opened it. I find it hard to believe that all that money and those diamonds have anything to do with my mum. It just doesn't seem possible.'

'Are you thinking that someone put the stuff in the case, and she knew nothing about it?'

She pushed her hands through her hair and blew out a breath.

'I don't know what to think. Once she was here, she was in her bedroom, and I left her to it. It's not as if I was going into the bedroom to make sure she was all unpacked. I just left her to do things herself, the way she always did. I don't even know if she opened the case. I'm just baffled.'

You and me both, I was thinking. But my gut feeling was that Cathy Evans knew perfectly well what was in the case, hence the reason she was hitching a lift back instead of attempting to take it on a plane. No other reason for her having a bag of cash and diamonds made any sense.

'And all the time your mother was here, was everything normal? Was her demeanour changed in any way?'

'No, not at all. She was the same as she always was. Happy to be here and to be with me, shopping, going out for a meal, and enjoying ourselves. But she was always glad when it was time to go back to the sunshine.' She paused, swallowed hard. 'I was looking forward to going out to Spain to be with her in a few weeks, then . . . it happened. The police came to my door and told me she was dead.'

We sat as the silence hung in the air, Gina in her grief and bewilderment, and Fowler and me raising our eyes, not really knowing what to make of it. But I believed Gina was telling the truth. Whatever had gone on to bring Cathy Evans over in a car with a stash of cash and diamonds, I didn't think Gina had played any part in it.

I looked from Gina to Fowler then back to her.

'Can we see the case?'

'Of course,' she said. 'Come. It's in the bedroom.'

We followed her out of the room, along the short hall to a bedroom, where the turquoise-blue hard shell case lay on the bed. It looked as though it had been in a crash, with a gaping hole in the middle of it where Gina had drilled through. We all stood looking at it, nobody speaking. Gina clutched her hair again as though she was ready to tear it out.

'Look at the state of it,' she said. 'I should probably never have touched it. If I'd known what was in it, I wouldn't have. But it was only yesterday that I decided I'd open it.'

'Why do you think that was?' I asked. 'I mean, why did you feel the need to see what was in it?'

'I don't know,' she said. 'Just curious, then it became like an obsession to get it open, and before I knew it, I was at it with a drill.' Her lips almost pulled back to a frustrated smile at how ridiculous it sounded. 'Stupid, I know.'

I didn't answer. I reached into the inside pocket of my jacket and pulled out a pair of surgical gloves, and Fowler did the same.

'Can we have a look?' I asked.

She nodded and we crossed over to the bed and pulled back the case a little more and looked inside, Fowler with his phone torch to see properly. We looked at each other. There were bundles of notes, fifties and twenties tightly packed and filling the case. I'm no expert but it looked like tens of thousands.

'If you lift a bundle out,' Gina said, 'you'll see the velvet pouch with the diamonds. At the top left side.'

Fowler picked up a bundle from the stack and sure enough there was a black velvet pouch with a little silk drawstring. He glanced at me as he opened it and very carefully emptied the contents onto the palm of his hand. Our eyes almost popped when we saw the jewels glistening under the ceiling light of the bedroom.

'Jesus!' I said. 'I don't know a lot about diamonds but these look bigger than anything I've ever seen.'

Fowler nodded.

'Me too,' he said. 'If they're real, they are worth a fortune.'

We both turned to Gina, who looked perplexed.

'What am I going to do?' she asked, spreading her hands.

There really was no answer to that.

CHAPTER THIRTY-THREE

We pulled out of Gina's street not really knowing if we were doing the right thing, but after sitting talking for a while with her and going over all her options, this seemed to be the first step. What do you do if you're sitting on a fortune in cash – proceeds-of-crime cash no doubt – and a dozen or so diamonds, also probably from crime?

I'd asked Gina what she wanted to do.

'You could go to the police and hand everything over,' I said. 'Tell the truth of how they got there and let them deal with it. That way your hands are clean.'

'I don't want to get dragged into a big police investigation,' she said. 'I had no idea that my mother was involved in any kind of criminal activity. I'm still shocked.'

It had been Fowler who came up with the idea.

'Why not get the diamonds valued by a jeweller, see how much they're worth?' He shrugged. 'I mean, finders keepers and all that. But once you do that, you are going down a different road altogether.'

Gina's face showed nothing. I looked at Fowler, a little surprised at what he'd said.

'The thing is, Gina, once you take the diamonds anywhere then you have handled them. If in time this did become a police investigation, then you wouldn't be able to say you'd just found the stash in your cupboard in a suitcase and didn't even touch it. You're completely innocent at the moment. You're not innocent if you take them and get them valued.'

'Billie's right.' Fowler glanced at Gina. He took a long breath, then went on. 'The thing is, this case has been in your cupboard for how long, Gina?'

'Over five months, I think,' she said.

'Okay,' Fowler said. 'And in all this time, even with conversations with your mother, there was no real interest in the suitcase or any impression that there was anything in there other than some personal things, right?'

She nodded. I could see where Fowler was coming from and the part of me that didn't always play by the rules agreed. Why hand all this over to the police if it seemed nobody was looking for it? It would just disappear into some proceeds-of-crime safe and never be heard tell of again. Gina seemed hesitant, then spoke.

'Are you saying I should just keep it?' She laughed. 'Like suddenly I'm rich?'

The thought hung there. I found myself glancing around at this neat, small terraced house and Gina's old car outside. She was a woman in her forties, working nine to five in a factory. How different her life could be if she suddenly found herself sitting on a fortune.

'Like a lottery win,' Gina said quickly. 'Only all the time I'm waiting for a knock on the door from whoever all this stuff actually belongs to.'

'It's tempting, I'm sure,' I said, then turned to Fowler. 'I know a jeweller who could value the diamonds for you. He would know what to do with them – I mean, in terms of moving them on, if they are genuine and worth a lot of money.'

'But I'd be breaking the law, you said, if I handled them.'

I clasped my hands and sat back.

'But we don't know for sure if the diamonds or the cash were all made from crime. I think it's a fair assumption that they were. But who can prove it? It's not as if anyone has come along to the police here or in Spain reporting it missing.' I paused. 'We actually don't know how your mother came about having these diamonds in her possession. I think if she was holding them for someone, you would have had a knock on the door by now. And if the money belonged to someone other than your mother, again, someone would have come calling.'

'Nobody over there knows me, though.'

'They'll know you,' I said. 'If your mum was holding this stuff for some criminal, they would know who you are, where you are. So maybe – and we will never know for sure – maybe your mother acquired all this stash from whatever she was doing on these trips. Maybe she left it here intentionally, so it would be far away from Spain, and unconnected.'

We sat in silence, and I could see Gina processing the information, and perhaps she'd already moved on in her mind as to how she would spend her windfall. Eventually she spoke.

'Well,' she said, 'I . . . I don't suppose it would do any harm to find out more about the diamonds, like, if they are genuine, and how much they'd be worth.'

I glanced at Fowler and could see the twinkle in his eye – the twinkle that said anyone can become a criminal in the right circumstances.

'I know a man who can tell you by looking at the diamonds if they are genuine, and advise from there,' I said. 'Do you want me to take them and ask him?'

It took her a long moment to answer, then she glanced from Fowler to me, swallowing.

'Yes,' she said. 'I think that's the best way.'

'This is all a bit dodgy, Billie,' Fowler said as we headed away from the estate and onto Great Western Road.

'A bit?' I half smiled. 'I think it's well past that.'

'Why are we doing this?' He glanced from the side of his eye.

I looked back at him.

'Maybe it's a rush of blood to the head, Dave,' I said. 'But you know what? That stash in the suitcase clearly hasn't been missed by whoever it all belongs to, so what's the point of handing it in?' I shifted in my seat. 'Yes, I know it's not what the police would expect you to do, but really, what's the point? The way I see it is this: Gina Evans has lost her mother because some brutal bastards murdered her in cold blood, and all because she was naive enough to end up being used as a drugs mule for someone way up the food chain. She's dead now. If you looked around you, Gina doesn't have a lot going for her. She's on her own, obviously not wealthy, working away to make ends meet.' I stopped. 'You know what, Dave? Sometimes people like her just need to catch a break. And if this is her break and it's not being hunted down by anyone, then, as you said earlier, finders keepers.'

He chuckled and shook his head.

'I can't disagree with any of that,' he said. 'But it's not right.'

'I know. And neither is battering a woman to death and dumping her body on a beach on the Costa del Sol.'

We were silent for a few minutes as we drove down through the city to London Road where my old friend, jeweller Avi Berg, had his shop. I'd called him before we left the house and he said he'd be glad to have a look at the goods.

Fowler parked the car and said he'd wait outside as I thought it was best for me to go into the shop by myself. Avi was the soul of discretion but the fewer people he dealt with, the better. Avi emerged from the back shop when the doorbell tinkled. He smiled.

'Billie! Always good to see you – even if this is a strange request.'

I smiled.

'I know, Avi. I know,' I said. 'I'll tell you a little bit about it. I just want to get a handle on if these diamonds are real.'

He lifted the bar of the counter, then went across and turned the sign on the glass door to *Closed. Back soon.*

'Come in,' he beckoned. 'Let's have a look.'

In the back shop he sat on a swivel leather chair at a desk that was adorned with bits of jewellery and scales and watches that were being repaired. Along the old wooden shelves his tools hung on hooks and one or two were on the desk. He gestured for me to sit, and I pulled up an old wooden chair. Then I carefully emptied the diamonds from the pouch onto a piece of black soft cloth he had on the desk. The spotlight turned onto them, and they glistened with blues and greens. They were beautiful, like tiny stars in the night sky. He looked up at me, his eyebrows going up, and then his mouth turned downward in concentration as he pushed the eye glass to his eye.

'Now, let me see.'

I watched, fascinated, as he picked each one up and placed them in his gloved hand then moved them between finger and thumb to examine them under the light, slowly, meticulously. He put each one back down to one side, picked up the larger ones and examined them closely, breathing softly. Then he took a deep breath, pushed out a sigh and sat back.

'Someone is missing a small fortune, Billie,' he said, his grey eyes shining.

'Seriously?'

'Oh yes. Seriously.'

'What can you tell me about them, Avi?' I asked.

'Firstly, I can tell you that the larger ones – they are three carats at least. They are not quite clean; that means they have to be worked on. These are like the kind we see mined illegally in Africa, but they're still worth a lot of money. You get them in London, anywhere really, but they are smuggled principally through Dubai.' He looked up at me. 'I take it there are no papers with them?'

I shook my head.

'I don't think so.'

He shrugged.

'Doesn't really matter. They are still very valuable for whoever wants to take them and cut them and make them saleable.'

'What kind of value are you talking?'

He picked up the four large ones and placed them in his hands.

'Each of these are worth about twenty grand. Less because they would be moved illegally and people get their cut. But alone, these would be about seventy grand for whoever sells them.'

'Jesus!'

He then looked at the small diamonds, his fingertips running across them on the blackness.

'These are smaller, but more refined. Someone has maybe worked on them. There are eleven of them here. I would think you would get six or seven grand for each of them, after the seller gets their cut.'

'That is a lot, Avi.'

'I told you, Billie. Someone is missing a fortune.'

'Have you ever had a whisper that someone is looking for these?'

He shook his head.

'I don't always hear everything, but it depends, I suppose, on how they were taken – say, if it was only one or two at a time over years. They might not be missed. There is so much coming into the country and across the trade continuously that it might not be noticed if one or two went missing every now and again.' He looked at me. 'I don't want to ask where they came from but whoever has them should either put them in a safety deposit box somewhere or get rid of them pronto.'

I told him the short version of what had happened and Gina's story.

'And she wants to keep them? Make money from them?'

'She's considering her options,' I said.

'Well, if I was her, the last thing I'd be doing is giving them to the police. Because if they've been in her house for months, then there's a real chance that nobody is even looking for them. Or if they ever were at any time, then they've given up, written them off.'

'And if she wanted to move them, Avi, would you help?'

'Yes. I will do that. In my usual, quiet, discreet way.'

I thanked him as he put the diamonds back into the pouch and told him I'd speak to her. I went into the front shop and phoned Gina, then I came back in.

'She asked if you could do that,' I told Avi. 'And if you could keep them in your safe for the moment.'

He nodded.

'Okay. I will make some phone calls and arrange things. It will be a few days.'

He showed me to the door, turned the sign back to *Open* and unlocked the door.

'I'll call you in a couple of days, and we can meet up, Billie. Good to see you.'

CHAPTER THIRTY-FOUR

Millie had come to the flat as arranged, and I was cooking pasta with meatballs – mostly to suit Lucas as it was one of his favourites. But a bowl of rich pasta would give us an excuse to open a bottle of red for dinner. Our weekly dinners had fallen away recently as various things were going on, so it was good to see her away from the office. And also, it was helpful to have Millie around as it distracted Lucas from incessantly asking when Danny was coming back. She played a board game with him on the floor, where his toys were scattered around, and he went from one to another while I cooked.

When we sat down to the table, I poured Millie a small glass and one for myself, and milk for Lucas. I still hadn't heard a thing from Scanlon, and it was like the elephant in the room as we were talking about everything except for the one thing that was preying on my mind.

'Okay.' Millie put down her cutlery. 'So, you haven't mentioned your favourite detective since I got here, Billie. Don't hold back on my account. I know you must be frantic.'

She spoke softly and was careful not to mention Danny by name as Lucas's ears would have pricked up.

I sighed, taking a sip of wine.

'I am a bit, actually,' I said. 'But I think if his condition had worsened, then maybe Wilson would have let me know. Or I hope he would.'

'Why not give Wilson a call?'

'I don't want to disturb him as he might be knee-deep in this investigation, and the last person he'll want to hear from is me asking how one of his detectives is.'

She shrugged.

'I'd still be phoning him, though. Or even sending him a message asking how he is.'

I thought for a moment.

'Actually, I might text Wilson, as I've got something to ask him. About Gina Evans.'

Millie gave me a confused look. When I'd got the call from Gina earlier to tell me about finding the suitcase, I'd left the office with Fowler in a matter of minutes and hadn't had time to tell her.

'I haven't told you this yet, Millie. So, strap yourself in.'

She picked up her glass.

'Will I need this?'

'Yep. And more, when you hear.'

Lucas had more or less cleared his plate and asked for an ice cream. I gave him one out of the freezer and sat back down as he trotted off to his toys and to watch television. Then I told Millie about our visit to Gina's house and the suitcase full of money and diamonds.

'You have to be kidding me!' Her mouth dropped open.

'Nope. I saw it with my own eyes. And Fowler too.'

'What the hell! And do you really believe that Gina knew nothing about it?'

'Yes. I think so. I know it sounds a bit dodgy but I believe she's telling the truth.'

'Do you think whoever all that stuff belongs to will hunt her down?'

'I think if they were going to do it, they would have done it by now. It's been five months.'

Millie took a gulp of her wine and sat back, staring into the middle distance for a long moment.

'I tell you what,' she said. 'If I was her, I'd get a cruise booked, then a very long stay somewhere far away from here and I'd never come back. She can live very comfortably for the rest of her life, and she's never even got her hands dirty.'

I chuckled.

'Except, it isn't her money. Or her diamonds.'

Millie grinned.

'Ach. Finders keepers. That's what I say.'

'Fowler said that too,' I replied. 'And I can't disagree with it.'

'Are you going to tell Wilson?'

'I think I will tell him a version of it.'

Later, after Millie had left and I'd put Lucas to bed, I sat in the living room feeling the weight of the silence now that the place was empty. I thought of going back into the hall cupboard to spend some more time looking over anything I could find of my father and mother's. It was strange the way this small room that had never entered my psyche all the years I had been back here was now a place where I could enter and suddenly feel immersed in another life – in my life before it all broke down, and also in the life that my father had led, of which I'd known nothing. I was about to get up and go there when my mobile rang on the coffee table and I snatched it up, seeing Scanlon's name on the screen.

'Danny!' I said, hearing the excitement in my voice. 'Is it really you?'

I could hear him smile.

'Every bit of me, Billie. How you doing?'

'Never mind me,' I said. 'How you doing? Jeez, Danny! I've been so worried. What's the situation. Are you okay?'

'I am now,' he said, sounding bright. 'It was a bit dodgy, though. Wilson said he told you I got shot.'

'Yes. He did. But he wouldn't say anything else. Just that you'd been operated on. God, Danny! What happened? I mean . . . can you tell me anything? Are you really okay?'

I heard him chuckle.

'One question at a time, Carlson,' he said. 'Sure. I'm okay. We're flying home tomorrow. I got caught in the crossfire is what happened. I wasn't in a shoot-out or anything, but just unlucky.' He paused. 'I'll tell you all about it when I see you. But the good guys won. And the bad guys are banged up and being prepared for extradition as we speak.'

'I can't wait to hear about it,' I said, excited. 'You mean, the top men in the whole set-up over there?'

'Yep. And that Marilyn and Steve couple. They just stuck everyone in once they got squeezed in custody.' He lowered his voice. 'They admitted it was them who arranged for Cathy to be killed. They told us everything, named names at the top, admitted drug running trips disguised as holidays. The pair of them will be going down for a long while.'

'Wilson must be thrilled.'

'Yeah, well, not that you would notice, Billie. You know what he's like. But he's well pleased the way it went. The only downside was me getting shot.'

'So how come you're getting home so quickly?'

'Bullet went through and lodged, and once they got it out, there was no real damage apparently. A nick on the shoulder bone, so I'll not be lifting weights for a while, but it's okay. I can move it a little and I'll be fine. I just want out of here.' He paused. 'How's the wee man?'

'He hasn't stopped talking about you since you left,' I said. 'I told him you sometimes go away to work, but he keeps asking when you'll be back. Wee soul. He loves you, Scanlon.'

'I love him too, Carlson,' he said. Then after a couple of beats. 'And you.'

'Don't start me filling up, Scanlon,' I said, trying to divert the lump in my chest. 'I miss you so much.'

'Well. I'm back tomorrow morning. So I'll be having a few days off. We can get together soon as.'

'You bet.' I paused. I wanted to say more, how much I'd worried and missed him, but all I said was, 'Can't wait to get you back.'

'I have to go now. I'm going to the hotel to get my stuff sorted and some kip, then flying early morning. See you tomorrow night?'

'If you're okay,' I said.

'I am. I will be.'

He hung up.

CHAPTER THIRTY-FIVE

I'd put a call in to Wilson early morning, and he told me he was at the airport waiting for his flight. He was curious as to why I was calling him, so I had to be careful how I put this to him. I didn't need to tell or ask him anything, but I wanted to fish to see if he would be interviewing Gina Evans as part of the investigation into her mother, now that they had nailed the case in Spain. I probably didn't need to ask that, as it would be standard for police to talk to the family of a victim to get as much background as possible. That would all have been fine if Gina hadn't discovered the suitcase with the stash in her bedroom after her mother left.

She'd asked me if she would have to tell the police about it, and I was vague with my answer. It could get difficult for her if she was interviewed because the police had no idea she had a suitcase full of money – but whether she could talk to the police in general terms about her mother and the case depended on if she could carry this off. Guilt on her part, knowing she had the case, could land her in trouble if she suddenly broke down and confessed. If she was going to be economical with the truth, then she would need to be able to carry it off. Even though she had committed no crime here – so far – it was still dodgy. I wondered how many people in her position would not even consider telling the police about the find. Loads, I suspected. I told him on the phone I wanted to talk to him about Jane McAllister and what had happened, and he agreed to meet me in a café down by Charing Cross.

Wilson looked knackered. He was sitting on a brown leather sofa with scuffed patches on its arms and with his crumpled suit and tired eyes, both he and the sofa looked like they had seen better days.

'Nice tan, Harry,' I said as I walked towards him.

'Aye, right,' he puffed. 'Like there was plenty of sunbathing.'

'How's Scanlon?' I asked, even though I already knew.

'He's all right. Good lad that. Just a shame that he got caught in the crossfire. It blew up and didn't pan out the way the Guardia Civil had told us.'

'What happened? Can you tell me?'

He shrugged.

'Yeah. We were mob-handed to bust open an apartment where the couple were holed up. Main man in villa. Everything was covered as far as we could see, plenty of cops tooled up. Even ours. But we were very much in the background. It was supposed to be softly, softly but somebody made us and alarms went off. Suddenly people came out of cars all guns blazing. Scanlon got hit. He's a lucky man. Any higher it might have spoiled his good looks. Lost a bit of blood, but he was all right once they got the bullet out.'

'Are all the bad guys in custody?'

'Yeah. Real result on that level. Much better than we hoped for. I love it when that happens.'

'Good.'

'So what about Cathy Evans? Was she deep into all this, drug muling and money laundering?'

'According to the couple, she was. She didn't suspect anything in the beginning, but she made four or five trips with them in the past two years and got well paid. She knew what she was doing.'

'What, they just paid her in cash?'

'And diamonds, apparently.'

'Diamonds? How come?'

'That's how they roll. There are so many coming in from Africa and moved on, there are always rough-cut diamonds. She made her money out of it no doubt.'

I wondered if the police had gone through her bank accounts as part of the investigation and found anything, but I didn't want to broach the subject.

'Seemingly one case is missing. The couple told us about how something happened out there on one of their trips. Some guy who had been delivering the goods and the cash went missing – with a whole load of money in a suitcase.'

'How could that happen?'

'Don't know. He said he got robbed. Can you imagine? Robbed. I think it's bullshit. He probably disappeared with the lot. He told them he left it for a few seconds while he sent a text on his mobile. The case was behind him at his feet, but the next thing it was gone. Apparently the place was busy and he couldn't see anyone. But it was gone. It's not as if he could call the cops.'

I hoped my face showed nothing. I was trying to work out where Cathy figured in this. If he was delivering a suitcase, how come she ended up with it, if that's what happened? If Harry knew right at this moment it was sitting in a bedroom in Knightswood, I'm not sure how he would react.

'At one point they said they thought Cathy was in on it, but she didn't even know what they were talking about. They believed her and it was just left at that.'

'Why did they kill her?'

'Because she was becoming a bit of a loose cannon, mouthy and getting pissed and talking loud in places she shouldn't have been, and once the big boys got to know about that, they just got rid of her.'

'Terrible, though. Naive woman to get involved in the first place, but what an end to get.'

'Aye. Well. There are all sorts in the murky world, and they're not all Scarface figures by any means. Some are green enough not to know what they're getting into. Others are middle-aged women like her being stupid enough to get hoodwinked and go along with making money. Well, it's a shame. But she should have known better. What did she think would happen if she kept it up?'

Cathy Evans hoodwinked, I was thinking. If only he knew.

I wanted to steer away from the conversation about Cathy being a drug mule. I looked at Wilson as he sat back and crossed his ankles.

'The guys in custody in Spain,' I said, 'are they the big shots or are they just part of the empire?'

'One of them, the guy who ordered the hit on Cathy, is high up, like one of their trusted lieutenants. He runs the mules out in Spain and moves the drugs on in the network, and the diamonds when they are brought in. He knows he's going down for a long time, and at the moment he might be looking at twenty years in a Spanish jail, so he's trying to get himself into a situation where he can be brought back to the UK for trial.'

'Even though the murder was in Spain?'

'Yep. Lawyers are talking about it with the Spanish, so we'll see what happens. I don't think Spain wants him or the others. It's not good for their image to have a constant trail of drug cases and gangsters all over the shop. Bad for tourism. Though everyone knows the place is full of people who seem to live the good life with no obvious means of support.'

I didn't mention the missing diamond ring that Jane had been wearing.

He scratched his stubble chin.

'I'm not convinced that she was totally innocent in all this,' he said.

'How do you make that out?'

He made a 'who knows' face and shrugged.

'Something about her bailing out so quickly. Would you really just do a runner if you saw what you thought was your best friend's body being carted out of the house? Would you not even think about calling the cops?'

I shrugged.

'It's hard to say, really. I'd like to think I'd call the cops, but if Jane suspected that she might be next, I can see why she ran.'

'Well, it didn't do much good, did it?' he said.

I wanted to sound him out about Gina Evans.

'Where does Gina fit in all of this?'

He looked at me, surprised.

'Nowhere that I can see,' he said. 'She was only the daughter of Cathy, and when she reported to the police at the time it was to tell us she was convinced her mother had been murdered.' His eyebrows went up. 'She wasn't wrong.'

'What happens to her now? Will you question her again? Has she been told about the arrests?'

'Not yet. My DI will be going out to see her later today, just to clear things up and let her know.'

I nodded, trying to keep my face straight. I wondered if Gina would be able to hold it together if she had a visit from the police.

CHAPTER THIRTY-SIX

I took a call from Avi after I left the café and was on my way back to the office.

'How're things, Avi?'

'All good, Billie. I've had some information from my friends in Amsterdam re the stuff.'

'How does it look?'

'Put it this way,' he said, 'I'm not a poor man as you know, but if I owned those diamonds, even the rough-cut ones, I'd be minted.'

'Really? They're worth a lot?'

'Oh yes.'

'Like, how much?'

'Over one hundred and fifty grand,' he said. 'Of course, anyone brokering the deal will have to get their cut. But it's a big win for the lady.' He paused. 'That's if nobody comes after her.'

'What do you mean?' I asked. 'Is the word out in those circles that some diamonds are missing?'

'My friend tells me it was talked about a few months ago, but not in recent times. In that world, Billie, so many diamonds are changing hands and coming from various places and lots of it so hot you can barely touch it that nobody sits and weeps over missing diamonds. Anyone dealing in them illegally knows another chance will come along soon.'

'Yes. But that doesn't mean they're not still looking.'

'They may be. But I didn't get that impression. And once the diamonds are cut and moved, there will be no trace.'

I was most impressed by the slick way he knew the game. It must have taken years of apprenticeship.

'So, what is the next move?'

'The diamonds are still over there. If the lady wants to deal, then they will deal.'

'Just like that?'

'Yes.'

'How?'

'Sometimes people would set up a bank account, and it would be transferred, but she might not want to do that. The other way is to go there and get the cash.'

'You mean, and travel back with it?'

'Yes. Or she could pay someone to bring it over.'

'How would that work out? How could she trust them?'

'People do it all the time.'

'Every day is a school day talking to you, Avi.'

'Sometimes for me it is too, Billie. Things change over the years. In the past it was all pick up and delivering money, but there are so many ways to hide bank accounts these days. But also there is the danger with that of someone finding a way into it.'

'Cash is king.'

'Yes.'

'Okay. I will ask her what she wants to do. I'll go and see her today and get back to you. Thanks, Avi.'

'Glad to be of help.'

The line went dead.

*

Gina Evans answered the door looking like she hadn't slept since I last saw her. She stepped back to let me inside.

'You all right, Gina?' I said as we went down the hall and into the kitchen.

'To be honest, Billie, I haven't slept,' she said, shoving the kettle under the tap. 'Tea?'

'Sure. Thanks,' I said. 'What's wrong? You just worried?'

'Yes. Petrified actually,' she said. She pulled mugs out of the wall cupboard. 'What if I keep all this stuff and then my life starts to fall apart? You know, if someone comes after me tomorrow, or in a few months or years, what happens? I could make a decision now that could wreck my life.' She glanced around. 'As you see, I don't have much. But it's mine, and it's paid for. It's legal.' She gestured to the hall and beyond where the suitcase was. 'But that stuff in there? It could make me rich, but it could ruin my life.'

I could see where she was coming from, and I'd be the same too. But I didn't want to tell her what to do.

'So, what are you thinking?'

'I'm thinking of going to the police. Handing it over.'

'After all this time?'

'Yes. But I didn't know it was there until a few days ago.'

'You think they'll believe you?'

'If they don't, what can I do? I feel I have to lay it on the line. Be honest. Be open. At least tell them. Then I know I'm in the clear.'

It was a huge opportunity to take the money and run, and so many people would take the chance to set themselves up for life. But she was scared.

'I can put some feelers out to the cops if you want.'

'Yes, but as soon as you tell them, will they not come breaking my door down like I'm a criminal?'

'To be honest, I don't know. But I can talk to someone I know.'

She poured water into the mugs with teabags, spooned them out and binned them, and we sat for a while, looking at the steaming mugs, not knowing what to say next. Gina wasn't up to this level of pressure. I could see that. She was just an ordinary woman who had worked honestly for everything she had. Sure, she needed a windfall like this – don't we all? – but did she really need everything that could go along with it? Whatever I really thought, I didn't want to advise her one way or the other. But she had to know just how much money she was sitting on.

'Gina,' I said. 'As I told you, I went to sound out a jeweller friend about the diamonds, see what he thought.'

'Yes. Did you do it?'

I nodded.

'Yep. He was very impressed by what he saw, and then he got a dealer friend in Amsterdam to look at them.'

'Really?'

'Is that okay?'

'Yes. I wanted to know. Thanks for doing that.'

'Gina. He called me just before I came here. Some of the diamonds are rough and uncut, but he said they are worth a fortune. He said even when they are cut and whoever was brokering a deal gets their cut, there is easily over a hundred and fifty grand there.'

Her face blanched.

'You're kidding.'

'Nope. That's what he said.'

'Oh my God! I don't know what to say. How did my mother get her hands on all that? I think I'm still in shock.'

'No wonder,' I said. 'But I'm just relaying the information. The rest is up to you. He would arrange for the deal to be done, and you'd either need to open a bank account or go and collect it yourself or get someone to do it for you.'

'Jesus. I can't think straight. It's overwhelming.'

'I know. I can understand. It's a life-changing amount of money, and that's not including the cash in the case.'

She sat shaking her head, then she looked at me and spoke.

'All my life, Billie,' she said, 'we struggled. My dad was an abusive waster and my mother had to get two jobs to pay the rent and put food on the table. I used to come home from school to the empty house and wait for her to come home. She worked so hard, and she was so tired, but she always, no matter what, found time for me, to sit and to take me places on the bus, to the seaside, or on caravan holidays. We had nothing. School uniforms had to be paid up. When my mum retired and she went abroad it wasn't because she had a lot of money. It was cheaper to live in Spain with no heating bills, and with her redundancy and retirement pension she was able to get the little apartment over there on long-term rent. I was glad she was living the life. And when she told me about the holidays, I didn't think too much about it. Now she's gone, and she never once even told me what she did. Why did she leave this suitcase with me? Why, Billie?'

I listened to her, feeling her pain.

'Maybe she planned one day to tell you about it, to give it to you. Like a nest egg. You really don't know how she got it. If she'd been doing these trips over a period of time, maybe that's how they paid her. Though it seems a lot of money for a few trips.'

I felt I had to tell her what Wilson had said about the missing suitcase.

'I'll tell you something, though,' I began. 'I talked to a cop I know who was on the investigation over there, and one of the men is talking big time. He told police that there was a suitcase with money and diamonds missing and one of their couriers said he got robbed. I've no idea what happened to him. Who knows. But apparently it just went missing.'

She gasped.

'Oh my God! You think Mum took it somehow?'

'I don't know. We'll never know. Maybe she was in cahoots with the guy. Maybe she stole it. But we will never know, Gina.'

'Why has nobody come looking for it?'

'Well,' I said. 'Maybe because it was so hot, they didn't want to pursue it. And at one point they apparently suspected your mother but didn't really take it seriously as she told them she didn't know what they were talking about. So, we will never know what the real truth is.'

Gina sipped her tea, and we sat in silence, listening to the tick of the kitchen clock on the wall and the hum of the dishwasher.

'I think I should talk to the police,' she finally said. 'I know it's a lot of money, and God knows, I would love to be able to live my life in the luxury that would give me, somewhere away from here. But I'm scared. I think I should hand it over.'

'Okay,' I said. 'But let me sound out my police contact first.'

I was driving back to the office before picking up Lucas from nursery when my mobile shuddered on the passenger seat, and I was delighted to see Scanlon's name on the screen.

'Scanlon!' I said, taking the call on loudspeaker in my car.

'You shattered?'

'A bit. Tired, but just glad to be home.'

He sounded a bit off somehow, distant.

'You okay, though, Danny?'

'Yeah, just a bit – how can I say? – a bit deflated. Like it's just all beginning to hit me.'

I knew exactly how that felt. When I got shot in New York as I'd tried to rescue Lucas, it was the adrenalin that kept me alive, but when I awoke from the operation the biggest downer floored me. It's a kind of post-trauma thing, when you're fired up and determined to survive, then it's over, and you have to get on with it, you just feel somehow depressed and deflated. I think for most of the time when Lucas was missing, that's how my life felt.

'I think that happens, Danny,' I said. 'After you've been through a big ordeal. It's just now sinking in.'

'I suppose.'

'Tell you what,' I said, 'are you going to bed, or would you be fit for some dinner at my house and an early night? I know Lucas will be jumping to see you. But no pressure, Scanlon. If you're knackered, maybe you just need a couple of days catching up on sleep.'

I could hear him take a long breath, then his voice sounded a bit tight.

'Aw, man,' he said. 'I could think of nothing better than just relaxing at yours and being with you and the wee guy.'

'Are you sure you're not too tired?' I said. 'I can order something in and come and pick you up after I get Lucas.'

'I'd love that, Billie. I really would.' He paused.

'Okay. Done. Just relax for a little while, and I'll call you when I'm picking you up.'

'Thanks, Billie. Can't wait to see you.'

'Me too, Scanlon. I was worried sick. We can just chill in front of the telly. If you want to stay, no problem. Lucas would love it.' I hesitated. 'And me too.'

'Okay. I'll wait for your call.'

The line went dead, and I found myself uplifted by the idea

of seeing him, taking care of him when he was down like this, the way he took care of me in the bad days when I could barely put one foot in front of the other. I couldn't wait to tell Lucas the good news. I should call Wilson about Gina, but that could wait until tomorrow.

CHAPTER THIRTY-SEVEN

'Guess what?' I squeezed Lucas's hand as we walked towards my car from the nursery.

'What, Mummy?'

'Danny's back!' I said.

He stopped in his tracks, his eyes bright and excited.

'He's here? Can we see him?' We got to the car and I opened the door and lifted him into the car seat. 'Can we see him, Mummy?'

I leaned in to kiss his cheek as I strapped him in.

'You know what, Lucas? We are going to get him right now!'

'Yesss!' His face lit up. 'That's a good idea, Mummy. I miss Danny.'

'Well, we are going to his flat and he's coming to our house for dinner.'

'Oh, wow, Mummy! I love Danny.'

'I know you do, darling, and he loves you too.'

Lucas looked at me.

'And I love Danny too,' I said, smiling.

I drove off in the direction of Scanlon's flat after sending a text saying I'd be there in five. From the back seat, Lucas was chanting, 'Go, Danny! Go, Danny!' the way the pair of them played around in the flat in a game.

We got to Danny's flat, and he was outside on the pavement with a small rucksack over one shoulder. His face brightened when he saw us. And when Lucas spotted him, he shouted, 'There he is, Mummy! Can I get out?'

We pulled up at the kerb and I jumped out and opened the back door to unstrap Lucas, who was already pulling the straps off his shoulders while I urged him to take his time. But he didn't listen and jumped out of the car and ran towards Danny.

'Be careful,' I said. 'Danny, just watch him. Don't let him jump on you.'

I ran and picked Lucas up in case he would slam into Scanlon and hurt his injuries.

When we got to him, Lucas flung his arms over Scanlon's neck. Then I hugged him and the three of us stood there in a group hug, and when we eased away, I could see tears in Scanlon's eyes. They sparked some from me too and I bit them back.

'Jesus,' I said. 'Look at the state of us. Come on. Let's get you home.'

Later, after Indian food and a mild chicken dish for Lucas, he curled up beside Scanlon on the couch and we told him he had been away and working but had an injury. He had a million questions, but I told him he had to just be careful not to punch or play rough until Scanlon was better. At one point Lucas went into his bedroom and came out with a doctor's uniform on. He tested Scanlon's pulse then gently pressed the plastic stethoscope on his chest and looked in his ears before pretending to give him medicine in an injection. Scanlon took it all in good part, looking happy to be here. I bathed Lucas and let him sit for a while with Scanlon, who took him to bed and read him a story, until I came in and tucked him in. It felt just about as good as it gets.

We sat on the sofa, both of us with our feet up on the low coffee table and a mug of hot chocolate in our hands.

'This is like being middle-aged,' Scanlon said, sipping from the mug and smiling. 'But tell you what, Carlson, it's the best I've felt all week.'

'Good,' I replied. 'I didn't want to give you any alcohol on top of the operation just in case it wasn't a good idea.'

'It would probably knock me out,' he said. 'It's like being completely exhausted. I hope this feeling doesn't last long.'

'Don't worry,' I said. 'Think about it. You've been shot, had an operation to remove a bullet, and then in a couple of days travelled home. Your system has had a kicking. You've got to just lie down to it.'

'Wilson says I'm not to turn up for at least two weeks,' he said. 'I'll go nuts.'

'You won't. You need to build your strength up and before you know where you are you'll be back on the streets fighting crime, like the caped crusader.'

He chuckled.

'I thought you were the caped crusader.'

'No. I just help out when he's busy.' I turned to face him. 'So, what happened over there that you ended up being shot? I know it was a bit of an ambush. But do you want to talk about it? Must have been terrifying at the time.'

'It probably would have been,' Scanlon said, 'if I wasn't in such a state of shock. I just remember feeling this stinging pain and a jerk on my shoulder, and then seeing the blood seeping through at the top of my Kevlar vest. Good job I was wearing that, because if I wasn't and the bullet was an inch or two lower, it could have been my heart.' He paused, as though back at the scene. 'But at the time it was just all action, me lying there and feeling the blood flowing from me and getting kind of weaker and stuff. I lost a load of blood, they said, and I'm lucky I made it at all.'

'Was Wilson at the scene?'

'Yeah, he was. Actually, he came with me in the ambulance.' Scanlon looked almost mystified at that, his eyes screwed up. 'Can you imagine Wilson, being all kind and caring like that?'

I smiled, then chortled.

'No. I can't actually. Are you sure you weren't hallucinating?'

He smiled.

'No. He was definitely there. He kept talking to me all the way to the hospital. Telling me it would be fine, that I was just faking it to get a day off at the beach.' He shook his head. 'But it was kind of nice, though, the way he was. Like he cared.'

'I think big Wilson does care,' I said. 'About his guys. He's just a tetchy old bugger who's seen it all and doesn't like all the rules he has to play by these days. But he's a good guy to have on your side.'

He nodded.

'You know what he said to me, Billie?' He sat back. 'He told me I had to make sure I pulled through this, because the force needs men like me.' He glanced at me, as though he couldn't believe it. 'I mean, he actually said that to me, that I was the future.' He grinned. 'The future. Me. It was a bit surreal, but I was honestly touched by it. I don't know much about Wilson's life but somewhere in there he's got a heart.'

I blinked, recalling some of the things I'd got to know about Wilson working with him, and in recent times.

'He's got a heart all right, Danny. I think he's a good guy. But he's at the fag end of his career really, and I guess when he suddenly finds himself sitting with one of his men in an ambulance, he might be asking himself if this is all worth it. You know what I mean?'

'Yes,' he said. 'I suppose so. He was good, coming into the hospital and seeing me, and pushing for me to get back home on the same flight as the guys and him.'

I nodded.

'Yep. You're here now,' I said, reaching for his hand. 'I'm so glad. I think he's right, Danny. Good men like you are the future. And who knows, one day you might be racing up the ranks of Scotland's finest.'

He laughed.

'If I last that long. We'll see.' He paused, squeezed my hand and turned to me. 'You know, Billie, at one point when I was in the hospital and it was quiet just before the operation, all I could think of was you and Lucas, and if I would ever see you again.' He swallowed. 'That's the first time I've ever had any doubts that I would survive anything. I just kind of lay there and felt choked and gloomy.'

I leaned across and kissed him on the cheek.

'Don't. You'll make me cry.'

He took a breath and composed himself.

'Anyway, I'm good now. It's over.' He yawned. 'Sorry.'

'Listen, just say when you want to crash out. I know you're tired, so you can just get into bed and sleep as long as you want.'

'You mean, you won't try to have your way with me?'

I smiled, shaking my head.

'I'd be scared you'd break.'

'Maybe tomorrow then.' He grinned.

'Maybe wait until you're feeling fitter. You know, you can stay here for a few days while you get back on your feet.'

'Thanks. Maybe just a couple of days. I wouldn't want to overstay my welcome.'

'Don't worry, pet,' I joked. 'I'll tell you when you've done that.'

We finished our drinks, then I said to him, 'Come on, let's get you into bed.'

Later, in bed, I lay watching Scanlon's lips flutter as he breathed in deep slumber. The wound on his shoulder was covered by an elaborate cushioned plaster. In the shadowy darkness he looked older somehow, bathed in the crack of light coming through the curtains. It was the first time I'd really considered that I might have lost him, and it made me more grateful that I hadn't, and there was a little tweak in my gut that told me that no matter what happened between us, I had to make sure that I never, ever let this man go.

CHAPTER THIRTY-EIGHT

Lucas was up and racing into the kitchen, where I prepared his breakfast. I put a finger to my lips to silence him, as Scanlon was surprisingly still asleep. Must have been all the effects of the last few days.

'Where's Danny?' Lucas asked, almost in a whisper as he climbed onto the breakfast bar stool.

'He's sleeping,' I said quietly. 'He's very tired. We mustn't make a noise in case we wake him.'

He looked at me, confused.

'Why is he sleeping, Mummy? It's morning.'

I placed a bowl of cereal in front of him and poured in some milk.

'I think he was working very hard. So we have to let him rest,' I said.

I had the sound low on the television and watched it without really taking any of it in. I was tired. Everything had been going around in my head for most of the night, between talking to Gina and the fortune stashed in the bedroom, and how to handle it. I hadn't mentioned it to Scanlon last night as I didn't want him having the pressure of knowing about it. I'm sure he would have said she had to report it, but I wanted to speak to Wilson first to see what he thought.

I picked up my mobile and tapped out a text to Wilson asking for a meet.

He texted back, What's going on?

I messaged him with a short, just something I want to run past you. I knew it would get his attention, and he replied, Typically cryptic, Carlson.

Scanlon suddenly appeared in the doorway and came shuffling into the kitchen, scratching his bed head.

'Everyone up but me!' he said, yawning.

'We didn't want to wake you,' I said. 'You went out like a light last night and barely moved.'

He yawned again and shook his head as he ruffled Lucas's hair.

'Hey, champ!'

Lucas turned to him with a big smile, his eyes lighting up.

'You were sleeping, Danny. Mummy said we had to be quiet.'

'Thanks, buddy. I was very tired.'

'You want some breakfast?' I asked Scanlon.

He gestured to Lucas's half-empty bowl.

'I'll have what he's having.' He sat up on the breakfast bar as I shook some cereal into a bowl. 'Food for champs, isn't it, Lucas?'

He nodded, spooning cereal into his mouth.

'Yep.'

I filled a mug of coffee and placed it beside him.

'How you feeling?' I asked.

He took a mouthful of Cheerios and gave Lucas the thumbs up of approval.

'Just kind of shattered. I've never felt this tired. I think I need to go for a bit of a walk this morning. Get some fresh air.'

'Sure,' I agreed. 'But you mustn't push yourself. Just take it easy. Lie around here for a while and relax.'

'You got a lot on?' he asked, sipping from the mug.

'A bit,' I said, feeling a twinge of guilt that I wasn't being straight. 'I'll call you towards lunch and see how you feel. If you want, we can go out, or I can bring something up.'

'We'll see,' he said. 'I don't want to be just sitting around, though. I can't cope with that kind of stuff.'

'Okay. I know how you are. A little walk will do you good. But then just chill and take in a movie on the telly.'

He nodded as he ate, and then started chatting to Lucas, who was telling him all about a great Lego build he had and asking if he would help him. Scanlon assured him he would when he came back from nursery. Lucas glanced at me wide-eyed, pleased that Scanlon would be here when he came home.

I told Wilson I'd meet him in a little café off Sauchiehall Street called Soups U, where I hadn't been for a while but sometimes went if I wanted to be sure I wouldn't meet anyone I knew. It was an old-fashioned Glasgow café with soup and sandwiches and all-day breakfasts, where you could be as far away from the chic coffee houses as you wanted to be and enjoy the banter of the characters behind the counter. One of the women once confided almost conspiratorially that if you ordered a roll and sausage in the morning, you got two square sausages on your roll. 'That'll do for me,' I told her, and I was pleased that I'd found a proper café that made me feel at home. The window looked onto Sauchiehall Lane and I saw Wilson coming down the hill, looking up to make sure he was at the right venue.

'You can dig the places up, Carlson,' he said, as he came into the café. 'What is this place? A greasy spoon?'

'Far from it,' I told him as he squeezed into the wall seating opposite where I was sitting. 'It's proper food,' I told him, handing him the menu. I leaned forward as he browsed it.

'And by the way, you get two square sausages if you order a roll.' I grinned.

He almost smiled.

'Haud me back,' he said. 'I'll definitely have one of them.'

The waitress, who looked to be a woman in her fifties with glasses and short hair, came to our table.

'What you having, loves?'

I reeled off two rolls and sausage and tea for two.

'Coming right up,' she said, going behind the counter and barking the order to the woman further down who was cooking.

Wilson glanced around, seeming pleased with the surroundings. This was clearly more his bag than the Starbucks or Costa coffee houses.

'Quite nice in here,' he said. Then he looked at me. 'So, what's the score, Carlson? You don't ever run anything past me, so I'm getting a funny feeling in my stomach.' He paused. 'By the way, have you seen Scanlon?' He gave me a knowing look.

'I have,' I told him. 'I cooked dinner for him at my place last night. He's okay, but very tired. He's straining to get back to normal, but he needs time to recover.'

'I told him to sit on his arse for a couple of weeks,' he said gruffly. 'But I knew he wouldn't listen.'

'He's going to have a quiet day,' I said. 'Just watching TV and maybe taking a stroll, he told me.'

'So, are you looking after him?' he asked. 'Not that it's any of my business. But I know you're close.'

I half smiled.

'He doesn't need looking after,' I replied. 'But yeah, I'll cook for him for the next couple of days. He's glad to be home in one piece, I think.'

'He's a lucky boy. It was a real shitshow out there. But we

won in the end. I hope the shooting doesn't put him off staying in the force.'

'No chance of that,' I said. 'He's a cop through and through.'

'So are you.' He smiled as the waitress came over and placed the food down on tea plates. 'You just don't want to admit it.'

I shook my head and smiled.

'I don't think so,' I said. 'Too many rules and too much red tape for my liking.'

'Aye, maybe it's the Spanish force you should be in.'

He picked up his roll, squeezed tomato ketchup onto the double sausage and then bit into it, nodding approvingly as he chewed it and washed his mouthful down with tea.

'This is good scran,' he said. 'I must tell the boys up the road.'

We ate for a couple of minutes in silence, Wilson dabbing ketchup off his lips as he ate hungrily.

'I'm starving actually. I seldom eat breakfast. Living on my own, you know.' He paused, mid-chew. 'I don't know why I'm even telling you that.' He looked a little awkward by his admission.

'No problem, Harry. Being a cop is not exactly the best way to make a marriage work.'

He nodded.

'Aye. Actually, I'm okay about it. I like being on my own. I've no regrets. It's been a good life. So different now, though – in the force, I mean. It's all changing.'

'Jeez, Harry, you sound like you've had enough.'

He sighed.

'I'll be honest with you, Carlson. Sometimes I look at it and I think it's time to sling my hook. Go play golf somewhere, or fish up north. Live a different life.' He half smiled. 'I might not look it, but I'll be fifty next year.'

'Oh, you look at least ten years younger.'

I grinned and he chuckled.

'Anyway, enough of the pish talk. What's on your mind?'

I swallowed a mouthful of food followed by a gulp of tea to give me time to work out how to word this.

'Gina Evans,' I heard myself saying.

He looked at me, a bit bewildered.

'Cathy Evans' daughter?'

'Yeah.'

'What about her? I sent my DI out to talk to her yesterday. Let her know about the arrests. He said she seemed a nice woman. Quiet. She told him she feels better now that there is recognition that her mother was murdered, which she said all along.' He looked at me. 'So, what about her?'

There was no easy way to say it, so I decided just to come straight out with it.

'You know she's my client, Harry – that she came to me in the beginning claiming her mother was murdered.'

'Yes.'

'Well, a few days ago – while you were in Spain actually – she called me up in a bit of a state.' I swallowed and glanced at Wilson, whose brows knitted waiting to hear what was next. 'She asked me to come and see her. So, I did.' I took a breath. 'And when I got to the house, she took me into the bedroom and showed me a suitcase.' I paused. Wilson's eyes pierced me. 'She said it was her mother's.'

Wilson nodded.

'Go on.'

'She opened it, Harry, and it was full of money,' I said, shaking my head, incredulous. 'I mean, absolutely full of money. Like, fifty-pound notes, all stacked. Must be a fortune.'

His eyes popped.

'Fuck me! Seriously?'

I nodded.

'Yes. Seriously. Must be . . . well, I don't know, but I'd say at least a hundred grand, maybe more.'

'Christ almighty!' He screwed up his eyes. 'Her mother's suitcase? Why was it there?'

'She said her mother must have gone away without it. That the morning she was leaving, Gina had to work, so she wasn't there when her mum left in the taxi. She said her mum must have forgotten about it.'

He gave me a pull-the-other-one look.

'Her mother forgot about a case full of money? Aye, right!'

'That's what she said, Harry. She said that when she phoned her mum, she told her not to worry and that she would get it when she came back next time. So, Gina just put it in the back of a cupboard and forgot all about it.'

'She didn't open it?'

'No. It was her mother's. She assumed it was just some clothes and stuff.'

He puffed out of the side of his mouth.

'So, she just left it there until when?'

'Until a few days ago, she said. She told me she just happened to notice it in the cupboard and took it out, but it was locked – one of those combination locks – and with her mother dead, she couldn't ever find out the code. So she forced it open and saw all the money.'

We sat for a moment not speaking and I could see the wheels turning in Wilson's head. He looked like he didn't believe it and no matter what else I said, it wouldn't convince him.

'I'm not buying this, Carlson,' he said. 'Who's going to believe that shite?'

'I know,' I said. 'But there's more.'

'What?'

'She took a few bundles out of the case and found a velvet pouch and when she opened it, there were diamonds in it.'

'Aw, come on. This is bullshit. Diamonds? At the back of her wardrobe? All this time and she knew nothing about it?'

'Yeah. Diamonds. She showed me them. One or two of them are rough diamonds. But the thing is, I don't know much about this stuff, but they'll be worth money, I was thinking, if they are genuine.'

'What did she do? I mean, why is she even telling you this?'

'I think she was just so shocked and didn't know where to turn.'

'What did you tell her? To get the fuck out of the country with the lot?'

I shook my head.

'No. To be honest, I didn't know what to tell her. I was shocked just at the sheer amount of money that must be there. And more than that, how it got there. Was her mother really into smuggling that much that she made this amount of money and chose to hide it over here? Was that really why she was murdered? All that stuff was going through my mind. I didn't know what to tell her.'

'Did you tell her to get in touch with the police?'

'I said to her that she needs to consider what to do, and it might be best to talk to the police. So, what do you think?'

He sat back and pushed a sigh out of puffed cheeks.

'Jesus, Carlson, I don't know what to think. Do you believe what she's telling you? That she knew nothing about this, about her mother's involvement?'

'Yes. I do.'

'What did she do about the diamonds?'

I didn't answer for a long moment. Then he looked at me and shook his head.

'You got them valued for her, didn't you, Carlson? You took them to some fence?'

I nodded. I couldn't lie to him. He could see right through me.

'Yes.'

'And?'

'The diamonds are worth the guts of a hundred and fifty grand.'

'And they were just sitting there at the back of her wardrobe for, what, a couple of months?'

'Over five months, she told me.'

'And nobody came looking for them?'

'Nope.'

He sat for a while, neither of us speaking. Then he picked up his mug of tea.

'So, what do you want me to do? Arrest her?'

I shrugged.

'I don't know, Harry. She doesn't know. She's sitting on a fortune, and she told me yesterday to talk to the police, that she wants to hand them in.'

'For fuck's sake!'

'That's what she said. I told her I would talk to you.'

We seemed to be sitting for an age before he finally looked at his watch and spoke.

'Tell you what, Carlson. If she hands this in in the middle of this enquiry, I don't know who is going to believe her, and what kind of shit she may find herself in. Bottom line is we got the guys who murdered her mother and Jane McAllister too. The only mention of money was one of the pricks saying money went missing, but nothing more than that. The money or whatever wasn't even part of our investigation.' He paused. 'And to be perfectly frank, I don't give two fucks about the money, or the suitcase. My case is wrapped up and these pricks are going down for a long time. This only complicates my life.'

Part of me was shocked but another part was glad that he wasn't going into her house guns blazing. I didn't know what he was going to say next. Then he leaned forward and shuffled as though about to stand up.

'Okay, Carlson. Here's the deal. I'm going to walk out of here and forget everything you just told me. I didn't hear it. All right? I've spent a lifetime chasing fuckers who murder and maim and steal from innocent people and leave victims littered all over the city. I've had enough, and I'm at the end of my career. Bringing this suitcase into the fray makes things difficult, and I have enough complications right now. So, I don't care what you tell her, but just don't involve me. But if I was her, I'd get my passport out and go as far away from here as I could, taking whatever I could make out of this and forgetting the life I had here. I know that's a fantasy, but that's what I would do.'

I didn't want to say anything, and I didn't know what to say, so I just looked at him. He stood up.

'I'm out of here. This conversation never happened, Billie. I don't want to hear any more about it. Okay?'

I nodded slowly, not quite believing what I was hearing, but totally understanding where he was coming from.

'Okay.'

'And tell your boyfriend I said he's to sit on his arse.'

He ran a hand across his mouth to make sure there was no ketchup lingering, then he turned and left.

CHAPTER THIRTY-NINE

I decided it was best to go to Gina's home to let her know how a senior police detective viewed her dilemma. That's if you could call someone sitting on a suitcase full of money and diamonds a dilemma. Plenty of people would be glad to be in that situation. But for Gina, it was a problem, and I wondered how she would take it when I told her what Wilson had said.

Gina had seen me parking outside her home and was at the door as I walked up the path.

'How you doing?' I asked as we went in and I followed her down the hall.

'Just the same,' she said. 'A DI came out yesterday to fill me in on the details of the arrest of the men who killed my mother. It was all very official, and he didn't say much.'

'How did you feel when he was here?' I said. 'That you were talking to a police officer, and you have a stash in a suitcase?' I half smiled and she rolled her eyes to the ceiling.

'I didn't say much. But I felt as though the guilt was written all over my face. I was glad he didn't stay long.' She motioned to me to sit at the kitchen table while she put the kettle on. 'So, did you talk to your police contact?'

'I did, Gina. Obviously I can't tell you who it was, but I gave him the details of the suitcase situation and how you were feeling.'

The kettle pinged and she poured water into mugs and handed me one as she sat down.

'And?'

'Well, I have to say that you might be surprised by what he said.'

'Really? How?' she replied.

'He said if you pitch up to the police station with a suitcase full of money and diamonds that are obviously the proceeds of a crime, you just don't know what you would be getting yourself into.'

She looked at me, surprised, and sat back.

'But I've done nothing wrong.'

'I know that, and you know that. But this suitcase belonged to your mother who has been murdered, and the police now have the people responsible for her death in custody. The fact that you have a suitcase that was brought here by her . . . well, it really complicates the investigation.'

'What do you mean?'

'Firstly, you would be questioned closely. And he said that nobody would believe your story.' I sipped from my tea. 'And I have to say, it is hard to believe – though I do believe it completely. You have to understand that the first instinct of the police would be to be all over this. And who knows, you might get arrested.'

'Arrested?' She stood up. 'What? I haven't done anything.'

'I know. But you have to think of it from their point of view. Who else has a case of money and diamonds? Only criminals or the mules who carry their stuff. Ordinary people like you don't sit on a case of money in their house for months. What he is basically saying is, they don't want to know.'

'What?'

'The bottom line is they are not interested. The investigation into your mother's murder is done and dusted. They have guilty pleas underway. This just complicates their lives.'

'I'm shocked. I can't believe it. What am I supposed to do now?'

I sat for a moment before I answered as she looked bewildered, her face flushed.

'Well, to tell you the truth, the cop I talked to said you should find a way to disappear with the contents of the case. He didn't want to know.'

'I find that hard to believe.'

'Yes. I know. And any cop at a police station where you turn up with this case will also find you very hard to believe.'

'So, what should I do?'

'You know the value of the diamonds and how much you stand to make, so it's up to you if you want to pursue that route.'

'I don't know where to start. Jesus! This is so confusing.'

'It's up to you.'

'How would I get the diamonds sold? I wouldn't know how to.'

'Look, I can put you in touch with someone who will do all that for you, and they would obviously take their cut. With the money in the case, you can take that or bank it over a few months or do something like that.'

'Then what?'

'You know what the cop said? He said disappear as far away from here as possible and start a new life.'

'Christ! What kind of cop is that?'

'A really good one. One of the best. He's seen and done it all, and he knows you would be making more trouble for yourself if you hand this in.'

We sat not speaking. Eventually Gina looked at me and swallowed.

'My head is all over the place. But the longer that stuff sits in my house, the more chance there is that someone will come looking for it. So.' She paused. 'Can you really put me in touch with someone who will take care of this for me?'

'I can,' I said. 'Are you sure that's what you want to do?'

'Ridiculous as it sounds, I feel right now I have no other option.'

'Okay,' I said. 'I'll talk to someone.'

'A crook?'

'He would call himself a businessman. But he can sort it, I'm sure.'

'Then what?'

'You ever wanted to go somewhere far away to live, like Australia, America or anywhere?'

'Always dreamed about it,' she said. 'And a cruise. I'd love to go on one of those cruises where you just go from place to place for about three months.'

'Well, this is your chance.'

When I left her house, I felt as though I was egging her on to do something criminal, even though she wasn't a gangster and she hadn't obtained the stuff from any crime that she had knowledge of. But what else could she do? And the part of me that doesn't give a damn about the rules thought of someone like her growing up the way she did, only to find her mother murdered by vicious gangsters far away from home. Who was to say she didn't deserve a break? I would make the call to Paddy on the way back to the office.

Paddy Harper listened as I talked to him on the phone and told him about Gina and the suitcase. Every now and then I could hear him snort in disbelief or chuckle at what he was hearing.

'It's sounds like a right fairy story, Billie,' he said. 'Do you believe her?'

'All I know is that she came to me to find out what happened to her mother in Spain, and now this. I think if she intentionally had a suitcase full of money and diamonds in the cupboard, she would not have been making a big deal of her mother's death in case it drew attention to her. She just doesn't seem the type to get involved in anything dodgy.'

'Well, she is now – involved in something dodgy. So where do I come in?'

I explained to him that I'd had the diamonds valued, and that it would be easier to do a deal if someone drove to Amsterdam and returned with the money.

'Does this Gina woman have enough trust in anyone that she will do that?'

'She trusts me, Paddy. And I trust you. What do you think?'

He took a long time to answer, and I could hear him letting out a long sigh.

'I don't think I would have a problem with that, Billie. It's a trip to Amsterdam, expenses paid, for whoever I send. I might even go myself.'

'And of course, I imagine she would want to pay you, Paddy, for doing it.'

I felt grubby even saying it, because this was making me part of the whole deal. But I was already in with Gina, so I had no alternative but to help her. The cop in me didn't like it, but then again, the best cop in the business had just told me he wasn't interested in anyone handing in a suitcase full of problems.

'Okay,' Paddy finally said. 'If you make an arrangement with

Gina to meet me, I can sort this all out for her. Give her my number.' He paused, and I could hear the brightness in his voice. 'I enjoy a wee adventure.' Then he hung up.

I called Gina and relayed all this information to her, and gave her Paddy's phone number. She listened and for a while she didn't say anything. Then eventually she spoke.

'Billie,' she said. 'I think I've made a decision.'

'You have?'

'Yes,' she replied. 'I know a bit about depositing money in the bank, you know, how you have to be careful about not banking too much at once?'

I stayed silent, but I knew where this was going. She went on.

'Well, I'm going to put some of this money into the bank over the next few days and weeks, and then, you know what I'm going to do?'

'What?'

'I'm going on a cruise.'

I felt a smile spread across my face.

'A cruise?'

'Yes. Actually, I looked online over the last couple of days – just imagining what it would be like, Billie, to have money, to have the means to live like that. And after you left, after you'd spoken to your police contact and with what he said, I think I'm going to do it.'

We were both silent for a moment, then I said to her, 'Good luck to you, Gina. Make sure you send me a postcard.'

She laughed, but it was a kind of hysterical, adrenalin-pumped laugh, then she hung up.

CHAPTER FORTY

It was the following day that the call came in from Christopher Fletcher.

'Billie?' he said. 'Hope I'm not interrupting you. Are you free to talk?'

'Yes, Christopher,' I said, then added, 'I thought you'd gone back to London.'

'Yes, I did. But I'm back to sort out some things at the house.' He paused. 'And also, I have Elizabeth's ashes. She spent her childhood in Scotland and she loved it here growing up, as her mother was Scottish, so she has roots here. That's why we bought the house. To be honest, I would rather we had stayed nearer London.'

I wondered why he was telling me all this. There was an awkward pause, then he spoke.

'You see, I wanted to scatter her ashes in Ayr. That's what she used to say she would always want. It's where she played as a kid, and the beach there is somewhere we used to visit years ago, long before we bought the house.'

'I see,' I said, not really knowing what to say.

I heard him take a breath.

'And, well, Billie, I wondered if you would possibly come down to Ayr and be there while I scattered the ashes?' He paused. 'But if it's something you're not comfortable with, I understand. It's just that there is nobody now. We don't have any family, and no real friends here. And the only person who got any way close to her in recent weeks was you.' He paused. 'Plus, I feel we are connected, with your parents being friends of ours . . .'

His voice faded a little and he sounded lost and desolate. I couldn't imagine what it would mean me standing down on some beach at Ayr while he scattered the ashes of someone I barely knew. But there was a connection, and it was Elizabeth who told me what had happened to my father. There was something there, and I couldn't just refuse.

'Er . . . yes, Christopher. I'd be fine to be there. As you know, I didn't know Elizabeth very well and we only met just before this tragedy, but I'd be fine to accompany you.' I felt as though I was babbling.

'Thank you, Billie. That means a lot to me.'

'Just let me know when you want to do this and I'll be there.'

'I will be in touch.' He hung up, and I sat for a few moments processing the weirdness of the idea that I was going to be doing this with someone who was a friend of my father and who knew so much more about him than I ever did.

I was glad of the wind whipping around me on the deserted promenade at Ayr Beach as I stood alone, watching the sea rough and boisterous, the mound of Ailsa Craig shrouded in distant mist, and I thought of Gina and wondered where she would be this time next week, next month, next year. I didn't even feel a flicker of guilt that I'd witnessed her plans.

I was glad of the alone time and the drive all the way down here to try and get my head around the last few days. I felt bad at not inviting Scanlon to come along for the ride as he was at a loose end and the trip might have done him good, but I'd told him this was something I had to do by myself, that this felt like some kind of landmark journey for me trying to come to an understanding about my father and the life he led, and I had to do it alone. I watched the seagulls diving and screaming, scavenging on the beach for whatever debris had been washed up. The place was empty save for a couple of cars and one or two people walking briskly, their faces set against the wind.

As I waited for Fletcher's car to arrive, I found myself looking back at day trips I'd made here with my parents, the picnics, the sitting with our backs to the shore wall, jumping over the freezing waves and running. I hadn't had any of these memories for such a long time; they had just been banished to somewhere I never looked back on until recently, until I found out so much about my father's life. I'd had many sleepless nights since then, thinking about it, and nothing would resolve the feeling of emptiness I had.

I saw a car slowing down on the promenade and parking up, then watched as Fletcher stepped out. He was carrying a grey cylindrical box which I supposed was his wife's ashes. I felt a little awkward as he came towards me, not quite knowing what I was supposed to do here.

'Thanks for coming, Billie,' he said as he approached me. 'I appreciate it.' He looked out to sea, and we stood for a few seconds, then he turned to me. 'All feels a bit strange really. You know, the very idea, the very fact that I'm here with you, after all this time; how I never knew you growing up, and here we are standing here waiting to scatter my wife's ashes. It's a bit surreal.'

I nodded.

'I know. I feel the same, Christopher. I was remembering days coming here with my parents, times we had, lots of memories that I have never looked back on because as a kid, well, the way things happened, I was suddenly in another country so far away from home, and I must have somehow trained my mind not to look back, because I seldom did as a child.'

He was watching me, studying my face.

'You look so like your mother, Billie,' he said. 'Every time I see you, I think of her, and of your father, and those days.' He paused. 'I wish I had contacted you years ago. I feel guilty that I did not. But with the service, my work, it was important that nobody knew what I did.'

'I wish you had too, Christopher. Although I don't know what difference it would have made knowing what happened to my father. At the age I was when it happened, I would have been too young to understand, and even a few years ago I still wouldn't have been able to comprehend it. But now I see it, and I can build the picture. And when I read a bit of his journal, I feel the presence of him in there. It's weird. He lived in a different world from the one I knew him in.'

He nodded, then looked at me.

'Yes. I understand that. So much of our lives were taken up moving around in the shadows. That's why Elizabeth and I had difficulty, in recent years especially. I regret that. I regret the way she died and will always blame myself because she was murdered because of me, and, well, maybe I should have moved out of the service earlier. But even by that time it was too late.'

The Adams apple moved in his slim neck, and I could see he was a little emotional.

'Well,' he said, sighing. 'There's no point in raking over it now, is there. I think we should get on with this while the tide is going out.'

'Yes,' I said, not really knowing what else to say.

I followed him down the slope onto the heavy sand and we picked our feet across until the soft wet sand stretched towards where the waves were lapping. We stood for a long moment, then he glanced at me and fiddled with the lid, unscrewing it to open it. He sighed.

'Neither of us were religious, so it's hard to know what to say here. Best just to get it over with. Elizabeth was such a free spirit. That's what attracted me to her in the first place.'

I watched silently as he stood with his back to the water and opened it. The fine powder and ashes swirled in the wind and then washed into the sea, little fragments of the woman who had brought all of this to me just a few weeks ago, and opened up a world and a truth I had no idea existed.

'Goodbye, my love . . .' he said as we watched the ashes disappear in the waves.

I took a step back, leaving him alone, and began walking up towards the promenade and he stood for a few moments looking out to sea. Then he joined me, and we didn't speak as we walked towards our cars. There was a little café along the prom a bit and we made our way there. Fletcher was driving back down to the house in Portpatrick, he told me, and then would do everything he had to do and head back to London. We sat in the café with a pot of tea by the window looking onto the beach.

I looked at him as he sat, his heavy coat unbuttoned, his face pale and lips thin. He suddenly went into his inside pocket and brought out a piece of white paper. He handed it to me as I looked at him curiously. I unfolded it and read it.

Dimitry Volkov. The name jumped out at me. His age, and then an address typed and then written in longhand.

'It's him?' I said. 'The man who killed my father? Is this where he lives now?'

He blinked and nodded.

'To the best of my knowledge, yes. That's where he lives. He has a grandson. He is with the child a lot, and my source tells me he may be looking after him as his daughter is alone, no husband.'

'How do you know this?' I asked. 'Have you just found this out since we last spoke? And why is nobody arresting him?'

He shook his head.

'It is something they will never do. When your father died, they immediately moved in and once the body was recovered it then became top secret. It was made to look like a suicide. That is how they worked. That is how we all worked back then.'

'It's so wrong, though. For the people left behind who never knew the truth. It's just wrong.'

'I know.'

He watched me sadly, sensing my frustration, but didn't answer. I looked at him.

'And why are you telling me all this now anyway, Christopher? Why are you giving me Volkov's address? What can I do?'

'I don't know.'

'I want to see him. I do,' I said. 'But I don't know how. Is it safe?'

He sat for a long time and didn't answer, then he spoke.

'I will help you.'

'Can you take me there?'

He nodded, said nothing.

'Why?' I asked again. 'Why now? After all this time?'

He looked weary and aged and desolate, his eyes downcast. Eventually he looked up at me.

'Because, Billie, I am on borrowed time, and it's the least I can do for you.'

ACKNOWLEDGEMENTS

It's always a thrill to be able to write these words of thanks to the people who have supported me over the years. It means I've reached the end of another book, and I'm ready to set my mind to the next one!

Big thanks, to my sister Sadie. She's a star, who's been on this road with me through good and hard times, and is my greatest friend. And to her big children Katrina, Matthew and Christopher, and their own children who make me feel blessed every day.

I have so many friends who turn out for me and encouraged me long before I was ever a published author. Here are just a few of them: Annie, Eileen, Mary, Phil, Liz, cousins Annmarie, Anne, and Alice and Debbie in London. My old journalist friends, Simon and Lynn, Mark, Annie, Keith and Maureen, and Thomas in Australia. And also the cherished veteran hacks, Brian, Gordon, Ian, David, Ramsay, Jimmy, Brian, Tom and Neil, Helen and Bruce. And to Tom Brown and Marie who are always an inspiration. Thanks also to my cousins the Motherwell Smiths for their huge support over the years. And back in the West of Ireland, Mary and Paud, Sioban, and Sean Brendain.

At Quercus, I want to thank the marvellous Jane Wood, who

saw the potential in my first Rosie Gilmour books all those years ago, and so began an incredible journey of nineteen books in four series. I will always be grateful to have had her expert advice, encouragement and friendship. And thanks to Florence Hare who understands the characters I create and whose advice helps drive me on. And to all the team at Quercus who push and promote my books, a big thanks. And, my amazing agent, Euan Thorneycroft, who works hard for me and whose advice I am grateful for over the years.

Of course, I wouldn't be doing any of this without the readers who invest in the characters in each series and give me feedback that encourages me when I'm sitting in the dark, figuring out a plot! Here's to the next one!